I MARRIED A DRYAD

Prime Mating Agency

REGINE ABEL

COVER DESIGN BY
Regine Abel

ILLUSTRATIONS BY
Vvevelur
Yuarsima

Copyright © 2023

All rights reserved. The unauthorized reproduction or distribution of this copyrighted work is illegal and punishable by law. No part of this book may be used or reproduced electronically or in print without written permission of the author, except in the case of brief quotations embodied in reviews.

The author expressly prohibits any entity from using this publication for purposes of training artificial intelligence (AI) technologies to generate text or images, including without limitation technologies that are capable of generating works in the same style or genre as this publication. The author reserves all rights to license uses of this work for generative AI training and development of machine learning language models.

This book uses mature language and explicit sexual content. It is not intended for anyone under the age of 18.

This book is a work of fiction. Names, characters, places, and incidents are either products of the author's imagination or are used fictitiously. Any resemblance to actual persons, living or dead, events, or locales is entirely coincidental.

CONTENTS

I MARRIED A DRYAD

He was her perfect match.

Fed up with the deadbeats and jerks infesting the standard dating pool, Maeve reaches out to the Prime Mating Agency, hoping to improve her luck. Her fear of ending up with some weird primitive alien is immediately alleviated when she's paired with a stunning Edocit. Smart, funny, sweet, and as hellbent in protecting the weak and the oppressed as she is, Helio exceeds everything she ever dreamed of. If only she didn't have to keep so many secrets from him.

Helio hadn't been actively looking for a mate, least of all an off-worlder. But the moment he lays eyes on Maeve, he's smitten… but also intimidated. Aside from the cultural shock their pairing is bound to give her, he's a mere bounty hunter, while she's a brilliant, high-ranking officer of the Enforcers, the elite intergalactic peacekeeping forces. Despite his insecurities, they're off to a great start… until tragedy strikes.

With the lives of countless innocents on the line, will the clash of their respective worlds tear them apart, or will they overcome adversity to prevail against evil?

DEDICATION

To those who acknowledge that Mother Earth is hurting and that we all must do our share to help her heal. Pretending a problem doesn't exist and focusing on casting blame will not make it go away.

To those who dedicate their lives to the protection of others. To the countless nameless heroes who relentlessly face danger as they work in the shadows to thwart evil in order to keep our homes and our children safe.

CHAPTER 1
MAEVE

Standing nervously outside of Kayog's temporary office on the Persea Space Station, I lifted a hand to knock on his door. Before my knuckles could even make contact with it, the Temern's muffled voice rose from behind the door and bid me come in. Startled, I took in a deep breath and entered.

As soon as my gaze settled on his face, annoyance instantly swelled within me. Judging by the amused smirk that the stiffness of his beak couldn't hide, and the mischievous glimmer in his silver eyes, Kayog clearly knew what a nervous wreck I was. It shouldn't surprise me, considering his empathic abilities were one of the key traits that made him so successful and popular in his field.

He gestured for me to take a seat in the guest chair across the table that served as his desk. I closed the door behind me and once more complied.

In many ways, my current behavior could be deemed irrational. There was nothing shameful about seeking the assistance of a mating agent to help find a life companion. And yet, I had seized the opportunity of my team patrolling this sector to seek

Kayog's services during my rest time as soon as I found out he was passing through the region.

The Persea Space Station was a popular entertainment hub that served multiple minor planets and moons in the sector, with very affordable direct transport for the patrons. Therefore, no one would question my motives for heading over there during my time off.

"My dear Maeve," Kayog said in his usual friendly tone. "Receiving a message from you pleasantly surprised me. How can I be of assistance?"

"Well, as you can probably guess, I'm here wondering if you could pull off the same miracle you did with Kaida," I said, once more feeling irrationally self-conscious for being here.

He shifted his maroon wings as he gently smiled at me. "For once, I'm afraid I had little merit as far as this pairing was concerned. They met each other without my intervention. Cedros recognized her as his Ejaya. I merely convinced her to give a marriage of convenience a try."

"True," I conceded with a nod. "However, you already knew right there and then that they would be a perfect match. Frankly, I never expected to come to you hoping to find myself a partner. But I'm tired of always ending up with deadbeats, idiots, unfaithful jerks, and pompous assholes."

Kayog winced, his feathery face taking on a sympathetic expression. "That indeed sounds like a series of unsavory characters."

"Unsavory is quite the understatement," I said dejectedly. "I've tried for a few years going through fancy meeting sites and dating agencies. The good candidates always end up getting snagged by some other bitch… pardon my French. But the bad ones are like freaking cockroaches. You get rid of one, ten more come out of the woodwork. I'm thirty-two. Yeah, I know some people will still call that young, but I'm ready to start building something solid and planning a future."

"A fair request," Kayog said, tilting his head to the side while giving me an assessing look. "But you realize I specialize in primitive aliens, right?"

I shrugged then nodded. "Yes, I'm fully aware of it. I won't lie that I never contemplated aliens. I wanted a human, like me. But seeing how happy Kaida is with her dragon has changed my mind. I never imagined that a union between two such different people, both anatomically and culturally, could thrive so beautifully. It made me realize that I may have been a little narrow-minded in my views of what a proper pairing should be."

This time, the Temern's expression took on an approving warmth as he nodded at my words. "People often miss out on great opportunities because they're not open enough to possibilities that fall outside of their comfort zone. However, it always makes me laugh when a candidate says they are open to aliens," Kayog added with an amused tone. "To me, *you* are the alien."

I snorted and nodded in concession. "Touché."

He leaned back against the narrow backrest of his chair, a common model designed specifically to accommodate bird folk and winged species. I squirmed under the intensity of his gaze. Temerns could only read emotions, not minds. And yet, in this instant, I felt like an open book, bared and exposed.

"Let me guess your criteria," Kayog suddenly said. "You want a male who is attractive, smart, has a sense of humor, is financially stable, is physically fit and fairly active, has no kids, no baggage, and no criminal record."

I scrunched my face, feeling somewhat called out by the way he had enumerated that very accurate list of traits. "Well, yes. Those traits make for a good foundation," I said, feeling slightly aggravated by the defensiveness in my voice.

"Basically, all the boring, generic, and useless things that have nothing to do with what you really need," Kayog said matter-of-factly.

I bristled at that comment. "What do you mean? Sure, handsome is a superficial factor. It is merely preferred, not compulsory. But the rest—"

"The rest is irrelevant," Kayog interrupted in a firm tone. "You want your soulmate, not a generic checklist. You want someone who completes you, elevates you, brings out the best that dwells within you, and for whom you can do the same."

I shifted in my seat, and chewed my bottom lip, forced to agree with his statements. And yet, in the back of my head, my analytic voice continued to whisper that this nonetheless required each partner to check a series of compatibility boxes.

"Do you know which was my best pairing?" Kayog asked, taking me aback.

I shook my head. "I'm guessing you will not say Cedros and Kaida?"

He smiled. "While they are a lovely couple, like I said earlier, I have very little merit in that success story. But no, my most successful pairing was between an Andturian named Olix, and a woman named Susan."

I lifted an eyebrow in surprise. As an Enforcer of the United Planets Organization's peacekeeping force, I had to familiarize myself with most of the species whose planets were members of the organization. When it came to primitive planets still under the protection of the Prime Directive, we didn't have to dive too deeply into their politics and culture. As we were not to interact with them, our job was merely to keep others from entering their space or messing with the local population. Communications with the indigenous people of those planets were strictly controlled and assigned to specific diplomatic liaisons within our organization.

"An Andturian? Wasn't a strict ban imposed on some development corporation that attempted to colonize their planet and oust the locals?" I asked.

"Yes. And that pairing prevented this turn of events," Kayog said proudly. "You see, Olix was broke, and his people were on the verge of starvation and of losing their lands. It wasn't for lack of hard work on their part. Many factors conspired against them, and in particular that corporation. He didn't meet any of the criteria Susan had originally hoped for in a mate, and she certainly did not correspond to what he had in mind for his spouse. And yet, not only did they end up falling deeply in love with each other, Susan was instrumental in turning their fate around while respecting the Andturians' way of life. On top of saving her new people, she also brought prosperity and hope to other women from her homeworld facing the same hardships that had forced her into this arranged marriage to begin with."

"Wow, it does sound like a perfect fairy tale," I said, feeling a sliver of envy.

I had become an Enforcer to bring peace and make life better for the weak and the innocent. What greater blessing and bragging right than your union with your soulmate also making you the hero of an entire people?

"It is," Kayog said with conviction. "Forget the criteria you *think* you want and open your mind to possibilities. Often, the most improbable pairings are exactly the ones that are needed."

I shifted again in my seat and licked my lips nervously. "Okay. Does that mean you already have someone in mind for me, but he's broke?"

I wasn't rich, but I had a comfortable enough nest egg if it came to that. I didn't need a billionaire. So long as he was a hard worker like that Olix had been, I had no problem supporting the right partner until he got back on his feet…

Assuming the male Kayog has in mind for me is even bipedal.

Kayog burst out laughing. "Broke? No, or rather, I don't know yet. I'm assessing you, although I have a suspicion."

"Oh?" I said, perking up. "Such as?"

"I'll tell you in a minute, after we've discussed a couple of other things," Kayog said, still staring intently at me.

I swallowed down my impatience and gave him a stiff nod.

"The first thing I have to say is that if I match you, you will likely have to leave the Enforcers," Kayog said factually.

My back stiffened. "WHAT?! Why? I don't want to leave the Enforcers! Kaida was able to stay. Why would I have to leave?"

"Kaida married one of the most powerful Shadow Lords of the Derakeens, able to open portals to any destination in the galaxy," Kayog said in a reasonable voice. "Your career would make it extremely difficult to have a healthy relationship with your mate unless he followed you around. But a homemaker husband would not suit you."

As much as that comment stung, I couldn't deny its accuracy. There was nothing wrong with either a male or a female taking care of the household. It was a lot of work. However, I did not believe a homemaker could have the adventurous and daring personality I wanted in a partner. It struck me then that I had never fully verbalized that trait in my list of criteria. I only ever mentioned someone fit and active.

Suddenly, I felt quite superficial about my requests. No wonder I'd been getting douchebags.

"I understand you are the hacker on your team?" Kayog asked.

My head spun at the sudden switch of topic. "No, I'm not a *hacker* but an I.T. specialist," I said with a frown. I always felt that hacker had a very negative connotation, even though my team often referred to me as such.

Kayog took on a taunting expression. "Which usually means hacking into enemy systems, taking over ship computers, and infiltrating networks, among other things."

I glared at him. "Yes, but only when necessary. I do it to save lives. To—"

"Why so defensive?" Kayog interrupted, while cocking his head to the side in the way birds often did.

"I'm not defensive," I mumbled, my face heating.

The Temern gave me an unimpressed look that made me

squirm. "You became an Enforcer to indulge legally in your passion for hacking," he challenged, as if addressing a naughty child who refused to confess to eating the cake even though her face was still covered in icing.

That struck a nerve. "It's not true! I'm just good at what I do!"

Far from convincing him, my vehement response only made me sound even guiltier.

"You *are* good, but you're not an Enforcer at heart," Kayog said matter-of-factly.

My back stiffened, and I almost jumped to my feet, barely remaining seated as I glared at him. "I resent that. I have devoted my life to the Enforcers! And I have been an exemplary agent."

"You have been," Kayog conceded in an appeasing tone. "But doing something well doesn't make it your calling. Kaida is a true Enforcer. You are a free spirit. You chafe at all the rules and restrictions, even if you follow them."

I wanted to argue and demand what the heck that had to do with finding me a man. But each of his words rang true… far too much.

Kayog smiled and took on an almost paternal expression. "Although it may feel like it to you right now, I am not attacking you, my dear Maeve. You have a beautiful soul, and you are an outstanding agent. There is nothing wrong with liking the things you do. You found a way to indulge in your passion that is both legal and beneficial to the community at large, which is commendable. But even if you leave the Enforcers, you can continue to do what you love without getting into legal trouble."

My heart leapt, the intensity with which this piqued my interest betraying how accurately he had assessed my personality.

"What do you mean?"

"You are a very interesting case, Maeve," Kayog said pensively. "I think I know your perfect match, but I must talk to him again to confirm my suspicions. I have only briefly interacted with him when I was helping his uncle handle some diplomatic issues on Trangor."

"Trangor? You think my perfect mate is an Ordosian?" I exclaimed, not having expected that at all.

Kayog laughed and shook his head. "No. He's not an Ordosian. His uncle is the Federation's Master Hunter Bron Kflen."

"Bron? The Edocit legend?" I asked, stunned.

Kayog nodded, a strange spark lighting his eyes.

"A Dryad hunter?" I repeated with a frown, unsure how I felt about it.

Kayog chuckled. "What? You're not a tree hugger?"

I once more glared at him, which only made him chuckle harder. "I've met a few Edocits. They're attractive. I know very little about their culture, except that they are quite advanced and have extremely strict rules about visitors to their homeworld. I don't have a problem learning a new culture and adapting within reason. But the hunter part is problematic for me."

This time, the Temern looked genuinely surprised. "Really? Why?"

"Like Enforcers, Hunters constantly travel for hunts," I said, matter-of-factly.

"True, but you could tag along."

"Right, but I would get bored with it in the long run," I said in an apologetic tone. "I don't mind killing critters from time to time, but doing that every day of every month for the rest of my life feels mind-numbing, even if each creature is different and requires different tactics. I like… puzzles, solving mysteries, beating bad people at their own game, catching them and bringing them to justice."

Kayog nodded approvingly. "Which is why Helio might be perfect for you. Unlike his uncle, he doesn't hunt creatures, but people."

"A bounty hunter?!" I asked, horrified. "That's even worse!"

"No, my dear. What he does is right up your alley. Helio specializes in search and rescue missions. He handles the cases too small for the Enforcers to take on, but either so complex their solution has eluded local authorities, or with so few clues or probable cause that no official law enforcement will take the case. Having someone with your skill set by his side would be perfect for Helio."

"Okay," I said slowly, my imagination running wild with countless possibilities. "That does sound exciting. So, you would need to talk to him to confirm if we're a match?"

"Yes, I would, although I'm pretty convinced you are a match. However, there is something you need to know," he quickly added, when my face lit up with excitement.

"What?" I asked, worry creeping into my voice. "Don't tell me he might be engaged or married?"

Kayog snorted and shook his head. "No. Or rather, that is highly unlikely. The last time we talked, there was definitely no one of significance in his life. The problem is that you do not qualify for the PMA program."

My jaw dropped, and I stared at him with a crestfallen expression. "What? Why?"

"The Edocits are not a primitive or endangered species," he explained. "As your union wouldn't benefit the UPO, directly or even remotely indirectly, I cannot enter it as a PMA marriage."

"So you can't help me?" I asked disbelievingly. Had he just dangled the promise of my happily ever after only to shout 'Syke!' once he had me hooked?

Kayog smiled in an indulgent fashion, looking amused by my outrage. "That is *not* what I'm saying, Maeve. *I* will help you, but merely as Kayog Voln, not as the Lead Agent of the Prime Mating Agency. That means you will not receive any dowry or enjoy any of the benefits usually afforded to the candidates. That includes traveling to him—or him to you—at your own collective expense."

Half the tension tightening my shoulders loosened, but I held off crying victory just yet. "That's fine. If we're a match, I can get to him, and I'm sure he can get to me. But what does that mean for the other rules?"

"Since the UPO doesn't take on any of the financial burden of your pairing, you're technically free to ignore all the rules," Kayog replied.

"But?" I insisted.

"But we have established them for a reason," he explained in a serious tone. "They genuinely help the couples establish strong foundations early on. Therefore, while I cannot contractually demand that you follow them, I strongly suggest that you do."

"Meaning giving this relationship a six-month trial and sex on the first night?" I asked.

Kayog smiled mischievously. "Yes. Don't make it sound like such a burden. Coupling with your soulmate is supposed to be one of the nice perks of any union."

My face heated. Although I'd brought it up first, it was super awkward talking about sex with Kayog. It felt like having the birds and the bees talk with your dad or grandfather. And yet, my stupid mouth couldn't leave it alone.

"Right, but Kaida didn't sleep with Cedros right away," I challenged.

"Her situation was very different. Kaida had entered into that union to avert a diplomatic disaster that could have led to an ugly war. *You* are willingly marrying the male I believe is your soulmate."

"But what if it doesn't work?" I asked.

Kayog took on a smug expression. "When it comes to pairings, I'm *never* wrong."

"But what if you are this time?" I insisted.

The Temern narrowed his eyes at me. "After I've spoken

with Helio and confirmed he is indeed your soulmate, should your union fail, I will personally pay for your relocation and find you a new match."

"That sounds fair," I said, pleased by the level of confidence Kayog expressed. Obviously, I *wanted* him to find me the perfect match. "However, I will have lost my job."

"Then don't quit. Once I've confirmed you're a match, request a sabbatical, if that makes you feel better. In the end, you *will* quit," Kayog said with a grin.

I couldn't help but smile. "So an Edocit?"

"Yes, my dear!" the Temern said in a sing-song voice. "Give me a couple of weeks to meet him in person again, and I'll be able to give you a definitive verdict."

"Two weeks?! That's forever!" I exclaimed.

Kayog burst out laughing. "Good things come to those who wait. Be patient, Maeve. Helio is worth it."

CHAPTER 2

HELIO

A human… Kayog had paired me with a fierce human female, who also happened to be a seasoned fighter, an expert hacker, and a galactic protector. It was like the Maker had designed her specifically for me. And according to the Temern, it appeared to be the case. I was beside myself with excitement.

In one of my far too rare chance meetings with Kayog, I had hinted at my potential interest in retaining his services. Hearing my uncle constantly praising the Temern and the Prime Mating Agency for the amazing work they had done with pairing Serena with Szaro, and preventing a diplomatic disaster, had made me want to see if he could also perform his magic for me. Unfortunately, the chances of him finding the type of mate I wanted and needed likely wouldn't come from one of the primitive species he worked with.

Therefore, receiving an impromptu message stating he had likely found my soulmate had completely taken me by surprise. I never thought he'd keep me in mind. People paid fortunes for the services of far less reliable mating agencies. And yet, the Temern had assisted us for free, merely for the pleasure of knowing he had helped form yet another happy couple.

I ran a nervous hand over my dark green hair, adjusting the placement of the tiny vines interspersed between the strands. I had willed the leaves to stand proudly, which would make me prettier—at least by Edocit standards. Sadly, I had no control over the tiny buds that grew on my vines. Powerful emotions made them bloom. That made us truly attractive, not to mention the enticing spores they released.

I could still control my sweat glands. They released a pleasant fragrance that could be relaxing, seductive, or behave as an aphrodisiac based on its concentration and whether I mixed it with other hormones.

Seconds later, my armband beeped with an incoming message from Kayog informing me they were on their way. My heart leapt, and I squared my shoulders, trying to look more imposing but not intimidating. I released a small amount of my seductive fragrance while debating whether to leave my arms hanging on each side of my body or clasp my hands behind my back. I was being ridiculous and overthinking everything. But I only had one chance of making a good first impression.

As promised, a giant black portal opened in the middle of my garden, only a few meters in front of me. Although I had expected it, I couldn't help but be impressed by this grand entrance. Kayog stepped through the portal, followed by three human females and a dragon-like male whose species I believed to be called Derakeens. As soon as the male appeared, he waved a hand in a dismissive gesture, and the portal collapsed.

While curious about my temporary guests, I couldn't pull my gaze away from my mate. She was even more beautiful in person than in the 3D hologram Kayog had shown me a week ago. She had the darkest, silky black hair falling to the middle of her back, with big, almond-shaped eyes of the same color. Her brown skin shared the delicate shade of the luxurious sculptures our artists carved out of Seilish trees. If not for the absence of *veris* on her skin and of vines in her hair, she could have passed for a daughter of the Seilish tribes.

To my utter delight, Maeve seemed just as fascinated by me as I was by her. The approving and appreciative way in which her gaze roamed over me lit a delectable fire in the pit of my stomach. Our eyes locked, and she gave me a timid smile, to which I responded in kind.

"Such a pleasure to see you again, Helio," Kayog said, breaking the magic.

I forced my gaze away from my woman to warmly welcome the Temern. "Greetings, Master Kayog," I said, pressing my right hand to my heart while slightly bowing my head.

To my surprise, instead of looking me straight in the eye, Kayog stared at my hair. His stiff beak stretched into a broad grin.

"You flowered!" he exclaimed. "If I didn't know better, I'd believe my charming presence stirred such a lovely response from you."

I chuckled, my right hand instinctively flying up to my hair and gently caressing the soft petals of one of the small buds on my vines that had indeed bloomed.

"While I won't deny that I do like you well enough, I'm sorry to say that another stirred such powerful emotions from me for this to happen," I said teasingly before casting a meaningful glance towards my mate.

She lowered her eyes timidly, seeming both flattered and embarrassed as she tucked a lock of her long black hair behind her ear. The younger human female of Asian descent behind her pressed herself against the Derakeen while smiling happily at my mate.

"Under different circumstances, my feelings might have been hurt," Kayog said in an amused voice. "But in this instance, I wholeheartedly approve. Helio, let me introduce you to the lovely Maria Maeve Riley, your bride. Maeve, please meet your betrothed, Helio Breisa."

"It is a tremendous honor to meet you, Maeve. You are even more beautiful in person," I said in all sincerity. "I can't wait to get to know you better. I have heard nothing but praise about the work of the Enforcers."

"It's an honor to meet you as well, Helio," Maeve said in a deliciously throaty voice. "From what I hear, you are also doing wonderful work protecting and rescuing others. I can't wait to get to know you better as well."

"And this is Kaida, Maeve's Enforcer teammate and friend, and her husband Cedros, who was kind enough to provide us with instant transportation here," Kayog said, once more breaking the magic.

Still, it shamed me to be acting like such a poor host. I nodded at the attractive Asian woman, with dark brown hair and eyes who he had called Kaida, and then at her husband, the Derakeen.

"Welcome to my home, Kaida. And thank you Cedros for bringing my mate to me in such a rapid and impressive fashion," I added in a friendly tone.

To my surprise, where Kaida smiled at me amiably, her mate sternly leveled his reptilian gaze on me. Covered in golden scales, he towered over me by at least a good head, his dark wings and the mix of golden and shadowy horns on his head making him look both regal and intimidating. Before I could dwell further on his cold demeanor, Kayog drew my attention to the third human female to traverse the portal with them.

"And last, but not least, please meet Isobel Biondi, the priestess who will preside over your union," Kayog said.

I was still baffled by what I believed to be Cedros acting as the disapproving big brother. He and Maeve clearly weren't related. However, as she was his mate's close friend, I could see why he could feel overprotective of her. Casting those thoughts aside, I turned to the priestess.

She beamed at me. Olive-skinned, with dark green eyes in a narrow oval face, the slender woman gracefully approached us while flicking a lock of her long dirty blonde hair streaked with silver strands over her shoulder.

Kayog chuckled, drawing our collective attention. "My dear Isobel, I believe this is one of the rare times you do not look distraught by an unusual pairing of mine," he said in a gently teasing tone.

The priestess blushed and gave the Temern a sheepish look. "While I never doubt the accuracy of your matches—proven countless times over by history—this is the first time I can clearly see that a couple is a perfect match. I don't know how you do it with the other pairings you do, but with these two, you'd have to be a machine not to feel the chemistry between them."

I couldn't help a grin before glancing at my mate. She, too, was looking at me. I never believed in love at first sight. Obviously, I wasn't in love with Maeve. But the instant chemistry and connection between us were undeniable. I could only pray that this wondrous energy would keep growing with each passing day.

In truth, I had worried she'd found my appearance unappealing. Although many species deemed Edocits attractive, the fact that vines, leaves, and flowers grew in various places on our bodies often disturbed off-worlders. They found various semi-diplomatic ways of saying that enjoying the beauty of a tree or a plant doesn't mean you want to bed it.

"Helio, Maeve, please stand face-to-face and hold each other's hands," Priestess Biondi said in a solemn tone.

Maeve met me halfway. The way she looked at me made me tingle in all the right places. I didn't consider myself remarkable in terms of Edocit beauty standards. I was attractive enough but not a stunner. Still, what she saw seemed to please Maeve. She certainly pleased me.

She placed her hands in mine, and I instinctively gave them a little squeeze. Despite their softness, her hands held me firmly. I liked that. The familiar pinching sensation stung my forearms as I willed my *veris*—the vines laying dormant just below my skin—to extrude and spread, wrapping around both our hands and stopping a little above Maeve's wrists.

For a split second, I held my breath, worried about how my woman would respond to this. Some off-worlders got freaked by our floral affinities and traits. Maeve looked down at our bound hands with an air of surprise quickly replaced by one of awe. That spread another wave of warmth through my chest, which instantly resulted in more buds flowering around our hands. My mate's lips parted with delight. Her eyes flicked up to lock with mine. The way she stared at me as if I was the greatest wonder in the world turned me upside down.

"Wow! That's lovely," Priestess Biondi said, her eyes glued to the white flowers of our binding vines.

My face heated with pleasure. "Thank you," I replied to her.

I didn't fail to notice the amused look Kayog was casting towards the priestess. Apparently, she was behaving differently than what he was used to. But then she did admit we were the first couple she could clearly see was a perfect match. However, where Kaida seemed to share the priestess' enthusiasm, the dragon still seemed a little distant, if not suspicious.

"We are gathered here to celebrate the union of this woman, Maria Maeve Riley, and this Edocit male, Helio Breisa, in the sacred bond of marriage. Such union must be entered into freely, with honest intentions, a genuine commitment, and not for financial gains or deceptive purposes," the priestess said. "Maria Maeve Riley, do you freely and willingly take this Edocit male, Helio Breisa, to be your lawfully wedded husband, for better or for worse, through good times and hardships, in sickness and in health, until death do you part?"

"I do," Maeve said in a breathy voice, as if she was trying to rein in a powerful emotion threatening to overwhelm her.

"Helio Breisa, do you freely take this woman, Maria Maeve Riley, to be your lawfully wedded wife, for better or for worse, through good times and hardships, in sickness and in health, until death do you part?"

"I most certainly do," I replied, my voice a little deeper than usual as my gaze remained locked with my mate's.

"Kaida Daigo and Cedros Qhelian, do you bear witness that this human female, Maria Maeve Riley, and this Edocit male, Helio Breisa, freely committed to be legally married to each other in accordance with human and galactic laws?"

"I do," Kaida said.

"I do," Cedros echoed.

"By the power vested in me by the Clerical College of Earth and the United Planets Organization, I declare you husband and wife. Helio Breisa, you may kiss the bride," Priestess Biondi said.

I unbound our hands so that I could draw Maeve closer to me. She came willingly, placing her palms on my shoulders. The heat of her touch burned right through the thin fabric of my shirt. With one hand on her hip, I cupped her nape with the other as I lowered my face towards hers. Lifting her chin, she once more met me halfway.

A bolt of lust exploded in the pit of my stomach the moment our lips touched. I swallowed back the moan that wanted to rise in my throat, reined in my urge to deepen the kiss, and clamped down on my glands wanting to release more seduction pheromones. Now wasn't the time. And yet, the way her fingers sank into my shoulders as if she, too, was fighting a strong physiological response to our kiss only made it harder.

I ended the kiss but didn't release Maeve right away. She

didn't seem particularly eager to move away from me either. But the thunder of applause from our witnesses snapped us out of our entranced daze. I moved one step away, and Maeve turned around to smile almost timidly at our guests.

Kayog approached us with a beaming expression. He didn't stop by our side but lured us a little further away in the garden. It made me smile, considering Priestess Biondi likely already knew what he had to say, and Kaida and Cedros had gone through the exact same process. Still, I appreciated him seeking to give us some privacy to discuss personal matters.

"Normally, this is when I give sugar-coated threats to the couple, warning them to honor the terms of the contract for fear of serious repercussions. Which I then soothe with promises of a fancy dowry on top of eternal love," the Temern said with self-derision.

Maeve snorted while I chuckled.

"No threats for us?" I asked, pretending to be crushed.

"Sorry, none for you," Kayog replied in the same amused voice. "You know which guidelines the PMA follows, but as you are not officially clients of the agency, we waive all standard bonding requirements. We proceeded to the human wedding only because it provides several protections for Maeve should things turn sour, as well as make things simpler from a human resources point of view with the Enforcers. As an Edocit wedding is permanently binding, we would have waived that requirement until the six months are over."

"Is that what you suggest? We should wait?" Maeve asked in a very serious tone.

"Yes, but only because of the spiritual and physiological aspect of such a bonding," Kayog said in a gentle tone. "There is absolutely no doubt in my mind that you two are soulmates. So do not worry about possibly regretting at some point that you performed the binding right away, should you decide to go that route. However, I believe it will be a lot more special if you save it for a little later, once you are truly in love."

"I agree," I said in a soft voice, which had Maeve looking at me questioningly. "Edocits do not just marry each other, they marry the land and the bloodline. You become a part of it as much as it becomes a part of you."

"Okay, that sounds a little intense," Maeve said cautiously.

I snorted. "I will teach you everything about us, and about your new world, Zailia."

"I look forward to it," Maeve said with an enthusiastic smile.

"Well, on this cheerful note, I will take my leave and let you make each other's acquaintance," Kayog said. "Thank you for reminding me how wonderful it is to simply match soulmates without a secondary agenda."

"What *is* your usual agenda?" Maeve asked, her Enforcer side peeking to the surface.

The Temern gave her an enigmatic look. "Isn't it obvious? Making people happy and keeping the vulnerable from being exploited."

Maeve snorted. "Spoken like a true politician. You seem to forget that I work for the UPO. While they do wonderful things for the galactic alliance, they are no saints."

Kayog smiled. "No one is, my dear. No one."

With these enigmatic words, he turned around to rejoin our other guests. We tagged along, stopping near Kaida and Cedros.

"Here's a little wedding present from all of us Enforcers," Kaida said while extending a prettily wrapped box to my mate. "It took us a while to figure out what a woman—who already has everything—and her bounty hunter husband could possibly want. In the end, Tedrick came up with this idea. Go on, open it!"

Feeling as curious as Maeve seemed, I stepped a little closer to my mate while she rather brutally tore the paper—which I took from her. As soon as she opened the box, her gasp echoed my shock. Within, a matching his and hers set of black bracers glimmered under the single sun of Zailia. A glance sufficed to recognize them as being designed by Xurgens—the most advanced species in the known galaxy. Nothing surpassed the quality of their high-tech products, from spaceships to weapons, to suits, and everything else in-between. This was a kingly gift.

"Are you kidding me?" Maeve whispered in disbelief. "These are insanely expensive!"

"Are you implying you deserve less?" Kaida asked in a teasing fashion. "Everyone pitched in, which made it quite manageable. And we had the design customized to meet your every need while running around chasing after bad guys. You'll want to read the manual."

"You guys are freaking amazing," Maeve said, her eyes misting.

The two women hugged, and my heart melted at the beautiful tableau.

"Thank you," I said once they released each other. "It is an extremely generous gift."

"It's our pleasure. Just keep our girl happy," Kaida said amiably.

"Indeed," Cedros said in a slightly dubious tone. Before I could respond, he also extended a box to my mate. "This is a present from Kaida and me. Open it."

"Seriously, guys, after this first crazy gift, I didn't need a second one," Maeve argued, even as she eagerly opened the box.

I remained baffled at the sight of four rows of narrow black stones next to a small tool that resembled a nutcracker.

Maeve's head jerked up as she gaped at them in disbelief. "Shadow obsidian stones?!"

Kaida and her mate simultaneously nodded.

"Yes. The first three rows are marked on the terrace of our dwelling on Dramnac," Cedros explained. "Those from the last row will open a portal to the Enforcers' HQ. The portal will form instantly, if you ever need it. Your bracer also has a direct line to me. Should you be in any type of distress, no matter how far you are, the signal will travel through however many relays are necessary to reach me, and I will come at once."

I didn't miss the way his dragon eyes flicked my way when he said "any type of distress." Did he think I would harm my mate in any way? I couldn't decide whether to be offended or amused.

"Thanks, Cedros. You two are the best," Maeve said warmly.

"Well, we're going to leave you now," Kaida said affectionately. "The team won't be the same without you. Don't be a stranger."

"I won't," Maeve promised, while giving her friend one last parting hug.

The whole time, Cedros's gaze weighed heavily on me. I once more bit back the urge to call him out on his suspicious attitude. Causing a fuss on my wedding day didn't seem like a good idea. Then seeing Kayog wrap his hand around his beak in the way bird folk often did, either as a sign of contrition or to repress a laugh, told me the situation amused him. I glared at the Temern, which only had his shoulders shaking from silent laughter.

"Goodbye, Helio. Take good care of my girl," Kaida said in a soft voice.

"I certainly will," I replied in a friendly but determined tone.

Cedros gave me a sharp nod then flicked his hand. A massive black portal opened in front of us with a swishing sound. For half a beat, dark shadows swirled before the center cleared to show a stunning terrace on what appeared to be the ledge of a cliff high in an opal-colored shimmering sky.

Our guests filed in. Cedros entered last before sending through a hover platform ladened with crates, no doubt containing my mate's belongings. Seconds later, the portal disappeared. Impressed by such incredible powers, I stared at the now vacant spot where the portal had appeared before turning my attention back to my mate. By the way Maeve was observing me, I could tell a million thoughts were going off in her mind. Thankfully, they didn't seem to be negative in nature.

"Your friend Kaida is charming," I said in a conversational tone.

"Only Kaida?" Maeve asked, raising an eyebrow with a hint of challenge.

"Her husband is quite impressive," I added in a non-committal fashion.

Maeve snorted. "That sounds like the diplomatic response of a politician."

I chuckled and bowed my head in concession. "You are correct. Do you want the blunt answer?"

"Always," Maeve said in a firm tone. "Give me an ugly truth any day over a pretty lie."

I nodded with approval. "In that, we are the same. I merely found that he was overly protective of you and excessively suspicious of me. Had he not been mated, and visibly happily so, I might have thought Cedros wanted you for himself."

Maeve burst out laughing, her disbelieving expression wiping out any lingering doubt I might have had about a potential bond between them.

"He's all but adopted me as his baby sister, and that's why he's being so protective," Maeve said, amused. "And those gifts are exceptional. Having a quick way out of a sticky spot is very useful."

"True," I conceded. "I can never begrudge you having such a powerful friend."

"That's all thanks to Kaida. We are part of the same Enforcer team. Kaida is Cedros's Ejaya. There's only a single female in the entire universe who can form this special bond with him. Shadow Lords like him, who fail to find their Ejaya before the age of fifty, usually go insane or die from blood poisoning that only her presence could have allowed his body to fight back.

Those two are so in love, it's ridiculous. Seeing what a perfect match Kayog had made for them convinced me to reach out to him so that he could find my perfect mate."

"And perfect he certainly found for you," I said with playful smugness as I waved my hand at my body.

Maeve laughed while giving me a shameless once over. "I don't know about perfect. Only time will tell. But you're easy on the eyes and clearly confident."

"It's just a front," I said in all honesty. "I can get quite timid in personal settings. I'm only tough and confident in a hunt or combat situation. But I'm glad that you like what you see. I think you are breathtaking."

She took on an embarrassed expression and demurely lowered her eyes while smiling shyly. "You flatter me."

"We agreed I would only say the blunt truth, remember?" I asked teasingly. "Therefore, it is not flattery."

Her smile broadened, and she locked eyes with me. "If you're trying to make me like you, you're off to an excellent start."

"Glad to hear it! Now how about I give you a tour of your new home, and then we can bring your stuff inside and get you settled in?" I asked.

"That would be lovely. This garden is incredible," Maeve said with enthusiasm. "You must spend a crazy amount of time just tending to it to achieve such perfection."

"Not at all," I said with an amused grin. "I do tend to the garden but not the way you think. I do not have to weed, prune, or any other such things. When I mentioned that marrying with an Edocit also means marrying the land, it was quite literal. We are one with the land. It tells us what it needs, and we provide it."

Maeve frowned, taken aback by my response. "I'm not sure I understand what you mean. When you say that it tells you what *it needs*, are you actually implying the plants talk to you?"

My smile broadened as I nodded. "That's correct. I can communicate with any plant, herb, flower, but more strongly with trees. We do not speak in words, although some of them will understand my spoken words. For the others, it will be more visual and sensory messages."

Maeve's jaw dropped. She stared at me in disbelief for a second before looking at the surrounding flora with the oddest mix of awe and worry etched on her pretty face.

"Are you saying that your plants are sentient? Are they looking at us right now and listening to our conversation?"

I burst out laughing. "No, Maeve. Or rather, not in the way you imply. Most of the flowers, bushes, small trees, and grass do not qualify as sentient. They cannot form thoughts or hold conversations. Their communications with me are nothing more than instinctive reactions in response to their needs."

I stepped out of my sandals so that I could walk barefoot on the grass. Gesturing for my mate to follow, I walked towards a bed of flowers by the pond.

"For example, this snakeberry bush is thirsty. I know just by the way the leaves hang down instead of perking upwards. Technically, it shouldn't be the case, considering the bush has direct access to the water from the pond. This tells me there is either a problem with the water itself, or something else in the soil surrounding the flower's roots. If I focus on the other flowers surrounding it, they are fine. Therefore, the water is not at fault."

Maeve gasped when the 'veins' around my feet and just above my ankles appeared to swell before the vine-like tentacles of my *veris* extruded from my skin and buried themselves into the ground.

I studied her features to see how she was responding to this display of one of my abilities. To my relief, Maeve did not look turned off, merely stunned.

"This allows me to directly communicate with nature on a wider radius," I explained in a soft tone. "I do not need to dig to see what is happening. My *veris* allow me to detect the pH imbalance in this area of the soil. It's too alkaline. But as that acidity is almost surgically localized, it tells me that the snakeberry bush is being attacked by a parasite. The spoolworm is usually the culprit, chewing its deep roots, making it difficult for the bush to drink sufficient water. The alkaline soil also makes it harder for it to get enough nutrients."

"Oh wow! So you have to connect to the soil regularly to know what plant needs help?"

I shook my head. "No. I have nothing to do in this instance. You see the small herbs with four leaves close to the ground?" I asked, pointing at them.

"You mean the shamrocks?" she asked.

I smiled. "We call them kinniks. While they resemble your clover leaves, they mostly serve as natural pest control. If you look closely, you will notice tiny bulbs beneath the leaves. They release spores that attract burnums."

"Burnums?" Maeve asked.

"Mmhmm. They are our version of a mole. The closest thing I could compare them to is a miniature Earth seal with six small legs. They have vicious claws that allow them to dig through the soil and hunt prey. Their favorite delicacy is spoolworm."

Maeve's eyes widened in understanding. "The kinniks call the little moles to the rescue?"

"Yes," I said with a grin. "As soon as they perceive the distress from the snakeberry, they release their spores. The soil is almost saturated with them. The burnums will be here soon. A properly designed garden is a self-sufficient ecosystem where each plant serves a purpose, with interdependencies that compel them to protect each other."

"Wow, that's nifty. But how do the kinniks benefit from helping the snakeberries?" my mate asked with curiosity.

I gave her an approving smile, pleased by her apparent genuine interest. "A variety of small creatures—mostly insects and some birds—feed from the berries. The leecha—which could be compared to a distant cousin of Earth's spittlebugs—particularly loves the berries. After they've eaten, they hide under the kinniks and spit back the skin of the berry in a pink foam as they cannot digest it. That foam overflows with nutrients for the kinniks, and the digestive acid within kills any weeds that could attempt to grow in that area."

"That's freaking brilliant!" Maeve exclaimed, staring at the garden with new eyes.

"It would take too long for me to go over how each plant and tree work in symbiosis. But we have a lifetime for you to learn," I said with a smile. "Just rest assured that everything here is safe to touch, eat, or fall asleep next to."

She narrowed her eyes at me. "Meaning that plants elsewhere could be dangerous?"

I chuckled. "Half of the planet will try to kill or eat you, unless you know how to stay out of trouble."

Although she frowned at me, Maeve didn't seem frightened by my bold statement, which tremendously pleased me. She looked around, glanced up at the sky, then back at me with a mischievous expression.

"If not for the two moons up there, I would have wondered if Cedros hadn't accidentally brought us to Australia instead of Zailia," Maeve said teasingly.

"Australia?" I asked, confused.

"A country on Earth where absolutely every creature is hellbent on killing you somehow," she replied in an amused tone.

"Sounds like my kind of place," I said before waving at the pond. "It is okay to swim in the pond. It contains freshwater. You'll notice tiny holes around some edges and at the bottom."

"Let me guess… Tiny fish live in there and maintain the pH of the water?"

I laughed. "Not fish, but crustaceans," I corrected. "They

only come out at night, and they also eat any bug or other biological debris that might dirty the water."

"Efficient!"

"Very," I said with a nod. "Now, before we go inside, I would like to show you the Mother Tree," I said, gesturing proudly at the magnificent tree in the center of the garden and walking in its direction. "She is a fenora tree, easily recognizable by the massive, but narrow roots that spread far and wide aboveground, as well as the braided trunk and the unusual knot. We merely refer to her as Myma."

"Myma? She? Her? You talk about the tree as if it's a person," Maeve said.

"Because she is," I replied matter-of-factly. "She isn't a person like you and I are, but she's sentient. Myma cannot hold a conversation or think in complex patterns like we do. Her communications are more basic. However, she feels joy, sadness, hurt, and anger, among other things. She will console, nurture, and heal you if you need it."

"Whoa!" Maeve whispered when some of the tangled roots of the tree shifted to make a passage for us.

My mate cautiously followed me until we reached the tree. I placed my hand on the smooth bark, the same soft brown color as my skin. My palm immediately tingled as Myma greeted me. Multiple *veris* extruded from the back of my hand and intertwined with the vines lazily wrapped around the braids of the bark. An affectionate smile stretched my lips as pure love seeped inside of me through our connection.

I turned to my female and slipped my free arm around her, drawing her next to me. "Myma, meet my mate, Maeve. Maeve, meet Myma."

My poor woman seemed a little unsure as to how to react to what had to be the strangest introduction. She gave me an uncertain look before turning her attention back to the tree. In that instant, I realized Maeve was wondering if I was teasing her by having her speak to a tree. To my delight, she played along.

"It is a pleasure to meet you, Myma," Maeve said with the appropriate level of deference one would show a mother-in-law.

Which, in many ways, is the case.

Myma emitted a deep, rumbling sound, startling my woman. She then shook her leaves, making them whistle in a happy chant while her buds bloomed with the same white flowers that adorned my hair whenever powerful positive emotions swept through me. My heart soared to have Myma so soundly express her approval.

"She likes you," I said with a proud grin. "Put your hand on her bark. Let her embrace you."

Looking awed and a little intimidated, Maeve nevertheless complied. Her lips parted in surprise as she undoubtedly felt Myma's greeting, seconds before her vines wrapped around Maeve's hand like they had done to mine.

"Whoa, what am I feeling?" Maeve asked with an air of wonder.

"Myma's love and affection," I said in a soft voice. "She's claiming you as her daughter."

"Daughter? Did she also claim you as her son?" Maeve asked.

"I *am* her son," I said calmly. "Although, technically, you could say that I'm her mother's son."

Maeve froze, her mind seeming to go blank for a moment while she processed my words. "What do you mean by that? As far as I know, Edocits actually have parents like humans, a male and female coming together to make a baby. You're not saying that this tree's mother gave birth to you, right?"

My smile broadened. "I'm saying yes and yes to both your statement and question," I replied teasingly. "I have an Edocit mother and father, who you will meet soon. But their Myma—

my Nyna—gave my final birth to me. Edocits only spend the first eight weeks of gestation inside their mother's womb."

Sensing my wish, Myma unwrapped her vines from around my hand, freeing it. I ran my fingers over the naturally artistic roping of the bark around her knot.

"We need a deep contact with the land and nature to properly develop," I explained. "Without it, I wouldn't have possessed some of the abilities that you will see me display in the upcoming days. Even the way I spread my *veris* to assess the needs of the plant would have been stunted."

Maeve swallowed hard, for the first time showing some sort of unease about my nature. "And how exactly does the fetus go from the mother's womb to the knot in the tree?" she asked in a concerned voice.

I stared at her for a moment, my occasionally irrational need to tease and needle coming to the fore. "You're wondering if I have a weird cock with a tip that opens up like a flower, grabs the embryo out of your womb like a grappling hook, and then yanks it back out?"

My attempt at remaining serious miserably failed at the sight of her horrified expression. I burst out laughing.

"No, Maeve. You do not have to worry about me sticking my private parts inside a tree to unload our offspring," I said mockingly. "You also don't have to worry about strange vines wiggling out of you when the little one is ready to come out."

"If you're trying to traumatize me and make me call Cedros to haul me out of here ASAP, you're sure doing a fine job," my mate said, glaring at me, although without genuine anger. "Now stop teasing me. What really happens?"

"At eight weeks, you will go into labor," I explained in a more serious tone. "It is nothing like human labor. You will not feel pain, and your part will be done in a very short time. The actual work is for the sprout. Although Myma will offer our offspring a bit of help, the sprout must make most of the effort to climb into the maturing knot."

"Our baby will walk and climb after only eight weeks of gestation?" Maeve asked with an air of disbelief.

"Yes," I said, amused. "Many species are born with the ability to walk within seconds of their birth. Don't humans have creatures that are born only partially formed and depend on their mother to nurture them while they go through their second phase?"

Maeve pursed her lips while nodding slowly as she reflected on my words. "Now that you mention it, a lot of birds hatch half-finished. Their parents must keep them warm while their feathers grow and feed them until they're mature enough to fly. But what you're describing sounds almost like kangaroos and koalas. Their babies come out almost at an embryonic stage, then climb into their mother's pouch where they finish growing. Your planet sounds more and more like Australia."

Although I chuckled, I continued to study her features to get a better sense of how she felt about this. "Does this disturb you?"

"Disturb? No, that's too strong a term. However, I admit I had not imagined that at all. I have some mixed feelings about it. A part of me thinks it's awesome that I won't have the swelling, back pain, discomfort, and a very long and painful labor. The other part wonders if I won't feel cheated from having had so little time bonding with my child, and if the child will even consider me or the tree his mother. And the last part of me worries about the safety of the fetus inside a tree. If there is danger, a flood, a fire, or any other natural disaster, as a pregnant woman, I can get out of there and find shelter. But what can a tree do?"

I smiled. "First, I'm relieved that your initial comment was not to say you don't want children. Second, it is not because you're not carrying the child for the remainder of the gestation period that you cannot bond with it. You can interact with the fetus the same way fathers do in most species. And as for danger, our future offspring can never have a more powerful protector than a fenora tree. The entire garden possesses its own defense system. And as an Edocit child bonds with the land, even more protectors will be on standby should he or she ever have need of it."

Despite her slightly dubious expression, Maeve nodded. In due time, there was no question we would discuss the matter further in depth. But there would be plenty of opportunities for that in the future. For now, I intended to spend the next few months making sure my female would fall madly in love with me and I with her.

"So, you were born from a tree like her, but not her. Correct?" Maeve asked.

I nodded. "Correct. I grew Myma from an offshoot of Nyna, the Mother Tree who birthed me. I still go see her from time to time in my parents' garden. But come, my mate. Let me show you inside the house. There will be plenty of time for us to further discuss offspring when the time is right for both of us," I said, giving Myma one last caress before I ordered the hovercart to follow.

Maeve cast an uncertain glance at Myma, clearly unsure how to properly bid goodbye to a tree. I bit the inside of my cheeks to hide my amusement, not wanting her to think I was making fun of her. It had to be strange to suddenly have to treat something you've considered an inanimate—or at least not sentient—life form for your entire existence like a person. Imitating me, my mate gave Myma a gentle caress with a farewell smile.

Tagging alongside me, she stared with undisguised curiosity and awe at the large structure of our dwelling.

"Your house is beautiful. It matches how I pictured the house of a wood elf. Well, except that your plants are far more exotic, and quite a few are rather luminous."

I puffed out my chest proudly. "You are not the first human

to refer to our architecture as elven in style. That prompted me to look up some illustrations. I couldn't believe they were a mythical species considering how elaborately their lore and culture have been defined."

"It's not really surprising since they are extremely popular in fantasy and paranormal storytelling. When humanity finally achieved interstellar travel, we discovered that many off-worlder species shared a lot of those traits. It still amazes me every time I encounter a new culture."

"Well, you're about to be served because our dwelling only shares parts of its aesthetic with the elves of human lore," I said mysteriously. I waved at the large, ornate doors in the form of an arch. "We build every house on Zailia with shift wood."

"Shift wood?" she echoed. "I thought it was some sort of plasticine or modeling clay, not actual wood."

I chuckled while shaking my head. "It's a common misunderstanding. Shift wood is a special type of wood that we harvest from nuvean trees. It bends and shifts its shape according to our will. It takes a great deal of coaxing, made a lot easier through bonding. Edocits become one with the wood. I embedded part of my DNA in the walls."

"Wow. So I guess you communicate with it the same way you do with the plants, with those vines you call *veris*?" Maeve asked.

"Yes, although it is mostly for healing, or if I want to use some of the more complex features of this bond. The house is alive. It will know if I am hurt and protect the people that I love from intruders."

Maeve froze, her gaze roaming over the house with the same uneasy expression she'd had when I told her about Myma. For the first time, I regretted how little information we publicly shared about our species and culture. But there were good reasons for that. Even though we had no real galactic enemies, sharing the extent of our closeness with—if not dependence on

—the land with off-worlders could leave us extremely vulnerable to biological warfare.

"How alive is the house? Is it as sentient as your mother tree?" Maeve asked.

I laughed and shook my head. "The house is not sentient the way Myma is," I explained gently. "It cannot eavesdrop on us or spy on our privacy, if that's what you're worried about. Shift wood is the equivalent of a smart home and acts the same way as the artificial intelligence integrated in your dwellings. The difference is that you build it with various materials and electronics. We grow ours over years alongside our mother tree and garden."

"So I guess you guys don't move around a lot, do you?" Maeve asked.

I snorted. "That we don't. You spend decades building your home. It is very much your forever home that one of your offspring will inherit and reshape as he or she sees fit. The others will start growing their own as of the age of eight."

"Eight? Isn't that too young to own a house?"

"It doesn't become a house for at least a decade," I replied reassuringly. "It is something they devote a few hours a week to, the rest of their time spent being a normal child. Come, let's go inside."

CHAPTER 3
MAEVE

Saying I was feeling some cultural shock right now would be the understatement of the millennia. I wouldn't say that I'd entered a real-world nightmare, but the initial fairy tale of my wedding to Helio was quickly losing some of its dreamy glow. Had we rushed too quickly into this marriage? Since the PMA rules didn't apply to us, should we have just dated the traditional way first?

Kayog is never wrong in his pairing. Why punish ourselves by delaying needlessly?

My husband was hot, charming, and appeared to have a mischievous personality that I rather liked. However, I had not expected there to be such major differences between our cultures. I'd run into so many Edocits while performing my duties as an Enforcer, all of them living seamlessly in a fashion similar to ours, that I always assumed their lifestyle and general society functioned the same way ours did.

I had no problem adapting to new things, but I suspected that a heck of a lot of them were about to get thrown at me back-to-back.

The tree baby business messed with my head. Too many

thoughts and emotions swirled within me at that prospect. I eventually wanted kids, and this certainly wasn't how I'd pictured it going down. Anyway, dwelling over it now served no purpose. Like Helio said, we had plenty of time to cross that bridge in the future.

The imposing ornate doors parting before us swept away those concerns as the large room took my breath away.

Once more, I got a powerful impression of having entered the magical world of the elves. The light-beige color of the polished wood made the open concept of the room look spacious and luminous. Swirly patterns in strategic places appeared carved directly into the wood, but I suspected those ornaments had actually been "grown" or "coaxed" by Helio's will. Some vines and flowers ran along certain walls. It gave a lovely natural feel to our surroundings without giving the impression of being inside a jungle.

"These flowers are lovely," I said in all sincerity. "I believe they are the same as the ones that flowered on you earlier. Does the fresh scent inside the house come from them?"

Helio smiled proudly, his deep green—almost black—eyes devoid of sclera, admiring the floral adornment of his home. "It does. And yes, they are. It is one of the visible signs of my DNA in the house."

"Right," I said, trying to silence my unease at this concept of a living house.

After all, Helio's point about it being no different from the A.I. in our dwellings made complete sense. However, you could turn off the A.I. of a smart home if it ever got wonky. The same couldn't be done with a 'living' entity unless you killed or drugged it.

I frowned as a different thought crossed my mind. "With so many fragrant flowers, do bees and other bugs come inside the house?"

Helio chuckled. "Bees, no. But the flowers draw a different type of bug, if I may use that term very loosely."

"That sounds like a problem," I said, my worry going up another notch.

"It's not," he replied reassuringly. "Alibelles are more like semi-sentient fairies than bugs. The nectar from the flowers is a wonderful treat for them. Under different circumstances, these flowers would be deemed parasites, as I didn't will them there or plant them on the wall," Helio explained. "They appear of their free will in the pattern they desire. But they do not leech the shift wood and act instead in symbiosis with it. They grow where the structure needs the most alibelle magic, which it automatically gets when they come."

"I see," I replied, not only relieved, but now quite curious to see one of those little fairies.

"As an added bonus, the flowers' fragrance actually behaves as a bug repellent," Helio said.

"That certainly is a bonus," I said with a smile.

To my delight, standard furniture filled the living area and dining room sharing the wide space. As expected, all of it was made of ornate wood, with colorful plush cushions on top. I loved how effortless, peaceful, and relaxing the decor felt. After so much time spent traveling aboard the Enforcer space ships, with their dull gray walls and dark floors, a little bit of color was more than welcome.

Helio then took me to the next room, adjacent to the living area and dining room.

"Whoa. That is one gorgeous indoor garden," I whispered, amazed.

"Actually, this is a healing room," Helio said in that sexy voice of his. "Like any garden, we design the healing room so that the mix of plants will ensure the health of each other. However, these large pods alongside the walls are equivalent to your medical pods. You lie down inside, and they half bury you in the soil while tending to any wound or illness."

Dark green, almost black, with swirling narrow leaves around the edges, it vaguely reminded me of a giant carnivorous plant.

"Wait, I've seen these pods before," I exclaimed while searching my memory. "But I seem to recall people using them for rejuvenation in fancy spas."

My mate snorted. "Right. Some off-worlders have been reproducing our healing pods for those properties. Non-Edocits will get some benefits from it, but nowhere near as much as we do."

"Is this what keeps your species looking so incredibly young even when you're one hundred years old?" I asked, fascinated.

He nodded. "It is. However, we do not use it for that reason. It is just a beneficial side effect. Once you and I have fully bonded, I will pass on some of my abilities to you. The healing pods will then work on you as they do with us. So expect to look the same way you do right now, well into your nineties."

"Whoa! I'll take a full serving of that!" I said greedily.

Helio burst out laughing before caressing my cheek with the back of his hand. The tender gesture and the affectionate look in his eyes did funny things to me. Too soon, he dropped his hand, gesturing instead towards one of the three wide benches recessed into the wall.

"These are focus seats," Helio explained. "We sit there for meditation, for communion with the land, or to telepathically project our consciousness. It allows us to see far and wide through the land without having to physically be there. I will show you later."

"Do you have to be in this room to use those telepathic abilities?" I asked, beyond intrigued.

He shook his head. "No. However, farseeing leaves us in a vulnerable position. It is therefore preferable to do it in the safety of the healing room, or with someone watching over us when in the wild to avoid nasty surprises."

"This sounds like a fantastic ability to have. I can't wait to see you putting it to use," I said, making no effort to hide my curiosity as my mind bubbled with a million potential applications.

"Soon, my mate," he replied, leading me to the next room.

My wistful smile instantly faded at the sight of at least three dozen life-size animal statues.

"A trophy room?" I asked, confused. "Kayog said you were a *bounty* hunter, not a hunter."

"He's correct. I take no pleasure in hunting creatures, although I participated in a few hunts with my uncle to protect an ecosystem they were endangering," Helio said. "But these are not the stuffed remains of creatures I killed, but realistic replicas of creatures I recovered or helped rescue."

"Oh! Were they pets?" I asked, my initial disgust fading as I looked at the creatures with fresh eyes.

"Some are pets, others are either valuable or dangerous creatures stolen by poachers or smugglers. Each possesses a unique story that resonated with me, which is why I immortalized them here. My uncle, Bron Kflen, tried to get me to follow in his footsteps as a hunter. But killing creatures isn't for me."

"You can make a very comfortable living as a Federation hunter," I argued, despite my relief to see we were on the same page as far as hunting was concerned.

"True, but I don't chase wealth. I make a comfortable living doing what I do, and it is a lot more rewarding for me in the long run," Helio explained. "Most of my bounties are private rescues. Many of the families I assist give me what they can afford. Some can't afford anything, but I won't deny them assistance because they can't pay me. However, bounties set by government officials, law enforcement, or large corporations more than make up for those other hunts."

I smiled approvingly. "I like that. Justice for all shouldn't come with a price tag."

"I'm glad you approve, my mate. But fear not, I make more than enough for us and our future family to live comfortably. We will never want for anything."

I snorted. "In case you have forgotten, I have a career of my own. I can work too to help provide for the needs of our household."

He smiled. "Yes, you can. But I hope you will choose to work with me instead. I'm long overdue for a reliable partner. And you, my dear wife, seem to possess exactly the type of skills needed."

"I'm pretty sure I do," I said smugly. "You have a few months to convince me."

"Then I shall!" he replied with a confidence I found super sexy. "Off to the next room we go."

The doors parted on what I instantly recognized as the master bedroom. To my undying relief, a normal, four-poster king-size bed sat at the back of the room. A series of pale green vines served as draping instead of traditional curtains. Like every other room we had visited so far, large windows allowed for plenty of natural light. Aside from the nightstands, a standing mirror, and a dresser, the room didn't have the sitting area or breakfast table I often saw in master suites. That didn't bother me as I only ever used my bedroom to sleep.

My gaze lingered on the exquisite furniture, all also carved out of wood. I chewed my bottom lip, wondering how to ask the question that popped up in my head diplomatically.

"I noticed that all of your furniture is made of wood…" I said carefully.

"And you're wondering how a tree man could cut down trees?" he asked in a teasing tone.

I responded with a nervous laugh, then sheepishly nodded, relieved that he didn't appear offended by the question.

"We mostly carve our furniture from deadwood or driftwood. The rest we grow using nuvean saplings; the same type of shift wood used to grow our houses," he explained in a gentle tone. "But we do cut down trees from time to time if their growth creates an imbalance in their ecosystem, or if they're too sick to be cured and risk infecting other trees. However, if they are semi sentient, then we will uproot and relocate them."

"That makes sense," I said with a smile. "So I guess you are a hardcore environmental defender, huh?"

"Of course," he said with a grin. "You won't find bigger tree huggers than we are."

I chuckled.

"It is not just a moral choice," he continued in a more serious tone. "Edocits literally depend on the health of our world. If the land of our mother trees is sick, any toxin or disease will transfer to our offspring during their gestation. We also root regularly—what you saw me do earlier when I sank my *veris* into the ground. Doing so with diseased soil would make us sick as well."

He turned around and waved at the bed. "When I wake in the morning, or sometimes right before going to sleep, I will root in bed. Outside, I did it simply to check the state of my garden. Here, I use it more like what humans call the Internet. It gives me information about the planet's health, allows me to glimpse what is happening in other regions, as well as grant me access to the latest news."

"That sounds really cool," I said, genuinely impressed. "But I must admit I don't quite understand how that works."

"Unlike when we are accessing global networks through a computer or connected device, I am not downloading information, but I'm projecting my consciousness outward so that I can directly see, hear, or feel things happening at that given location."

"Oh wow! So it's almost like astral projection?"

Helio nodded. "Yes. That would be an apt comparison. Which is why we avoid doing it in the wild as our body remains vulnerable during that time. As long as there is a healthy natural plant in that area, we can project to it."

"Only healthy?" I repeated. "It doesn't work with the sick ones?"

"It would work, but we could come back with a virus, just like when you access an infected site," he replied.

"I see," I replied with a slow nod. "So keeping your world as healthy as possible reduces the risks of you projecting yourself straight into trouble."

"Among other things," he replied with a smile. "Now let me go show you the rest of the house."

After the initial introduction to the mother tree and the living house, I had expected a lot of weird rooms with freaky features that would have me scrambling for the exit. I had needlessly worried. Just like the master bedroom, the other rooms were very similar to human dwellings, with four other bedrooms, three hygiene rooms—four if you included the ensuite in the master bedroom—and a gourmet kitchen where I could picture myself getting creative.

The tour completed, Helio brought me back to our bedroom and helped me unpack my things. He had given me half of his spacious walk-in wardrobe. The few civilian outfits I had to hang in there made me feel slightly embarrassed.

Until now, I hadn't realized just how little socializing I actually did. I devoted most of my time to the Enforcers. The few times I had dated, I'd reused my five favorite outfits, considering most of the males I met rarely deserved more than a couple of dates for me to know they were not worth my time. Therefore, I felt no actual need to fill up my wardrobe.

"I want to take you to the town square," Helio suddenly said as soon as we finished unpacking my stuff. "But first, I want to have a look at the weather and activity there. It will only take a moment."

The mischievous way in which he spoke those words instantly made me suspicious. Then my jaw dropped when he removed his loose shirt. My blood heated at the sight of his muscular chest.

Like most Edocits, Helio didn't possess the bulky and brawny shape of a bodybuilder. He was more slender, with the defined muscles of a swimmer or fitness model. On his chest and sides, beautiful swirly patterns appeared to be embossed on his skin. On his arms, thick, ropy veins almost gave the impression of being roots poking at the surface.

By the smug and teasing way his lips stretched, my brand-new husband had noticed I enjoyed the view. It should have embarrassed me to be caught blatantly ogling him, but I felt no shame whatsoever. Anyway, he had clearly staged it, undoubtedly to prompt that specific reaction from me. For a reason I couldn't explain, an unnaturally strong connection had instantly formed between us.

To my surprise, Helio walked to the bed, and lay down on the left side before spreading his arms. My lips parted in a mix of shock and awe when the vines dangling as curtains from the posters of the bed began stretching towards my husband. From the root-like veins in his arms and feet, *veris* extruded to connect with the vines. But the ones entangling with the vines from his hair left me speechless.

His face went slack. Contrary to what I expected, he didn't close his eyes. They only took on this far away air one had when daydreaming. To my shame, my dirty mind immediately latched on to the fact that he looked bound to the bed. Saying it turned me on would be quite the understatement. I would love to have my way with him while he was this helpless. And although I didn't consider myself submissive in the slightest, the thought that he could restrain me in a similar fashion with his *veris* while getting his freak on had me tingling in all the right places.

The smug smile returned to his face, but this time with a sensual edge. "Enjoying the view, my mate?" he asked in a deep, rumbling voice.

I barely repressed a shocked expression. "I thought your consciousness was gone."

"You did not answer my question," he replied tauntingly.

"Yes, you're definitely easy on the eyes. And there's something quite sexy about you being bound like this," I replied in the same taunting fashion.

"It will be even sexier once I have *you* bound like this," he whispered, his voice dipping lower.

My ovaries instantly did a backflip while a bolt of fire exploded in my nether region. I shifted on my feet and squeezed my legs together to silence the dull throbbing his words had awakened. I was looking for a clever comeback but failed miserably. Thankfully, Helio spared me by shifting the topic.

"To answer *your* question, part of my consciousness has indeed left. The square is buzzing with activity, but it's not too crowded. You're going to love it."

"Wait, you can see the square right now?" I asked, baffled.

"Yes," he replied, his speech a little slower, not quite slurred. "I project my consciousness through the trees in the square. So long as we have contact with the soil, we can communicate and see far and wide, feel the air through it. So I can also tell you exactly what the weather is over there, down to the quality of the air."

"From what you said earlier, I thought you were blind to what was happening to your body and its surroundings," I said, confused.

"That's true if we go very deep, or if we project ourselves at a very great distance. Otherwise, we are aware of our surroundings. However, the farther away we go, the longer it takes for us to return and reclaim full control of our body. Therefore, we must do it in a safe environment. If a wild beast was coming at me, by the time I returned—and assuming it wasn't already butchering me—I would likely be too groggy to properly defend myself for the first critical moments."

I approached the bed and sat at the edge to have a closer look at the way the vines had connected with my husband.

"You can touch," Helio whispered.

I gave him a timid smile but didn't hesitate. I carefully ran my fingers over the ropy veins of his forearm whence the tendrils connected to the vines.

"This part feels almost like tree bark," I said in a soft voice, as if speaking to myself. "But then the rest of your skin is so soft. Does it hurt?"

He shook his head, his movements still slow as if he was half asleep. "No. My root ducts are only hard right now because I'm partially shifted to make the connection. Once I disconnect, they will soften like the rest of my skin."

As Helio spoke, the vines binding him detached from his *veris*, which retracted into his skin. I observed the phenomenon with wonder.

"I love the feel of your touch on me," he whispered, the tender way in which he said it turning me on far more than if he had done it in a lustful fashion.

Feeling my cheeks heating, I smiled then pulled my hand away. He stared at me for a moment with an unreadable expression before sitting at the edge of his bed, next to me. He paused there for a second, as one does after waking in the morning while trying to get their bearings.

Then another thought struck me. "So you could see everything happening through the trees," I said pensively. "That means any other Edocit could do the same. How do you ensure no one encroaches on your privacy? Doesn't that make it easy for anyone to spy on anyone else? This planet has vegetation just about everywhere."

He smiled as he carefully rose to his feet. I imitated him.

"You ask a valid question. But no, privacy is not an issue when at home. Remember that I infused my home and garden with my DNA. The floor will deny access to intruders or to anyone with evil intent. It is hard to put in words, but the trees and the plants must consent to be used. They will close themselves to negative energy like the one emanating from malicious people."

"Well, that's a relief. But that still means you have to behave in public spaces or risk someone stumbling in on you at an inopportune time," I said, still feasting my eyes on my husband.

He gave me that boyish grin laden with an underlying naughtiness that made me tingle again. "Have no fear, my mate. The day I decide to get frisky with you outdoors, I promise no one will be able to spy on us."

I snorted, both in amusement and to hide my embarrassment. "Glad to hear it," I teased. "You're quite the flirt."

To my shock, Helio's brown skin darkened, a fascinating phenomenon. Although I was mixed, born of a Black Cuban mother and a White Irish father, I'd taken on my mother's darker shade. While I felt my cheeks heating when I blushed, the redness didn't show through my skin. But Helio's entire upper torso and face grew a couple of shades darker for a few seconds. I was too amazed to otherwise react.

"Actually, I'm rather shy," he said while scratching his nape in the most endearing fashion. "And yet, for some reason, I don't feel that way around you."

"Good. Nor should you," I replied with a smile before gesturing at his chest with my chin. "Your markings are truly beautiful. Are they scarification tattoos?" I asked.

Helio looked down at himself. He then glanced back up at me and shook his head. "No, they're not tattoos. They are called yevins and are natural. We are born with them, but they become more visible with age. They are like your fingerprints. The pattern is unique to each Edocit, but some segments are common to every member of a given bloodline. If you know how to read them, they also reveal the age of the person."

My eyes widened when he took my hand and placed it on his yevins. I didn't pull away and traced the swirly patterns in a slow movement. He observed me quietly, a Mona Lisa smile on his lips. My fingers continued to roam the embossed tattoos on his skin even as I lifted my head to study his features. Our eyes locked, and he held my gaze unflinchingly.

After one last caress on his markings, I dropped my hand and shook my head. "You're not shy. Bold suits you better."

The same unreadable expression flitted over his handsome face. "Too bold?" he asked, a barely noticeable sliver of worry in his voice.

I shook my head again. "No, not too bold. You're bold in a sexy way. Shy does not match your personality, at least in my humble opinion." I tilted my head to the side as we continued to stare at each other, an undefinable communication passing between us. "It's so strange. We've only just met, and yet I feel like I've always known you."

His face melted in the sweetest expression that made me want to close the short distance between us and snuggle. "I feel the same."

I felt sorry when he started putting his shirt back on.

"Come, my mate. Let's go to the square before I truly grow too bold," he said, that mischievous glimmer coming back in his eyes. "I want you to discover your new home."

"Lead the way, husband."

He chuckled, took my hand, and led me out of the house.

CHAPTER 4

HELIO

I stopped in front of my personal shuttle on the small landing pad on the east side of the garden. The impressed look on my mate's face had my chest swelling with pride. Maeve let go of my hand to come closer to the vessel and delicately run her fingers over the hull.

"This model is called a Skiff," I explained while she continued to examine it.

"What material is that?" Maeve asked.

"Wood," I said, immediately amused by her stunned expression. "It is myrdian wood. It's very light but becomes as hard as titanium once properly treated. The fanned tail at the back, and these adornments alongside the nose are actually onoya leaves."

"Wait, as in the onoya solar panels?" Maeve asked, incredulous.

I chuckled and nodded. "Yes. The ads don't lie when they say these are the cleanest solar panels you can get anywhere. They literally are tree leaves. The onoya sheds them twice a year. That's when they are ripe to use as solar panels. When you peel off the outer skin of the leaf, a bit like the layer of an onion, you find a translucent layer right beneath it. It's the onoya leaf's epidermal cells. Once it's directly exposed to oxygen and light, there's a chemical reaction that hardens the leaf, which then greedily absorbs the energy from the sunlight."

"And converts it into electrical charges," Maeve finished for me.

"Exactly. Everything about this vessel is of organic origin. When we retire it, we recycle or compost every single part."

She gave me a teasing smile. "You will get no arguments from me that few planets are as clean and environmentally conscientious as yours. I can see why your organic products are so fancy and costly."

"We have the finest plant-based and organic products in the galaxy. They are our main trades. Our entire ecosystem is designed to avoid the need for artificial pesticides or fertilizers," I explained while opening the shuttle.

It was low enough on the ground that we didn't need steps to climb in. The limited space only had two seats, and a small area behind them to store bags or a few medium-sized containers. After we finished putting on our seatbelts, I started the skiff and took off.

"You seem so knowledgeable and passionate about plants and the flora," Maeve said while studying my features. "How did you end up as a bounty hunter instead of following one of the more traditional careers for an Edocit?"

I grinned. "My mother used to take great pleasure in blaming her brother for my aberrant behavior. As a child, Uncle Bron was my hero."

"Right, the Master Hunter from the Galactic Hunters Federation," she said. "That's a prestigious role and title. But then he was a legend when he actively hunted."

"He was," I said with pride. "The only reason I know so much about onoya leaves as solar panels is because it's the family business on my mother's side. When they were teenagers, Uncle Bron and my mother would help their parents gather some of the fallen leaves for the panels. One day, a wild harstag mare was getting attacked by a Sayeef while giving birth."

"A Sayeef?" Maeve repeated questioningly.

"It's what humans would call a doppelgänger or a mimic," I explained in a serious tone. "Sayeefs can take on almost any appearance, although nothing that would significantly increase or reduce their natural mass. They have a limited speech capacity when they take on the form of a sentient being."

"So they are intelligent, not monsters?" Maeve asked.

"No, they definitely are monsters. They will parrot a few sentences, always the same things in a loop. Usually, they are the words heard from their last victims calling for help. And once you come to assist them, they kill you, then eat you."

"Whoa! You guys have a lot of these roaming around?" Maeve asked with an unimpressed expression devoid of any actual fear.

"Thankfully no. They are rare occurrences. There is a spike of Sayeef sightings whenever a major tragedy occurs in a given area," I said. "When Edocits are grievously injured, subjected to torture, or in great distress, we can project our consciousness into the trees or certain plants. It helps dampen the pain and slows down our vital functions to give our bodies a chance to survive longer or until help arrives. But if help never comes or arrives too late, a Sayeef may spark."

"Oh, God!" Maeve whispered with compassion. "Is it the spirit of the dead that has risen that way?"

"No," I said, shaking my head. "Or rather, we do not believe so. Our scientists have studied the phenomenon and believe it's more a matter of residual energy, not the actual soul of the deceased. That theory has been reinforced by Sayeefs appearing in areas where no Edocit died, but the locals endured extreme pain and trauma during a tragic event."

"Sheesh. At least I'm happy to know what to look for,"

Maeve said. "But sorry for interrupting your story. So your uncle took on that Sayeef?"

I smiled. "Don't apologize. I love telling you about my world. And yes, Uncle Bron battled that Sayeef with no actual weapon. Those creatures are vicious. My uncle prevailed but barely. He spent an entire week in a healing pod. When he finally got out, the harstag and her foal were waiting to thank him outside his garden."

"Oh wow! He knew the mother?" Maeve asked, flabbergasted.

I chuckled. "No. But harstags—and many other creatures on Zailia—can root like we do. She found him that way. Her intentions were good, so his garden answered her calls and led her to him."

"That's amazing! But now, you can guess my next question. What's a harstag?" Maeve asked sheepishly.

I laughed. "They are beautiful creatures, more or less a cross between a forest horse and a reindeer. They are mounts with a slightly higher intelligence level than Earth's dogs. I was planning on taking you out riding one of them."

"That would be fantastic! I love riding, and those harstags sound wonderful," Maeve replied, beaming at me.

I loved how her face glowed whenever she was happy. My mate was truly beautiful.

"I'm guessing that incident made your uncle decide to become a hunter?" she asked.

"Yes and no. It was more the triggering incident. Had he failed, not only would that mare and her young have died, but chances are, so would he and my mother," I explained. "He never wanted to be that helpless again, so he learned how to hunt and developed a taste for it. For an Edocit, it was an aberration."

"How so?"

"We cherish and protect life. Killing, especially for sport, is antithetical to our nature. When I asked my uncle about it, he said he didn't hunt for the pleasure of killing, but for all the harstags in the world."

Maeve's eyes widened in understanding. "He kills to protect."

I nodded. "That's why he joined the Galactic Hunters Federation. They do not hunt for sport. All of their hunts are either to relocate vicious predators who roamed outside of their territories, or to cull the excessive population of predators that threaten the balance of the ecosystem."

"Like those hunts on Trangor," Maeve said in understanding.

"Correct."

"And how did that make *you* a bounty hunter?" she asked.

I smiled. "Uncle Bron was my hero. Every time he came to visit, I would hound him with a million questions about his adventures and heroic rescues. Watching him climb the ranks and earn an intergalactic reputation as the greatest hunter of our times only made him even more godly in my eyes. So, I followed in his footsteps, only to realize I took no pleasure in killing monsters, even for a good cause. At that point, I was completely at a loss as to what I wanted to do with my life. I had trained in hunting and tracking. That didn't leave me with too many options unless I went back to school."

"Ouch. That must have been tough," Maeve said with commiseration.

"It was, especially with my parents constantly in my ears, telling me to come home. Mother wanted me to join her family business, and Father wanted me to work with him as a nuvean wood sculptor. According to him, I am gifted when it comes to bending wood to my will," I said with a hefty dose of self-derision.

"Well, considering how you shaped your house, I would agree with your father," Maeve said softly.

"*Our* house," I gently corrected.

She smiled. “So, how did you end up becoming a bounty hunter?”

“Circumstances. The son of a family friend went missing,” I said with a frown, reminiscing. “It’s not uncommon for juvenile Edocits to run away at the peak of their hormonal transition. Correction, it’s not so much that they run away, but more that they wander off in a dazed trance for a short while.”

“What causes that?” Maeve asked, confused.

“The same hormones that cause their down leaves to grow in large quantities in their hair also flood their system. They’re essentially almost constantly high during that period,” I explained.

“Oh wow! I knew the leaves that grow on the vines of an Edocit teenager’s hair were a potent drug. We’re constantly hunting down pirates trafficking them. But I did not know it also ran in their blood.”

“We keep that part as quiet as possible, or our young would be hunted even more furiously than they already are,” I said with disgust. “Our law enforcement stopped searching for him after a week, leaving it as an unsolved case when they failed to find him. Since I had tracking training, his parents asked for my help. It took a while to discover he had been taken off world by a visitor. By the time I could track them down, the boy was but a shadow of himself. Between his down leaves being steadily harvested and his blood drained, he never fully recovered. He’s younger than me but looks twice my uncle’s age.”

“Oh, God! That’s terrible,” Maeve said, a mix of sympathy and anger at such injustice warring on her beautiful features.

“Freeing him and bringing his abductors to justice was the greatest feeling in the world. I’ve made it my life’s goal since then to take on the cases that law enforcement will not or has given up on,” I said factually.

“That’s quite commendable. I can definitely see myself

helping you in that endeavor," Maeve said, looking at me with something akin to respect that touched me deeply.

"I would love that," I replied with a smile.

In that instant, I hated the distance between us. Had we not been flying, I would have pulled her into my embrace and kissed her.

"I keep babbling about myself instead of pointing out the beauties of your new world as we fly over it," I said in a sheepish tone.

She laughed. "Don't worry, I've been stealing glances at the landscape. Zailia is truly beautiful. However, I noticed a large group of giant flowers, like the size of a building."

"They're not giant flowers, they're actually buildings," I said, amused. "More specifically, they are dwellings. Some villages build flower-shaped homes, each themed around a specific species of flowers. This was the standard architecture of our ancestors and still is for certain Edocit tribes. People of my generation build more modern dwellings. But I'll take you to visit one of those villages."

"Looking forward to it!" Maeve said with enthusiasm.

We continued chatting amiably until the tall walls of Veloya, Zailia's capital and principal city, appeared ahead. Maeve gasped at the sight of the giant pillars smoothly curving towards each other to connect in a loosely netted dome over the city.

"Welcome to Veloya, my mate," I said. "These giant columns are nuvean trees."

"Oh, my God! This tall?!" she exclaimed.

I snorted. "Yes, nuvean trees can grow up to fifteen meters in height. Only masters could bend such ancient trees to their will. Right now, the spaces between the trees are open," I added as we flew by such an opening to the parking tower. "If you look closely, you will notice discreet generators along the sides of each pillar. When it rains or snows, the generators create energy fields to seal those openings and keep the elements out."

"That's clever," Maeve said approvingly as I settled our shuttle inside one of the parking slots of the tall tower annexed to the city.

We disembarked and took a lift down to the ground.

Once again, my chest filled with happiness at the wonder on Maeve's face as she took in the city. As with my dwelling, most of the buildings and structures were all built out of living nuvean wood. Their walls curved in impressive organic designs before reconnecting seamlessly. Their deep roots ensured each building's timeless longevity, so long as the land remained healthy. Branches grew out of the roof of many of them, their limbs spreading skyward, their leaves rustling in the soft breeze. Some of them boasted blooming buds, making it look like colorful crowns of flowers adorned them.

"This is breathtaking," Maeve whispered out as she took in our surroundings.

A proud grin stretched my lips. "I'm glad you like it. I want you to fall in love with your new world."

"I don't think anyone could help but fall in love with Zailia. Everything is so beautiful, so harmonious, it feels like I'm walking through a living work of art," Maeve said.

"We like to think that Zailia is indeed a living work of art," I replied.

Taking her hand, I led her down one of the city's many paths, some of which were lined with flowering bushes and shrubs.

"Our city is constantly changing," I continued. "Obviously, the seasons play a big part, but also the fauna that shelters within. These slightly glowing sculptures in those branches over there are actually bird's nests."

"Oh wow! So that's all the chirping I'm hearing right now."

I nodded. "In about two or three more weeks, the young will all have left their nests. The parents will then abandon them for a breed of caterpillars to feed on."

"Oh no! They are so beautiful!" Maeve said with a sorry expression.

I chuckled. "Don't be sad. They will build new ones next year. But the caterpillars do us a favor. Those nests are high in protein and contain all the nutrients the caterpillars need before forming their cocoons. If not for them, we'd have to climb up and take down all those nests before they began rotting. The stench would be horrendous."

Maeve scrunched her face. "Okay, maybe it's a good thing, after all."

"It is! The chrysalises are beautiful, especially at nightfall. They hang like those long ornaments humans put in your holiday trees, and glow from within."

"They glow?!"

"Yep. They make for the most romantic setting at night. That's why you see so many terraces built a short distance from those trees. And when the chrysalises hatch, little alibelles come out. We turn it into an event, with our younglings running around with sticks covered in spiced honey puffs to feed them."

"That sounds magical. I can't wait to see it," Maeve said enthusiastically as we circled around the large fountain in the center of the city.

"It will happen in about one month and last two or three days. I'll bring you," I said, giving her hand a gentle squeeze.

We traipsed through the streets of Veloya, stopping by various stalls of the open market and entering some shops along the way. To my surprise, Maeve seemed particularly interested in the clothing stores.

"My wardrobe is limited," Maeve said sheepishly. "I mostly have clothes suited for work or undercover missions, and very few casual, feminine, or elegant outfits. I've never been big on colorful clothes, but the Edocit fashion has me rethinking everything. Those maxi dresses your women wear are gorgeous. It reminds me of a mix of Moroccan caftans and the sarongs Asian Indian women wear on Earth."

"We love our colors. Our dresses will look lovely on you," I said sincerely.

We eventually settled on one terrace for a romantic dinner as the sun lowered on the horizon. Across from the elevated dais of the terrace, we had a perfect view of the square. Aside from the other patrons also dining on this terrace or those of neighboring restaurants, a crowd had gathered around the square, some people sitting directly on the ground.

"What's happening?" Maeve asked.

"Dancers from the Utzac tribes are going to perform," I said with a thrill in my voice. "They are a different Edocit breed than mine. You will see the anatomical differences as soon as they come out. It should be any minute now."

As if summoned by that comment, the hammering of drums resounded over the square, accompanied by the haunting sound of a flute. Then the couple came out of a tent camouflaged by a curtain of the sagging leafy branches of a yaster tree.

Typical of their breed, the Utzac couple had very dark skin, like the shadow trees our folklore claimed the first of their kind had emerged from. The female had bluish-green hair, which matched the long leaves that formed a wide skirt-like train around her legs. The male had a reddish-orange mane and shorter skirt of leaves to cover his modesty.

"They are magnificent! I can't decide if her skirt reminds me more of a peacock's tail or a French can-can skirt," Maeve said, her eyes glued to the Utzac female.

"A peacock is an apt comparison," I said, impressed. "It is not a crafted skirt. The gown, as we call it, is an extension of her. Those leaves grow naturally on Utzacs just like the vines in my hair. The small antlers on her head, and the bigger ones on the male, are also integral parts of their anatomies. But contrary to your peacocks, the female Utzacs have the biggest 'tail' in the shape of their gown. The color of its leaves constitutes a significant part of her appeal."

"That's amazing! And what of the male?" Maeve asked.

"As you can see, his gown is fairly short, barely a loincloth. But the size and shape of his antlers make him more attractive."

"Agreed!" Maeve said with a bit too much enthusiasm. "Don't mind if I admire the view."

I gaped at her in shock, only to see her pinching her lips in a failed attempt at repressing a smile. I scrunched my face at the mischievous sideways glance she was giving me.

"You brat," I mumbled. "Have no fear. I'll get even."

She chuckled before taking a sip of wine as she turned her attention back to the performers. I marveled at the impressive Utzac dances. With powerful movements, bold steps, and decisive waves of his arms in time with the music, the male aimed to display strength and virility. The female interspersed her fluid and elegant movements with sharp flicks of her hands followed by enticing gestures representing both seduction and grace. The two of them moved in perfect sync, their intricate footwork appearing effortless as their bodies told a story of love and passion.

Entranced by their performance, we barely noticed the server bringing us our food. A thunder of applause saluted the dancers once they finished their first choreography. We dug into our meals before they began their second set.

"I know it's silly, but I was wondering how much meat I was going to find on Zailia, considering how environmentally protective your people are," Maeve said sheepishly while cutting a piece of the juicy steak before her. "I'm quite the meat lover."

I laughed. "We're very much omnivores as well. Although, in hard conditions, we can root and survive for extended periods of time from the nutrients and moisture in the soil, and from the rays of the sun."

"You guys are every shade of awesome," Maeve said, looking impressed.

"We are!" I said smugly. "But we do not breed and slaughter animals for our meat. The vast majority is cell-based meat, cultivated and grown in giant vats. It's environmentally clean and cruelty-free. That said, there is a minimal amount of hunting and fishing allowed, under very strict quotas and only to maintain the balance in certain populations that could otherwise threaten their ecosystem. We usually reserve hunting to specific tribes."

"Well, that's certainly the tastiest lab-meat I've ever had," Maeve said before taking another large bite of her steak.

We finished our meal having an amiable conversation a few minutes after the dancers ended their performance. Holding hands, we headed back towards the shuttle tower and ran into a group of juveniles hanging by the fountain in the square. They made some teasing kissing sounds our way, the young males flicking their hair and taking on seductive poses for Maeve.

I glared at them with pretend anger, knowing they were just playing. My mate burst out laughing, then gave the bold young male an assessing look.

"You're very pretty, but saplings are far too green for me. I like my male mature," Maeve said in a flirty voice while pressing herself against me.

I grinned smugly at the juvenile and, letting go of Maeve's hand, I wrapped a possessive arm around her waist instead. His friends chuckled, some making mocking noises at him for having been rejected. He pressed a hand to his chest as if an arrow had struck straight into his heart.

"You wound me!" he said in an overly dramatic tone that had us both laughing again. "But very well. If you would not have me, oh fairest of flowers, at least accept this token of my affection."

The little wretch then plucked a large down leaf from the vines interwoven in his full head of hair. With a flourish, he extended the leaf to my mate. Even from where I stood, I could see how healthy and potent the leaf was. At least fifty more such leaves gently rustled in the wind around his face—a substantial fortune on the black market, and even more so on the pleasure barges that allowed their trade.

Maeve stiffened at the unexpected offer. She stared at it in shock for a second before giving me an uncertain look. I smiled and nodded encouragingly. Although taken aback and slightly confused, she took the leaf with a timid smile of gratitude.

"What about me?" I asked the sapling in pretend outrage. "You have offended my honor by flirting with my mate."

"Apologies. Her beauty made me forget my manners," the brat said with the most insincere repentant expression.

I couldn't help a laugh, echoed by Maeve, as he once more made a spectacle of plucking another leaf from his hair and giving it to me. His friends snickered as I took it from him.

"I forgive you this once. But see that you behave in the future," I said, winking at the young male as I resumed walking.

Still grinning, Maeve waved at the juveniles who waved back at us.

"They are all so beautiful," she breathed out with awe. "You Edocits are quite a stunning species."

I smiled. "Thank you, my mate. But yes, they are beautiful. Saplings reach the height of their beauty during puberty. They are a delight to look at."

Maeve snorted and looked dejected. "Well, humans are the exact opposite. Our arms and legs look too long for our bodies. Our faces erupt in pimples. We start getting those unpleasant, sweaty body odors. Girls receive the unwelcomed monthly visit of Aunt Flo. Hormones have us acting up in every possible way… Basically, not great all around."

I chuckled with sympathy. "Wow, none of these sounds pleasant. But who is Aunt Flo? And why does she only visit girls?"

"It's a code name for women's menstrual cycles," Maeve said with an expression that made no mystery of how she felt about this physiological phenomenon.

"Oh, right," I said with even greater sympathy. "Our females do not have that. The main change for our juveniles is that they are basically high for the duration of their puberty. The peak happens at around the age of the saplings we just met—fifteen to sixteen years. It will gradually fade by the time they are nineteen or twenty."

"Is that why they were so jovial?" Maeve asked with curiosity as we followed the path to the tower.

I nodded. "Did you notice that their eyes were slightly glazed over?"

"No," Maeve said, shaking her head. "But I did wonder if they were a little tipsy."

"It's not surprising," I said with indulgence. "We don't have irises or pupils like humans. Therefore, it is harder for people to realize it as you can't see the dilated pupils. And our saplings do not consume alcohol. There's no need. They already spend their teenage years in a naturally induced state of euphoria."

"Do you know them?" Maeve asked while casting a glance at the leaf still held between her fingers. "They were quite charming."

"No. I've seen them around a few times, but I do not know their names. Our people are naturally friendly, and even more so juveniles going through puberty," I explained. "It is not uncommon for them to give away one or two of their down leaves to adults. It's a gesture of friendship, and in your case a welcome to our world."

"That was super sweet of him," Maeve said, looking touched as we stepped inside the lift of the tower. "I didn't really know how to react, considering how they are exploited for it."

"It is only inappropriate to ask when one hasn't been offered," I said, which had her frowning in confusion. "I only asked because he offered you one," I added with a chuckle, guessing at the reason for her reaction. "He would have given me one regardless, as not doing so would have been deemed rude. But we were playing a game. He expected me to ask."

"Wow, this seems a little complex. I'm going to keep you right next to me as I learn the ways of your world not to screw up," Maeve said.

I laughed. "I approve of this course of action."

The way she smiled did strange things to me.

"So, we're supposed to get high on young Edocit down leaves?" Maeve asked in a dubious tone as she lifted the leaf to look at it up-close.

"No," I said in a tone that brooked no argument before snagging it from her.

I placed it inside my pocket with the leaf the juvenile had given me.

"Hey! That's mine!" she exclaimed.

"It is. But you're not consuming it now," I said before kissing the tip of her nose. "We're on our way home for the night. And I want you to be clear-minded when you decide how you want to spend the rest of the evening."

Maeve's eyes widened, her lips parting in understanding. Then the oddest mix of lust and shyness descended over her features. The potent wave of desire that surged through me left me reeling. I didn't know what expression my face had taken, but whatever it was, it made Maeve's dark eyes smolder.

My mate licked her lips nervously and tucked her hair behind her ear. "Right. Wise thinking," she said.

The doors of the lift opening dampened the overwhelming sexual tension that had erupted between us. I placed my hand on the small of her back to nudge her forward as we exited the lift. The way Maeve's breath hitched in her throat sent my blood rushing to my loins.

Maker, this female has far too great power over me.

CHAPTER 5
MAEVE

The journey home took forever, or so it seemed to me. I barely noticed the beauty of Zailia at night. And yet it was magnificent. In truth, I could barely focus on the casual conversation Helio was mostly carrying for us. To say I was hot and bothered would be the mother of all understatements.

The way he had said he wanted me clear-minded to decide how I wanted to spend the rest of the evening left little to the imagination. Obviously, I appreciated such thoughtfulness on his part.

For the first time, I resented that we didn't fall under the strict rules of the PMA. Every other couple didn't have to make a decision about what would happen on their wedding night. They were contractually obligated to consummate their union. Helio and I had no such constraint. We could wait a week, a month, or even a freaking year if we wanted.

My husband was hot as all hell, and I was beyond itching to get down and dirty with him. I had no problem embracing my sexuality, but I also wasn't the type to jump in bed with someone on a first date. However, this was not just a first date, it was our wedding night. Technically, nothing prevented us from giving in to our desires. The chemistry between us was undeniable. The way Helio looked at me, you'd think he wanted to devour me—which I would more than welcome.

Stop overthinking everything!

Yeah, my previous matches with the popular dating agencies had left a few scars. I needed to remind myself that this wasn't a random pairing with some sleazy douchebag looking to wet his dick or for a side piece. This was the male the infallible Kayog had deemed my soulmate.

The sight of our garden temporarily silenced the conflicting emotions bubbling within me. As we began our descent, countless little magical lights floated around the vegetation. Large luminous bulbs hung from the trees, like glowing Christmas balls. I remained speechless as Helio landed the skiff on the pad.

I got out of the vessel, transfixed. "It feels like I just stepped inside a fairy tale," I whispered, afraid that speaking too loudly would chase away the little lights that I could now see resembled some kind of miniature dragons.

They only possessed two front legs attached to a plump upper body, and no back legs. Their long tail ended with another luminous sphere. Surprisingly, most of the light emanating from them actually came from their diaphanous wings, whose shapes I couldn't quite define. They definitely weren't draconic, but not quite insectoid either.

"Well, you are my princess. So I guess we are living a real-life fairy tale," Helio said in a soft voice while slipping his arm around my waist in a gentle caress.

The way he looked at me seriously messed with my head. It wasn't the naked lust he'd displayed earlier in the lift, but a possessive pride, filled with hope and awe that made me feel more wanted than ever before.

A little fairy dragon came buzzing near our faces. No, buzzing wasn't an accurate description of the sound of their wings. It was more of a soft swooshing, almost like the sound of the breeze against a silky fabric. Helio lifted a hand, and the tiny creature, the size of a lip balm stick, landed on the side of my husband's index finger. It held on with its tiny hands, its big glowing eyes examining me.

"This is an alibelle," Helio said in an almost whispered voice. "They are here to welcome you."

"Welcome me?" I asked with curiosity, in the same hushed tone.

"Mmhmm. Myma told them about you," he said, bringing the creature closer to me. "Their ears are very sensitive, so we avoid speaking too loudly in their presence."

I nodded, grateful for that information as I brought my hand near his. The alibelle immediately flapped her long wings to come settle on my hand instead. Apparently deeming this an open invitation, the countless alibelles flying around the garden all flocked to me. Had they rushed me like a swarm of locusts, I probably would have fled screaming. But they slowly descended all over me like feathers, some landing on my arms and my shoulders, and others hanging on to my hair. I had to be quite the sight, lit up like a Christmas tree.

When I peered up at Helio to tell him how magical this was, the look on his face took my breath away.

"My beautiful mate, the land welcomes you. You are home. You are part of us now," he whispered with such affection my skin erupted in goosebumps.

Careful not to knock any of the little dragon fairies, he cupped my cheeks with both hands then leaned it to kiss me. It felt like lightning had struck, setting my entire body ablaze. I moaned, my hands settling on his shoulders as he deepened the kiss. The alibelles took flight but didn't go away just yet. Instead, they swirled around us in a luminous vortex as Helio drew me closer against his firm body.

The dull throbbing that had dimmed upon entering this magical garden came back in full force. I wrapped my arms around Helio as our tongues danced with each other. In response, my husband began caressing me with an intensity that hinted at repressed urgency.

For the first time, he became bolder in the way he was touching me. One of his hands settled on my behind, pressing me against his pelvis, while the other glided up my back to rest on my nape. A deep moan rumbled through his chest as his kiss grew even more passionate. My breasts felt heavy and my nipples achy as his length stiffened against my stomach.

Dear God! Even through the fabric of his pants and of my dress, I could feel how well-endowed he was. Instead of frightening me, it had my inner walls contracting with anticipation as moisture pooled between my thighs.

I gasped when Helio suddenly fisted my hair at my nape and yanked it back, holding me firmly so that I couldn't turn away. His forest green eyes devoid of pupils or sclera appeared to softly glow as he stared at my face with something akin to a feral hunger. My stomach did a series of backflips as I drowned in the endless depth of his eyes.

He didn't need to speak for me to understand his silent question. All my earlier thoughts of 'should we or shouldn't we' now seemed completely silly. He was my husband. I wanted him, and he wanted me just as much. I smiled, my hands sliding down to cup the round globes of his firm behind, and I ground my pelvis against his.

Helio inhaled sharply through his bared teeth, his canines lengthening into a set of fangs I didn't even know he possessed. That and the hissing sound he had made resonated directly in my nether region. I gasped once more when he picked me up, my legs instinctively wrapping around his waist and my arms around his neck.

He continued to look at me like a wolf would his prey as he carried me into the house. Above our heads, like a million fireflies, the alibelles danced, and the leaves of the mother tree rustled in an almost melodic whistle. This level of sentience should have creeped me out, but it didn't.

The land was celebrating our union.

My husband kissing me voraciously reclaimed my full attention. I'd never kissed someone with fangs before. Their sharp tips grazing against the sides of my tongue sent a thrill coursing down my spine. I barely heard our bedroom door opening behind me, too busy savoring the sweet taste of my man, vaguely reminiscent of mulled wine.

I shivered when his right hand holding the back of one of my thighs slipped under my skirt and glided up my bare back as he was putting me down on my feet. Helio broke the kiss and finished pulling my dress over my head. Another shiver washed over me as I stood naked but for my sexy lingerie and my medium heel sandals.

I was comfortable with my body. Regular training as an Enforcer kept me fit. Sure, like everyone else, I had some things I considered as flaws, but nothing that would make me squirm under his stare. As a B cup, I always found my breasts a little too humble, and my waist didn't have an accentuated enough dip before that feminine flare at the hips that gave women that sexy hourglass shape. But Helio's gaze was roaming over me with a possessive lust that made me feel like Aphrodite herself.

"You are stunning, my mate," Helio whispered, his voice so thick with desire it came out almost like a growl.

My nipples hardened against the lacy fabric of the tiny triangles of my see-through bra. Feeling emboldened, I pulled his shirt from his pants and caressed a path up his well-defined abs while lifting the shirt. He raised his arms to ease my task.

I never finished ridding him of the garment.

The sight of the embossed tattoos on his chest—in beautiful lighter swirls than the rest of his skin—made my mouth water. As he finished removing his shirt and tossed it somewhere in the room, I vaguely noticed that his armpits were as smooth and hairless as the rest of his body currently exposed.

I pressed my lips to his chest and gently brushed them over the tattooed bumps. Unable to resist, I poked out my tongue to trace the swirly patterns while caressing his sides. To my surprise, his skin didn't have the saltiness my brain had expected. It had the same sweet spiciness as when I kissed him but with a hint of cinnamon.

Helio's chest vibrated with a purr as I licked the small buds of his left nipple. The heat of his palms explored my back before unclasping my bra. I stopped caressing him only long enough to let the garment slide down my arms. Cupping my nape, my mate forced my head up to reclaim my lips and drew me against him.

A moan rose from my throat at the searing heat of his bare chest against mine. Without interrupting the kiss, Helio picked me up again and carried me the short distance to our massive bed. I kicked off my sandals moments before he lay me down on the most divine mattress. I began scooting back, but he grabbed my ankle, stopping me even as he climbed on the bed.

He kissed me again, gently pushing me against the mattress. As soon as I was fully lying down, he raised my wrists above my head while our tongues continued to mingle. Helio's hands gently caressed the inner side of my arms as they glided back down towards my shoulders. Wanting to touch him as well, I moved my hands, but he immediately pinned them back down onto the bed. He broke the kiss to give me a stern glance that made it clear I was to remain still.

I wasn't submissive, and yet that resonated straight in my core, and I began tingling in all the right places. Apparently satisfied that I would behave, Helio lowered his head again, but not to reclaim my mouth. Instead, his lips roamed over my face, tracing each of my features as a blind person would see with their hands. I shivered when they reached my neck, always so sensitive, and they parted so his fangs could graze my skin.

A bolt of desire exploded in my loins, and I fisted my hands above my head not to reach for him. Like many women, I'd always fantasized about getting bitten by a vampire. There was something so primal and sensual about it. What would it feel like to have his fangs sinking into my neck while his length pounded into me?

I moaned and bit my bottom lip as he continued his journey down to my chest. My stomach quivered as his tongue teased my areola. God, how I loved the way he caressed my body, his touch so insanely silky. I was so used to males having calloused hands, I never expected to enjoy this kind of softness. While one hand kneaded my left breast, his thumb flicking its hardened little bud, Helio nipped at my other nipple before soothing the sting with his tongue.

Throbbing and aching with need, I almost held my breath when his spare hand finally wandered further south. My abdominal muscles contracted when his fingers brushed over the tiny triangle of my thong. A spasm shook my legs, and a frustrated moan escaped me when he continued to trace the seam of my sex over the thin fabric, his touch so light you'd think it was merely a breeze teasing me.

Helio chuckled even as he sucked on my nipple. Lifting his head, he released it with a popping sound to look at me with a taunting expression. Did he want me to beg him? I was so hot and bothered, if he continued to tease me like this, I would have no qualms begging. Needing proper friction, I lifted my pelvis for greater contact with his hand. To my surprise, instead of pulling away as I'd expected him to, Helio pressed his palm on my sex and slowly rubbed me a few times over my thong.

"Please," I whispered as my abdominals contracted painfully.

He gave me a predatory smile, his fangs peeking between his lips. The fire burning in the pit of my stomach cranked up another notch. His dark green eyes, now looking almost pitch black, remained locked with mine as he finally slipped a hand inside my underwear. My back arched, and I cried out when he touched my clit at long last. After the initial teasing, I'd expected him to torture me some more, but Helio immediately went to work, massaging my little nub the right way.

He had me nearing the edge in no time. To my dismay, he halted abruptly. I jerked my head up to look at him in disbelief. Before I could say a word, he yanked down my thong, and his mouth picked up where his fingers had left off.

The next sound that came out of me was a shout of ecstasy as I climaxed. Even as I flew high, Helio licked and sucked on my clit with fervor while two of his fingers moved inside me. Just as I was coming back down to reality, my husband curved his fingers, repeatedly zeroing in on my sweet spot with deadly precision. Another orgasm swept me away.

Feeling dizzy, my body trembling from the waves of bliss, it took me a moment to realize Helio was no longer touching me. I opened my eyelids, the room spinning slightly before my eyes, to find Helio standing at the foot of the bed.

He looked like a pagan god with the vines tangled in his hair, the slight glow of his dark green eyes giving his face an even more otherworldly aura. Breathing audibly through his parted lips, the tips of his fangs showing, my husband looked on the verge of losing control over the passion that raged inside him. The delicate vines that ran the side of his shoulders and the length of his arms appeared thicker and even longer. But it was his hands detaching his pants that held my attention.

My breath caught in my throat as he lowered them. Like the rest of his body, there was no happy trail or other form of pilosity around his nether region or down his legs. I barely noticed the narrow vines swirling around the sides of his thighs and down to his ankles. His thick cock standing proudly erect held me enthralled.

He had two testicles, like a human. While the general shape of the shaft held similarities, the lower half had a series of beady bumps on the underside that promised some unusual sensations. The upper half seemed draped in long ridges up to the base of the head, itself vaguely shaped like the closed bud of a flower. Despite that, no vines lurked around in that general area. His cock appeared entirely made of flesh.

I licked my lips nervously as Helio climbed back onto the bed, now fully naked. My pulse picked up and my breathing came in short and shallow bursts as he settled between my thighs. My inner walls contracted in both anticipation and fear. As wet as my husband had gotten me, it would be a tight fit.

To my relief, he didn't push himself in right away. He kissed me again, and we exchanged tender caresses, which quickly grew more urgent. When he began rubbing his length against my core, I knew the moment had come.

Although he aligned his tip with my opening, he didn't penetrate me just yet. Helio paused and locked gazes with me. Once again, I didn't need him to speak to know which question he was asking. I smiled and spread my legs wider to make my consent clearer. He smiled back, his handsome face taking on such a tender expression I could almost feel it wrapping me in a warm cocoon of endless affection.

"My mate…" he whispered against my lips.

He reclaimed my mouth at the same time as he gently began pushing himself inside of me. As expected, my body resisted his invasion. To my pleasant surprise, it didn't hurt or burn as Helio moved with careful shallow thrusts. However, I felt the oddest sensation when, halfway in, the tip of his cock seemed to narrow each time he pulled out, and open up just as he finished pushing in, as if to propel itself deeper inside. The whole time, Helio kissed and caressed me, whispering sweet words of affection and encouragement.

Too focused on trying to understand the strange sensations inside me, I almost felt cheated when my body yielded at last—and yet too soon. Helio took in a hissing breath, his grip tightening around me. Eyes closed, his forehead resting against mine, he remained still to allow me to adjust to his girth. The way his muscles contracted beneath my touch revealed the intense effort he was making to rein himself in.

He finally opened his eyes and looked at me with such burning desire that my toes instantly curled.

"Do you have any idea how good you feel?" he whispered in a throaty voice.

I never got a chance to respond as Helio crushed my lips in a possessive kiss as he slowly began moving in and out of me. God almighty! I had been so focused on the way his glans opened and closed inside me as he was pushing himself in that I had paid little attention to the draped ridges and string-like bumps lining the length of his shaft.

Did I ever now!

Each stroke had me drowning in far too many sensations for my mind to handle. An endless string of moans flowed out of my throat, half of them swallowed by Helio's voracious kisses. He picked up the pace, rubbing against my sweet spot with a relentlessness that quickly had me seeing stars.

I cried out, my inner walls contracting around his length, and my nails digging into the small of his back. In response, Helio threw his head back and shouted. In my blissful daze, I thought he had climaxed as well, but soon realized my mistake. Something had apparently broken inside of him, and my husband unleashed his passion on me.

Spreading my legs wider, he started taking me faster, deeper, and harder. A volcano was raging inside of me, each stroke sending me flying even higher on the wings of ecstasy. Helio's hands were everywhere, caressing me and restraining me even as his cock wrecked me. As another orgasm crashed into me, my husband finally joined his voice to mine as his own climax swept him away.

He shouted my name, and slammed himself in deep, his

hands tightening in an almost bruising hold around my waist. I felt his seed shoot out inside of me in a powerful stream. Lips parted, eyes closed in an air of pure bliss almost too painful to bear, my mate looked magnificent. The buds in his hair flowered, and a violent shiver shook his body.

Looking back down at me, he pumped his hips a couple more times before lowering himself over me again. He captured my lips with something akin to adoration. Still buried deep inside me, he turned us around so that I would rest on top of him. Feeling both wrecked and wondrously sated, I rested my head on the swirly patterns adorning his chest. I listened to the thundering sound of his heart as he protectively wrapped his arms around me.

“I am yours, my mate,” Helio whispered.

I smiled.

CHAPTER 6
MAEVE

I woke up feeling wonderfully sore, not in a painful way, but in the 'I had the craziest and wildest night' kind of way. Helio certainly deserved the badge of the best lover in the universe. Not only was his body a work of art, but he also knew how to use it to make mine sing. We had a few additional romps during the night. I wouldn't have minded another one this morning, but my husband was already gone.

I stretched, loving the caress of the silky blankets on my bare skin. The delectable aroma seeping into the room revealed Helio was likely preparing breakfast for us. I jumped out of bed and made a beeline for the hygiene room.

Like everything else in this house, Helio had designed this room to give the impression nature surrounded us. The separate shower resembled a natural waterfall encased in brown stone walls. The tub, carved directly into the floor, could have passed off for a hot spring. Under different circumstances, I would have gone straight for it. I loved lingering in a hot bath while reading a book.

This morning, however, I was too impatient to see my husband again. I jumped into the shower and did quick work of washing. The raining water on my body reminded me all too well the expert way in which Helio had touched me. To think I had been so worried about this pairing.

A part of me feared that this was indeed a fairy tale and way too good to be true. Although Kayog had a flawless record, and despite the perfect happiness that my friend Kaida and Cedros now enjoyed, shouldn't there be some initial challenges and friction? Helio and I had hit it off so smoothly from the start that I kept waiting for the other shoe to drop.

Sure, parts of his culture would take some getting used to, but nothing to write home about. I'd interacted with enough alien species that it took a lot to unnerve me or freak me out. Edocits also were an advanced species, well-liked and respected by the other members of the galactic alliance. Maybe that partially explained why I hadn't been confronted with as many cultural shocks as Kaida had faced.

Stop comparing yourself to others and looking for trouble where there is none.

I'd never considered myself a negative Nancy or a prophet of doom. However, I'd had such horrible luck with the dating scene that I struggled to reconcile the fact that this was turning out to be such smooth sailing so far. No creepy jokes, poor manners, misogynistic remarks or behaviors… Helio had been the perfect date, perfect lover, and an all-around wonderful companion. I could see myself falling in love hard and fast for this male. And it shamed me to admit that it frightened the hell out of the control freak in me.

Dismissing those thoughts, I hastily dried myself, brushed my hair, leaving it still a little damp, and hurried back to our room. Feeling a little naughty, I slipped on a thong but no bra under my spaghetti string short summer dress. For all my complaining about my humble breasts, I took great pride in their round and perky shape. One glance at my reflection in the mirror put a mischievous smile on my lips. The light fabric of the yellow dress was opaque enough not to be too revealing, but thin enough to show a hint of my nipples poking at it.

I'd never been big on makeup, in no small part because it didn't really have its place in my job. But I also wanted Helio to fall in love with the natural me. Plus, from what I had observed in the city last night, Edocit females didn't use any of these artifices to enhance their beauty. I slipped on a pair of open toe sandals and went to look for my man.

As expected, I found him in the kitchen. Shirtless, barefoot, and wearing nothing but black shorts, my husband was a feast for the eyes. He was putting the final touches to a rather lavish breakfast. On the dining table, small quantities of various spreads, thinly sliced cooked meats, breads, cut fruits, and other things I couldn't quite identify had my mouth watering.

"There she is!" Helio exclaimed as soon as he saw me.

The way his face lit up with genuine happiness and seeing the buds in his hair bloom upon my arrival had me melting from the inside out. Damn, it was nice to feel so wanted by such a gorgeous male. The tenderness in his eyes quickly gave way to a smoldering expression when he took in my appearance. My girly bits instantly tingled.

He put down a pitcher containing a reddish liquid I assumed to be juice and circled around the counter to come to me.

"You're so beautiful," he said, as if he couldn't believe I was real.

My pulse slightly picked up as he drew me into his embrace. I lifted my face to receive his kiss. It was brief and tender.

"Did you sleep well?"

Despite the gentle and unassuming way in which he asked, the intensity in his gaze told me what he truly wanted to know.

"I had a magical night and slept like a baby," I said while pressing myself against him.

Helio smiled back, a sliver of relief flitting over his features. That he could even think I might not have enjoyed our night together blew my mind. He tightened his embrace and kissed me again, this time with a hint of restrained passion. His palms glided up my back, and his thumb rubbed the area where the clasp of my bra should have been under my dress. An approving purr rumbled through his chest. He broke the kiss and studied my face with an air full of promises.

"Someone is being a temptress this morning," he whispered teasingly.

"Maybe," I replied in the same tone.

"I approve," he said.

He kissed my lips one last time, rubbed his nose against mine, and then took my hand to lead me to the table.

"Before I let you lure me into temptation, let *me* tempt *you* with a few local delicacies, in this Edocit version of a brunch."

"Everything looks so good," I said while settling down in the chair he had pulled for me.

"It is!" he said with conviction. "These are some of my favorite dishes. I hope you will feel the same."

"I'm sure I will," I said while greedily eyeing the bounty before me.

He brought the last couple of dishes and set them down on the table. For the next hour, he took me on a delicious culinary experience with samples of sweet and savory traditional Edocit breakfasts.

By the time we finished, I felt overly full. Frankly, I couldn't believe how much I had consumed.

"Handsome, smart, funny, a fantastic lover, and an amazing cook," I enumerated while giving him a seductive look. "Do you have any flaws?"

"None whatsoever," Helio replied smugly.

I chuckled and gave him a playful tap. However, I didn't miss the way his skin had darkened slightly from embarrassment at the compliment.

"Today, I want to take you on a harstag ride through the

forest. Then we could stop at the river for a swim and have a picnic," Helio offered.

"Sounds like a plan! You had me really intrigued yesterday with that story about the harstag your uncle saved," I said with enthusiasm.

"Good! Because we will specifically ride that young harstag —now adult—and his mate," he replied with a grin.

"Awesome!" I exclaimed before glancing down at my dress. "I should probably change into a pair of pants."

"Absolutely not!" Helio said in a tone that brooked no argument. "You're absolutely perfect as is."

The way he undressed me with his eyes, and especially how his gaze lingered on my chest, had my toes curling again.

"Are you sure?" I asked. "I wouldn't want to shock the local population."

He snorted. "Your outfit is hardly shocking, merely enticingly sexy. Edocits do not wear many layers of clothes. It is not uncommon for both males and females to walk around shirtless, and often only wearing some type of loincloth or shorts. We dress more in the city where off-worlders can come and go as they please. But in our villages and residential areas, we are a lot more laid back."

"I should at least get a bathing suit if we're going to swim," I insisted.

His gaze smoldered. "What for? We'll be alone, and we're past the point of being prudish with each other."

"Very well then," I said, excited at the prospect of our little adventure.

To my surprise, after we finished putting away the remaining food and cleaning the kitchen, Helio didn't put any shoes on. He retrieved a medium-sized basket from the cooling unit and then lured me outside to the garden.

My gaze immediately zeroed in on the magical creatures grazing by Myma.

"Oh, my God! They are magnificent!" I whispered.

"Come say hello," Helio said with a smile in his voice.

I let him lead me to the two harstags. They looked like the offspring of a horse and a deer. Above the short coat covering most of their bodies, a fluffy fur climbed up their collar and formed a bushy mane along the sides of their faces. An impressive set of antlers recurved over the head of the male, while a smaller and more delicate one adorned his female companion. On closer inspection, what I first thought to be small leaves on the sides of their cheeks, shoulders, and flanks turned out to be small green scales interspersed around the narrow vines that swirled around their shoulders and down the length of their legs.

They emitted a neighing sound in greeting as we approached. Not appearing in the least intimidated or wary, both boldly came towards us. The female had a lustrous brown coat with light beige and yellow fur, whereas the male had a charcoal coat with a reddish and yellow mane. I raised a hand towards the female's face. She pressed her muzzle against my palm, while the male did the same with Helio.

"Maeve, please meet Sefa and Laros," Helio said, showing the female and then the male. "My friends, meet my mate, Maeve."

He passed his arm around my waist, drawing me against him as he spoke those words.

"You are both so beautiful," I said with awe. "I'm honored to meet you."

Laros gently bumped his muzzle against my shoulder. God, they were gorgeous! I didn't know to what extent they understood my words, as Helio had compared their intelligence level to that of a dog. But their warm welcome was undeniable.

My eyes widened in surprise when Helio placed his palm on Laros's shoulder, and the vines from his forearms extruded to intertwine with those of the harstag. Laros nodded with a soft neigh, as if in acknowledgement of whatever communication had passed between them. I looked at Helio questioningly.

He smiled. "I am showing him the path I would like him to take us on," he explained, his voice a little slurred, like when he had projected his consciousness from our bed to the city last night."

His *veris* detached from Laros, and his eyes lost that glazed over quality. To my shock, it was Laros's turn to extrude his *veris*, but this time from his ankles to the ground.

"Whoa! Animals root, too?" I asked, flabbergasted.

Helio chuckled and nodded. "Yes. Most lifeforms on Zailia can. Everything and everyone are bound to the land here. Most exceptions are certain insects and fish. But every aquatic mammal can. Laros is scouting the way before heading out. He will take us to the area where we'll have the most privacy."

"Right… You guys can see every nook and cranny, so long as there's a tree," I said, scrunching my face.

He burst out laughing. "I know what you're thinking, but no, it will not happen. If there is already a couple or group engaged in activities that would require privacy, they will have requested the local fauna to deter anyone who would seek to go peek into the area."

"Deter them how?" I asked, still suspicious.

"You will get shut out," Helio replied matter-of-factly. "It feels like you're pushing against something made of rubber. It will bend a little but not give. Then you know it is already occupied by people who require privacy."

"Oh, okay. That's not too bad then," I said, my wheels still spinning.

"It's not too bad, but?" Helio asked. "Something seems to trouble you."

I gave him a sheepish look and nodded. "Yeah, there is. The Enforcer in me cannot help but think of how people could easily exploit this to hide criminal activity."

He smiled and shook his head. “It would not. If you recall what I was mentioning yesterday, unless the flora shares your DNA—like all the vegetation in this garden does with me—it will not respond to you if it perceives negative intentions on your part. And even when it is part of you, it may challenge you. All the trees, plants, and bushes in the wild are neutral land. They will never assist me in doing evil. But they will shelter my privacy with my mate.”

“Well, that’s a relief. And sorry, working in my field for so long has made me quite suspicious of every potential loophole.”

“Don’t apologize, my mate. It is not a flaw. It merely makes you cautious, something that will come in quite handy once you become my full-time partner in bounty hunting.”

I laughed at this bold statement but otherwise didn’t respond. If things kept going as well as they were right now, I could definitely see myself officially leaving the Enforcers to become his partner.

“If you are ready, let’s get going,” Helio said.

I nodded and watched him secure our picnic basket on Laros. “No saddles?” I asked.

Helio frowned. “No, we never used those. They irritate the harstags’ backs. Is that a problem for you?”

I shook my head. “I’m used to bareback riding,” I replied smugly.

“Good girl,” Helio said. “Unlike horses, harstags have a natural padding above their spines. So the bones of your lovely behind will not cause them any discomfort.”

He leaned in and kissed me. I almost groaned in frustration when it ended too soon. When he followed me as I went to stand by Sefa’s side as if to help me climb onto her, I gave him a ‘Are you kidding me?’ look that had him raising his palms in surrender with an apologetic expression.

Yeah, I was showing off a little as I effortlessly hoisted myself onto the female harstag’s back. She certainly was tall, but slightly shorter than a horse. I grinned smugly at my husband, who bowed with a flourish in acknowledgement of my skill. I chuckled as he went to get onto his own mount.

To my shock, the vines on Sefa's shoulders extended towards the middle, knotting together into a sort of rein. It wasn't very long. In fact, a handle would have probably been a more accurate description, like the ones on the bull ropes Cowboys used back in the day when rodeos were still legal.

"The vine handle is just to help you keep your balance if needed, especially if she starts galloping, or if you would like to make her stop. Otherwise, just let her go. She knows the way," Helio explained.

"Understood!" I said.

And just like that, we were off. He hadn't been kidding when he said Sefa's back was naturally padded. It felt like sitting on a comfortable cushion. As we approached what looked like a leafy version of a three-meter-high cedar hedge fencing the humongous backyard, a large section of the hedge parted in the middle. My jaw dropped as two panels opened like massive doors, letting us out of the courtyard.

Helio burst out laughing. "No, my darling, the hedges didn't move on their own. They sit on a pivoting platform. The drooping branches hide the large planter beneath them. The security system automatically activates them through the facial recognition system."

"Okay, that's a relief. I mean, I realize your plants are partially sentient, but seeing them just get up and walk is a step a little too far for me to handle just yet," I said, still recovering from the shock.

"Uh, oh! What will you say then the day you see an arzig?" Helio asked with a mischievous glimmer in his eyes.

"A what?" I asked.

"An arzig," he repeated with a chuckle. "It's a carnivorous

plant that literally gets up on two feet and walks to a new location if prey is too scarce where it is."

He burst out laughing when I just gaped at him. "Have no fear, my mate. While they are nasty little things, they don't go after people. We're too big for them. The younger ones will go after insects and small rodents. Mature ones could go after something as big as a young pup or Earth's rabbits."

"Sheesh, I'm liking your planet a little less," I said with an exaggerated air of distress, which made him laugh further.

He accurately understood that I was merely teasing him. I didn't scare easily. God knew I'd fought some crazy shit in the line of duty. But then, the day we met Cedros and the shadow creatures that had invaded the research lab remained one of the freakiest ones.

As we rode through the forest, the beauty that I had admired from afar as we flew to the city now revealed its true face to me. Everything felt more alive, the colors fairly similar to Earth's flora and yet more vibrant, more saturated.

Helio pointed out the various trees and exotic plants that surrounded us. Some had thick trunks like baobabs and others were narrow but towering, with their limbs stretching far up in the sky. Amidst these wonders, one tree took my breath away. He called it a Weeping Fairy. The trunk truly had the seductive shape of a woman, with a set of limbs lifted up like the arms of a woman invoking the gods for mercy. A handful of very long leaves hung at the tips of those two limbs, almost like a drooping bouquet of long feathers. At the base, a network of roots twisted and turned in intricate patterns that almost looked designed rather than random. And on top of those roots and up the base of the trunk gradually fading out, the most unique moss shimmered in the sunlight like countless diamonds.

"It is the pollen that falls from those bushy leaves at the top that creates these shimmering pearls once they soak up some moisture," Helio explained.

"Thus the fairy's tears that gave it this name," I said in understanding.

"Exactly."

The sweet aromas of the blooming flowers, both on the ground and many on the trees themselves, filled the air all around us. I could spend days just feasting my eyes on the perfection of this world. My husband was the ultimate guide, pointing out the various fruits and berries that we encountered, most of which surprisingly turned out to be safe to eat. He had hilarious anecdotes about almost every single one of them, from personal experience during his youth to legends and folklore of his people.

In between all that, I marveled at the unusual creatures that scurried about. Many of them shared similarities with forest creatures of my homeworld. But it was as if they had been thrown into a mixer and matched according to a different combination. From birds with butterfly wings, to bunnies with owl heads that laid eggs, Zailia was a treasure trove of the magical and unusual.

The thick forest eventually thinned, the trees parting to reveal a vast clearing leading down to a wide river. We dismounted close to the treeline. Still barefoot, Helio rooted with the ground, his forest green eyes glowing slightly even as they darkened. His face went slack for a few seconds.

When he refocused on me, a predatory smile stretched his lips. "You are all mine now. No one will disturb us."

CHAPTER 7
HELIO

Maker take me, I couldn't keep my eyes off her. We'd only just met, but I was utterly obsessed. She was so beautiful, so perfect. And Maeve's wretched little dress was doing everything in its power to break whatever willpower I still possessed and that kept me from throwing myself on her.

While I had always had a healthy sexual appetite, I'd never been so hungry for anyone as I was for my mate. Thoughts of our first night together had blood rushing to my groin. I wanted to throw Maeve to the ground, bind her in vines, and have my unbridled way with her.

However, the burning desire currently torturing me had to take a back seat. I wanted Maeve to fall in love with me. She needed to know that my attraction to her went well beyond just lust. Granted, she seemed to welcome my attentions. The enticing outfit she had chosen, not to mention her deliberate decision not to wear a bra, hinted that she was trying to seduce me. Still, we needed to spend more time getting to know each other better, and not just in a physical sense.

I pointed out a huge leaf shaped small boat by the shore. "I hope you don't get seasick. Our ride is waiting."

Maeve fell into step with me as we began walking down the small incline towards the shore.

"So it truly is a boat," Maeve said with the same enthusiastic curiosity she had displayed since her arrival here. "From where I stood, it looked like a giant leaf."

"Because it is," I said with a grin.

Maeve eyed me suspiciously, her gaze flicking back and forth between the boat and me. "I can't decide if you're pulling my leg or if you're being serious. Next thing you know, you'll tell me it's actually a creature with little webbed feet underneath that will paddle for us."

I burst out laughing. "This could indeed have been what I had said. We have turtle-like creatures who serve as rides between the Thousand Islands region. Instead of their backs being shaped like a dome, it is a bit more like a bowl in which they usually carry their young. But this small boat is truly a leaf. It has been bio-engineered so that it can grow in that specific shape. It also has a simple organic artificial intelligence that allows it to follow a direct path between here and the hidden cove."

"Well, that's nice," Maeve said approvingly. "What kind of propulsion system is it using?"

I chuckled. "It's not paddling with little feet underneath, but it has a long tail to propel it forward like a fish."

Maeve stretched her neck to look at the back of the boat, impressed by the long, blade-shaped leaf she could indeed see underwater behind it.

"All aboard," I said, extending a hand towards her.

"That is probably the thickest and sturdiest leaf I've ever seen," Maeve said pensively while giving me her hand as I helped her in.

We settled next to each other on one of the two long benches made of the same thick leaves. They were comfortable enough for a brief ride. But for much longer distances, travelers often used cushions.

"So I'm guessing this is not your boat?" she asked.

I shook my head. "No. It is public property. There are many of them scattered along the river, each one set on a specific path. If you get by the shore and it's gone, then you know someone has already claimed the private area you might have been coveting. Anyone who projects here will know right away that the boat is gone. It does not prevent them from coming here, but they're less likely to do so if they need privacy. They wouldn't be amused by having us return right in the middle of them being naughty."

Maeve laughed, her face taking on that mischievous expression I loved. "That would definitely be awkward."

I brushed my mate's hair from her face, pushing it over her shoulder. After kissing her forehead, I wrapped my arm around her waist. She leaned against me with a contented sigh.

"I've spent all of yesterday running your ears down about Zailia and the strange Edocit culture and world. I'd love to know a bit more about you, Maeve Riley. How did you become a hacker and an Enforcer?"

Maeve scrunched her face at me and opened her mouth to respond. But before a single word could come out, a notification on her com went off. Stunned, she looked down at her armband, and her eyes widened in disbelief before she burst out laughing.

"What is it?" I asked when she shook her head with an indulgent smile.

"It's from Cedros," she said with a chuckle. "He's checking in on me to make sure that I'm fine."

My jaw dropped, and I stared at her, feeling slightly outraged. "What the fuck? Why wouldn't you be?"

Maeve smiled and rubbed my chest in an appeasing fashion. "Don't be upset. I think it's super sweet. Wouldn't you want to know if your baby sister is fine after you've dropped her light years away in the lap of a stranger?"

I grimaced as if I had eaten something foul. Yes, I probably would. As much as the dragon's implied distrust annoyed me to no end, I couldn't be mad at him for being protective of my woman. It reassured me to know that she had someone this powerful to look after her should anything ever happen to me.

"Right," I conceded in a grumpy tone.

Maeve chuckled and gently kissed me. Unable to keep a disgruntled face, I smiled and caressed her hair. She quickly messaged him back saying she was fine, although it would probably take a while for it to reach him across the great distance that separated us.

"To answer your question, yes, I am a hacker, but I don't like being called that," Maeve said with a shrug. "I've always been extremely curious. The best way to make me do something I shouldn't is to forbid me to do it," she added with a sheepish grin.

I burst out laughing. "That sounds like a rather unhealthy habit."

She grimaced and nodded. "Yeah, I know. For the record, I'm stubborn but not reckless. My parents were always secretive about everything. It was extremely annoying. So yes, I would snoop because I knew they were lying to me about many things."

I frowned, my curiosity piqued as I tried to figure out what could have possibly prompted such a behavior from her parents. "Were they doing illegal things?" I asked in a gentle voice devoid of condemnation.

Maeve shook her head. "It turns out that my father used to be a spy. He got grievously injured during a mission, and his identity was exposed. Although he escaped, they forced him to retire. On top of that, he had to get both a face and name change."

"Wow! I guess that meant severing whatever ties he had with

anyone he had ever known, including relatives," I said in a sympathetic tone.

She nodded. "The one constant in his life was my mom. She used to be his handler. She resigned after this whole mess happened, and they got married."

"And from this union, a beautiful little girl named Maeve was born," I said while caressing her cheek.

"A bratty, nosey girl, you mean," she replied with self-derision. "The thing is, we lived far too comfortably, with my dad being an accountant and my mom being a secretary. Their few friends who came visiting looked more like Navy Seals or Men in Black than your usual white-collar worker. It also didn't help that they always had some long meetings behind closed doors. Why would you have private meetings when you're supposed to be hanging out with your friends? Why not wait until you're back at work?"

"You don't sound so much nosey as observant and with a great analytical mind," I said with admiration. "How old were you?"

She smiled gratefully, like one does when you think the person is just complimenting you out of politeness. "I can't deny that I was indeed observant for a twelve-year-old. I love computers. As an only child, I had nothing better to do than to poke around where I shouldn't. So, as you can guess, I started snooping and found out they both still worked for the government. It wasn't highly classified stuff, but they were contacts for other agents at lower security levels passing through the area."

"I'm guessing it didn't take long for you to get caught," I said in a sympathetic tone as our boat was turning the corner around the rock formation that framed the entrance of the large cove ahead.

"Not long is quite the understatement. Try right away," Maeve said with a traumatized expression. "But the system didn't show me I'd been discovered. So I cluelessly kept poking around until my father barged into the room. He got so furious. It was the first time he'd ever gone off on me like that. I actually thought he was going to strike me, which he had never done before."

I frowned. "But he didn't hit you, right?"

She shook her head. "No. But that probably would have hurt less than him saying he had lost any trust and respect he ever had for me."

I flinched, imagining how deeply those words must have cut her, being her dad's only little girl. "So you left it alone, hoping to get back into his good graces?"

"Hell no!" Maeve replied, looking at me as if I'd said something absurd. "It hurt terribly, but it also made me even more suspicious. Why did he get so angry just over a bit of snooping? What was he hiding? I started imagining the worst things."

I tilted my head to the side, staring at her with undisguised curiosity. "Such as what?"

"All the craziest theories you could come up with," Maeve said with self-derision. "Obviously, I thought they were criminals. Then I wondered if I wasn't their child. What if they had kidnapped me? Sure, I had my mother's darker skin. But I didn't look like her, and I especially looked nothing like my father."

"Right," I said, nodding slowly. "They had completely changed his appearance."

"Yep. I asked my hacker friends for help. Turns out they were all conspiracy theorists," my mate said, anger seeping into her voice. "I resisted their suggestions at first. But eventually, they convinced me to let them help me break into my parents' computers."

"No!" I exclaimed, horrified.

"Yeah," she said, looking dejected. "Luckily for my stupid ass, Dad had already set up a trap for them. He knew so much more about what I was up to than I ever imagined."

"Makes sense for a professional spy," I said in a commiserating tone.

She nodded. "Contrary to what they'd led me to believe, my so-called friends weren't twelve-year-olds like me. They were grown adults whose job it was to recruit and train naïve young people like me to do their dirty work."

"Blast..." I whispered, anger rising within me. "I hope they got what they deserved."

So many of the bounties I ended up working on stemmed from this type of people without scruples taking advantage of the innocence and trust of others.

Maeve snorted. "They sure did, and then some. My little stunt involuntarily helped to get many members of that underground group arrested. That's when my parents finally told me the truth. Dad said that important lives depended on the secrets he and mom kept. They needed to be able to trust me not to jeopardize the lives of those people and our own by snooping where I shouldn't."

"Ugh, talk about a heavy burden on such a young child's shoulders," I said sympathetically while caressing her back in a soothing fashion.

"It was *a lot*. I felt lost and confused. Even though I'd been questioning the reality of my life, this by far exceeded anything I could have ever imagined. Still, it felt great knowing that they truly were my parents, and they weren't villains but heroes."

"I can imagine. So how did that take you down the path of becoming a hacker?" I asked with genuine curiosity. "I would have thought this near tragedy would have turned you off from this path."

"Honestly, I might have if not for the way my parents handled the situation," Maeve said pensively. "First, they promised to no longer lie to me. If they couldn't share certain things, they would just say that. Second, they offered to have me properly trained as a hacker by someone they trusted, so long as

I didn't use it to do anything illegal. They also made me promise never to betray them."

I pursed my lips as I pondered on the approach her parents had chosen. "As much as that initially surprised me, I can see the logic of their approach. If you were determined to continue on developing your hacking skills, the chances of you once again associating with dangerous or unsavory people would be too high. By forbidding you, they risked you doubling down and following an even darker path than the one you have been treading."

"Exactly. This way, they controlled what I did while keeping me and everyone in their organization safe," Maeve said. "And thus I became a hacker."

"Clearly you enjoyed it."

"Fuck yeah!" she said with an almost malicious grin. "It was a lot of fun helping break into hate groups, exposing illegal auctions held by flesh traders, and discovering terrorist plans before they could enact them. However, this kind of work had too many restrictions."

"What do you mean?"

"I wanted to go all out doing what I do, legally. My work wasn't illegal, but it was all undercover stuff, which I hated. My mother was the one who suggested I joined the Enforcers. I love my parents, and they love me. But a secret life isn't for me. I don't want to live under a false name, be forced to limit my number of friends, or lie to everyone about who I truly am. I want to openly speak of my career and not have the secrets for the kids I hope to have one day that my parents had to have with me."

"Are you still in contact with your parents?" I asked.

She nodded. "Yes. We talked from time to time. However, our video conferences are few and limited by necessity."

I almost said that, even if she couldn't spend much time with her parents, mine would welcome her with open arms. It was indeed true—they would absolutely love her. However, it felt a little insensitive to bring it up now. Still, I was reconsidering my initial plan of waiting a couple of weeks for us to get to know each other better before introducing her to my family.

I nodded and gave her a sympathetic smile. "Yes, I can see that. I'm sorry it must be so. Nevertheless, you must be very proud of the sacrifices they make in order to keep others safe."

She smiled with a wistful expression. "I am. They made me who I am and taught me that some of the greatest heroes are actually the ones who remain in the shadows."

"I couldn't agree more," I said with enthusiasm. "But the only shadow we'll be dealing with today is the one under the tree when we have our little picnic. For now, behold Sanya's Cove!"

Maeve looked around at the paradisiac beach that sprawled before us. Thick trees lined the beach, encircled by a tall rocky formation that provided us with complete privacy. A few birds chirped in the trees, their voices rising above the joyful singing of the narrow waterfall.

The small boat finally came to a stop by the flat rock that served as a dock. As soon as we disembarked, Maeve cast a worried glance at our ride.

I smiled and slipped a possessive arm around her waist. "Don't worry, my mate. It will not leave without us. Time to go for a swim. But first, let's get the privacy issues out of the way."

Holding my mate by the hand, I walked up to the grassy area closer to the trees. Once in position, I began extruding my *veris* so that I could root. Maeve's eyes immediately flicked down to stare at my feet. As usual, I studied her expression for any sign of unease. Considering she never showed any disgust the previous times I had done it, I shouldn't still feel so relieved by her merely displaying curiosity.

Not wanting to linger here longer than necessary, I quickly broadcast the request for privacy to the local flora.

"There. If anyone tries to peek in this area, they will be

denied. No one gets to enjoy your beauty but me," I said provocatively while removing my shorts.

To my delight, Maeve grinned, her eyes smoldering as she immediately undressed. Maker, my female was perfection! We entirely stripped, placing our bracers on top of our clothes. Holding hands again, we ran into the water, laughing like children.

Despite the desire burning inside me, we didn't actually get naughty in the water. Instead, we started playing by chasing each other. With her being an Enforcer, I had known Maeve would be fit and a great swimmer. However, I had not expected her to be this fast or this agile. Every time I thought I'd caught her, Maeve would wiggle free with the swiftness and ease of one well-versed in wrestling or hand-to-hand combat. And yet, not once did she use anything that even remotely flirted with violence.

On top of further increasing my admiration for my woman, it reinforced my conviction that she would be my perfect partner as a bounty hunter. Someone so competent and well-trained was a true blessing from the Maker.

I couldn't remember the last time I'd had this much fun or felt this carefree. Everything always felt so natural with Maeve. But then, this was still our honeymoon. Our first fight would reveal much about how solid the foundations we were currently laying were. Hopefully, it wouldn't happen anytime soon.

Growing increasingly out of breath, and determined to capture my little siren, I swam as hard as I could after she'd once more escaped me. Seconds before I reached her, I extruded my *veris*, keeping them at the ready. Maeve had been playing me with devious intelligence, making me exert needless effort, and using my strength against me to break free. As soon as I caught her leg, my mate dove and balled herself up, knowing I would follow. She'd used that tactic a couple of times before, with a slight variation that always ended up with her using my chest as a springboard to propel herself forward. Already out of breath from the chase, the pressure on my chest systematically depleted my reserves of oxygen, forcing me to go back to the surface before I could give chase again. Naturally, she was long gone by then.

But not this time.

Instead of following her, as soon as my hand closed on her ankle, I wrapped my *veris* around her shin. Kicking back towards the surface, I yanked on her leg, drawing her after me. Realizing I had ensnared her, she didn't fight, coming to me before jerking her legs down to force my upper body under water. But I'd prepared for that. I released her ankle while slipping my other arm around her waist and drew her tightly against my body. Before she knew what hit her, Maeve was caught in my vise, my *veris* from both arms wrapping around our waists, binding us together.

"Cheater!" Maeve exclaimed, our legs moving underwater to keep us afloat.

"Absolutely not! You didn't state any rule before our little game," I said smugly.

"What?! I shouldn't have to! It should have been obvious!" Maeve exclaimed, looking like she couldn't decide if she was more amused than outraged by my shamelessness.

"Tsk, tsk, Ms. Enforcer. You, better than anyone, know that unless a rule has been written or verbally stated and acknowledged by all parties involved, then they are deemed non-existent," I said with an insufferable smugness.

Even as she wrapped her arms around my neck, Maeve scrunched her face at me. "Oh, I see how it is. Remember that you started this. When I give you your impending payback, I don't want to hear any whining."

I chuckled and rubbed my nose against hers. "Challenge accepted, my mate. I look forward to getting spanked by you."

"The pleasure will be mine, not yours," she said menacingly, although her voice became seductive while her gaze lowered to my lips.

"Lies," I whispered before claiming her mouth.

A bolt of lust set my loins on fire. My mate's heated response almost made me lose control, but I had other plans for us first. Forcing myself to break the kiss, I release the vines binding us together and released her.

"Let's get out of the water," I said.

Her gaze burning with unsated desire, my mate nodded. Swimming side by side, we headed back to the shore.

CHAPTER 8
HELIO

The hunger that had tormented me all day and had temporarily abated during our game was now raging with full force inside me. By the way Maeve was looking at me, she was all in. But I once more reined myself in. The minute we emerged from the water, I took her hand and led her after me towards the phyre trees a short distance from where we had left our clothes and picnic basket. I chuckled at her confusion when I didn't pull her back into my embrace.

"I want to make you try something," I said as sole explanation as we came to stand under the tall tree.

Despite its height, its branches hung low, laden with the landmark fruits of my homeworld.

"I noticed these little bulbs in your garden," Maeve said pensively when she saw me reaching for one of them. "I thought they were some kind of Christmas balls—although there's obviously no Christmas here—that you had adorned the tree with. But is that liquid inside?"

I smiled and nodded. "These are definitely not decorative balls, be it for Christmas or any other holiday. They are fruits called phyre gourds."

I gave her one before picking a second one for myself. She held it up in front of her face, turning it this way and that in awe.

"Wow! It feels like a peach to the touch but looks like a translucent pear. And yet this is clearly organic!"

"It is," I said with a grin. "It is entirely edible, except for the stem. Although the skin is translucent, almost like a thick layer of amber, it is quite sturdy. Pull the stem like this to open it. And then, you can drink the content straight up."

Maeve first gaped at my open phyre gourd with disbelief before looking back at her own. After deftly pulling off the stem, she brought the gourd to her face. She smelled it, her eyes widening with approval at the sweet scent. She took a small, careful sip to taste. This time, her eyes nearly popped out of her head in shock and, to my utter relief, in delight.

"Oh, my God! It tastes like pina colada!" Maeve said. "Are you telling me these gourds grow naturally like this, with that cocktail inside?"

I laughed. "They grow naturally like that. But this is not a cocktail yet. When they are yellow, the juice inside is very thick. It is not ripe yet but can be used for various desserts or jam preparations. When it is ripe, the skin becomes translucent, and the cream inside becomes liquid like this. But if you wait a couple of weeks longer, the juice will become fermented and take on a dark reddish hue. That's when it has become an alcoholic beverage. It is deceptively mild to the taste, but it will hammer you when you least expect it."

"Sheesh! Thanks for the heads up," Maeve said before taking another long gulp.

I started heading back towards our clothes while we finished drinking our gourds.

"This drinks like a smoothie," Maeve mused out loud while walking by my side. "Does the fermented version become thicker?"

"No. The more mature it gets, the more liquid it becomes."

I crouched next to our clothes to rummage in the pocket of my shorts, and I retrieved one of the two leaves the young sapling had given us in town last night. Maeve slightly recoiled upon seeing it.

"We will eat the skin of the gourds along with last night's unexpected gift," I said with a mischievous grin.

To my surprise, Maeve appeared uneasy. I gave her a questioning look. She shifted on her feet and tucked a strand of her damp hair behind her ear.

"I don't do drugs," she said in an apologetic tone. "I've never done any of those things. First, because I guess I'm too much of a control freak to allow some substance to take it away from me. And second, because it's a requirement for my job."

I smiled and drew her to me. She came willingly, and we embraced each other.

"First, you never have to apologize for expressing your right not to want to do something," I said in a gentle voice. "Second, while off-worlders use Edocit down as a recreational drug, we use it as a relaxant and as a sensory enhancer. It is not addictive, and it does not cause loss of control."

"A relaxant?" Maeve echoed, taken aback. "I knew it was not addictive, and that the euphoria it provided was so amazing that it was why people pay exorbitant prices to get it. I never heard of it described as a relaxant."

"That's because people eat a full down or two," I said. "In our juveniles, the concentration is very high, so the effects are more than doubled. And if you consume them on an empty stomach, it will affect you even more strongly. Which is why I gave you the phyre gourd to drink and eat first, and why I brought a single leaf for us to share."

"I see," Maeve said, looking pensively at the leaf before glancing at my hair. "Do you eat your own leaves?"

I nodded. "Yes. Most of us find the juveniles' down leaves too strong for the day to day. It is good when you want your senses heightened, like when you're about to be naughty with your mate," I added, my voice dipping as I wiggled my eyebrows suggestively, making her chuckle. "But when I just want to relax, I may simply eat one of my own leaves or drink them as tea. It is akin to taking a warm bubble bath or getting a massage."

"Well, that sounds practical," Maeve said teasingly.

"It is," I replied, before casting a look at the down leaf. "We do not have to consume it, since it makes you uncomfortable. I promise to make you feel plenty, even without it."

To my surprise, Maeve appeared to hesitate. She chewed her bottom lip while staring at the leaf. "Hmmm… If you say it won't make me lose control, maybe I can try it."

I frowned, taken aback by this change of heart. "Maeve, you don't have to do this. I will never ask you to go against your principles or wishes. You don't have to try to please me. I'm not offended. I want you to fully enjoy everything we do together, and only do them because you also want it, not because you feel compelled to."

She smiled and gently caressed my face before resting her palm on my shoulder. "Thank you for saying that. But you really don't know me if you think I would ever do anything against my will just to please someone else. My mom would tell you I have inherited the Irish stubbornness of my father. And he would tell you that I've inherited the Cuban 'You better not fuck with me' ways of my mother. I'm willing to try it because I trust you. If you tell me it will only enhance what I feel without making me lose control, then I believe you."

A powerful wave of affection rushed through me as I looked at my beautiful mate. "You do not know how much this means to me. I may not be perfect, and I will fall short at times. But I will never betray you or mislead you. You will always have nothing but the truth from me."

Judging by the powerful emotion that flitted over her

features, I realized I had said something she had needed to hear from me. It had not been calculated, but it certainly struck me that, in light of the way she had been brought up, lying and secrets would be the biggest betrayal for her. Thankfully, that was one thing she would never have to fear from me.

We exchanged a slow, deep, an incredibly tender kiss. Maker, I was truly falling for this woman. As soon as we broke the kiss, Maeve yanked the down leaf out of my fingers. Just as she was about to take a bite out of it, the chime of a com notification resonated from our pile of clothes.

"This must be a joke!" I hissed, glaring at our clothes in disbelief. "If it's your Derakeen again—"

"No, no, no. Don't even go there," Maeve said, giving me a stern look. "First off, Cedros may be overprotective, he's not a stalker. You don't have to worry about him harassing us. Second, my com does not ring like that. You are the one getting a call."

My brain froze, and my jaw dropped at the sudden realization that she was indeed right. But who in the world would call me right now? They knew I was on my honeymoon and not to be disturbed.

I scrunched my face at the mocking way in which Maeve was smirking at me. "Right. Sorry about that," I mumbled, my eyes throwing daggers in the general direction of my shorts.

"Aren't you going to answer that?" Maeve asked with an insufferably taunting expression.

"No. They should know better than to bother me during our bonding time. Anyway, it stopped ringing," I said dismissively. "Now, where were we?"

My mate smiled seductively and leaned against me when I drew her closer to me. "I believe I was about to take a bite of that down leaf you've been waving in front of my face. Someone promised me some particularly enhanced sensations."

"That someone meant every word and certainly intends to

deliver," I said in a purring tone while pressing her pelvis against mine. "Go on, my love. Bite."

My com going off again just as Maeve was going to take a bite had me cursing in the most unfashionable way. To my relief, my woman burst out laughing at my aggravation rather than being offended by my foul mouth. I was generally quite polite until you pissed me off.

"Whoever it is, they are rather persistent," she said in a sympathetic tone. "It's okay. Go on and answer."

I frowned, my teeth clenched with indecision. No one should bother me during this special time with my mate. Everyone knew they were to leave me alone for the next week or two. Had they forgotten, or was there truly…?

I never got to finish that thought. The trees lining the beach began shaking their leaves in an ominous sound that left no mystery that something serious had happened.

"What's going on?" Maeve asked with worry as she glanced around us at the trees.

"An emergency signal," I said while rushing to my shorts to retrieve my com.

I felt my blood drained from my face at the sight of the message.

"What is it?" Maeve asked upon seeing my expression.

"A sapling is missing," I said with the familiar anger rising through me every time such a thing happened.

Maeve flinched, an air of commiseration settling on her beautiful features. "Oh, no! Do you know who?"

"The name isn't familiar. A sixteen-year-old male, Strasa Melayan," I replied absentmindedly while scanning through the message. I flipped to the next page, and my heart seized. "No!"

"Oh, my God!" Maeve exclaimed upon seeing the familiar face on the interface of my com. "That's our boy! That's the teenager who gave us those leaves! We saw him less than 24 hours ago. Isn't that too early to deem him missing? Surely, he just spent the night at one of his friends' houses?"

Although those were fair questions, the hope in Maeve's voice showed she suspected there was cause for concern. But she wanted to cling to the illusion that he might still be fine.

I quickly skimmed through the rest of the message, my heart sinking a little more with each word.

"Unfortunately, he did not spend a night with a friend," I said in a grim tone laced with anger. "They were the first people his family contacted when he failed to come home. Apparently, the security cameras show him getting on board a Nazhral ship which departed last night. The boy is off-world."

I spat the last words, feeling both outraged and helpless. While I didn't always take every bounty sent my way, handing them over instead to other hunters, I never turned down a case of an abducted youngling. I didn't know the boy, but our brief interaction last night had created a bond, which made the prospect of not searching for him even more unacceptable.

This was not how I envisaged spending the first few days following my marriage. But I could never live with myself if I didn't do everything in my power to save the youngling. I swallowed hard and gave my mate a wary glance.

"As I had mentioned to you previously, I have asked my bounty hunter friends to take up any fresh cases that might pop up during our honeymoon," I said cautiously.

"Fuck that!" Maeve exclaimed, sounding a little outraged. "Our honeymoon can wait. This is *our* boy. *We* find him."

The weight of the world suddenly fell off my shoulders. I beamed at my woman, affection and gratitude filling my heart. To think I had feared she would have argued against me taking on the case instead of focusing on our relationship.

"You truly are my perfect mate," I whispered before pulling her into my embrace and kissing her deeply.

Although she melted against me, the kiss was as passionate as it was brief.

"There'll be plenty of time for us to enjoy quality time together," she said gently once we parted. "I could not enjoy the wonders of your world while I worried about that youngling."

"Agreed," I said, silently thanking the Maker—and Kayog—for giving me my soulmate.

"How did they know where we were?" Maeve asked while we quickly dressed. "I thought they couldn't see us through the trees?"

"They couldn't see us. They sent a general call to find me. The trees knew where I was because I asked them for privacy. When they shake their leaves like that, it warns you that someone is urgently trying to contact you. You *never* use that for play or for something trivial. When it happens, you know you must respond immediately."

"Well, that's practical," Maeve said as we hopped back into the boat to return to the shore where the harstags were still patiently waiting for us. "If you didn't know the youngling, who sent you that message?"

"Captain Ethra, the head of our law enforcement," I said. "The minute I saw it was from her, I knew it wasn't just a case of a youngling wandering off because of an excess of euphoria. I have a great relationship with her. There are too many cases that she wished her team could tackle, but it would stretch their resources too thin. I am one of very few Edocit bounty hunters. When our younglings get abducted, she trusts more in one of us searching for them than any off-worlder only in it for the credits."

"That's quite understandable. I cannot imagine how his parents must feel right now," Maeve said with commiseration.

"They will be devastated for sure. As soon as we get home, we'll take the skiff to their house so that we can get as much information from them as possible."

"Is there any chance he might have voluntarily gotten on board that ship?" Maeve asked.

"The way Captain Ethra worded her message, Strasa wasn't forced to board the ship. Or if he was, his abductors did it in a way that fooled everyone. But you know as well as I do that there are countless ways to influence someone into acting against their will," I replied.

Maeve nodded, her wheels spinning as she reflected on the case. "Considering the history of your people and based on our brief interaction with that young male, I'd be shocked if he actually ran away without leaving a note to his parents or at least communicating after his departure. I could be wrong, but he didn't strike me as the type to put his parents through this type of heartache."

"Our younglings do not run away," I said forcefully. "They wander off under the effects of their hormonal imbalance. But as soon as they regain self-awareness, they immediately communicate with their parents to reassure them. Our world isn't perfect, by any means. However, it is almost physiologically impossible for our youth to be miserable or unhappy, and certainly not to the point of wanting to run away. Plus, we need frequent contact with *our* land."

"Hopefully, his parents will have some answers to give us somewhere to start," Maeve replied. "Do they have anything on the ship and its destination?"

"I'm sure they are trying to track it. But flesh traders are usually very good at vanishing," I said with disgust. "Ethra can only divulge so much before the family officially grants us permission to access everything in the case. She told me what she knew would make it impossible for me to resist getting involved."

"Good. I imagine it's just a legal formality, right? His parents won't object to our assistance?"

"They will more than welcome it," I said reassuringly, as our small boat finally reached the shore.

The harstags came to meet us before we'd even finished disembarking. Laros knew me well enough that a single look at my face told him we were in a hurry. We hopped on their backs, and the harstags immediately started galloping back home. I thanked the Maker once more to see how comfortable my mate was sustaining this harsh pace without a saddle. You'd think she'd been born riding Sefa.

As soon as we got home, we went inside to put on some more appropriate clothes. Despite our impatience to go meet Strasa's family, showing up in such casual attire would be disrespectful.

Minutes later, we were airborne. Thankfully, they lived in a hamlet close to my house. After a short flight, we initiated our descent, landing right outside of their imposing residence. A crowd of villagers had gathered outside, undoubtedly to support the family. Before we even set foot on the ground, the front door opened on a tall male whose resemblance to the young sapling made it clear he had to be his father.

The crowd parted to let us through, eyeing us both with curiosity. The male I presumed to be Strasa's father barely spared a surprised look at my mate before returning his attention to me.

"Helio Breisa?" he asked, his voice filled with hope.

"Yes. That's me. You must be Strasa's sire?" I asked while circling to the front of the shuttle to join Maeve and approach him.

"Yes, yes. I am Imreth. Thank you for coming so quickly," he said with obvious relief, although the underlying grief couldn't be mistaken.

"This is my mate, Maeve. She is an Enforcer of the United Planets Organization," I said, waving at my woman before taking her hand.

An impressed gasp rose from the crowd, who stared at my female with renewed interest.

Imreth's eyes widened in a mix of surprise and heightened hope. "An Enforcer? That is great news indeed. But please, do come in."

We followed him inside, only to find his wife sitting at the table, her attractive face drenched in tears, and the vines and leaves in her hair withered from sorrow. He quickly made the introductions.

"My beloved, this is Helio, the bounty hunter Captain Ethra told us about. And this is his mate, Maeve, a UPO Enforcer," Imreth said.

Maeve slightly flinched at the hopeful way in which he repeated her association with the galactic peacekeeping force. I kicked myself, realizing how mentioning her being an Enforcer could have been misleading to the couple. I'd merely meant to let them know she was qualified to assist in the search, and not just some gawker here to listen to some juicy gossip. Instead, I feared they assumed this meant the Enforcers were taking on the case. But this was too small for them to get involved.

"Helio, Maeve, this is my mate, Niphne," Imreth continued, apparently oblivious to our discomfort.

The female rose to her feet, her palms still resting on top of the dark wood table, as if for support. She leveled her brown eyes, a few shades darker than her hair, on my mate.

"An Enforcer?" Niphne asked, her face lighting up with the same hope it had triggered in her husband.

"Yes," Maeve said in a gentle voice. "I am an Enforcer, but I'm not here in that official capacity. I met your son last night in town. He's a delightful young man. So naturally, hearing of his disappearance, I volunteered to help. Whatever skills I have gained in my line of work, I gladly put at your disposal to help bring Strasa back home safe and sound."

To my relief, although the couple seemed a little disappointed that the entire organization wasn't taking up the case, the glimmer of hope continued to burn deep in their eyes.

"Whatever the capacity in which you are here, all that matters is that you *are* here," Niphne said, her voice shaking with emotion. "We are no longer alone trying to bring our baby back home. We do not know what to do, or even where to start. We need help."

"And we are here to give it," I said in a reassuring tone.

"Please, have a seat," Imreth said, gesturing at two of the fancy chairs on the opposite side of the table from where his mate had been sitting. "Can I offer you some refreshments?"

Maeve and I both shook our heads as we settled down on the plush beige cushion of the dark chairs.

"No, thank you," I said. "Could you tell us everything that has happened? Last we saw your son, it was around 7:00 o'clock in the evening. He was standing with his friends by the fountain in the town square."

Imreth nodded with an angry expression. "It's all my fault," he said, his eyes glistening. "I should have insisted on being there with him."

"While he hung out with his friends?" I asked, confused.

"No, I meant for the meeting he was having with an off-worlder friend," he said, clearly angry with himself. "Strasa left his friends around 8:00 PM. He was supposed to meet with the off-worlder earlier, but she had been delayed."

Maeve and I exchanged a look. This was sadly a much too familiar tale with flesh trader cartels trapping young males and females into falling in love with beautiful off-worlders, with promises of a lavish life. They would get them to pack up and leave, only to realize that the person they believed to be their soulmate was in fact a complete fabrication. By then, it was already too late. They'd either be sold on the slaves market or forced into prostitution in some brothel. In Strasa's case, they would drain him until there was nothing left of the beautiful and charismatic young male he had been.

By the defensive expression that settled on Imreth's face, I could guess what my own revealed as I looked back at him.

"It's not what you think. We were not being careless or indifferent," Imreth said. "Strasa and Saydi had been talking for over a year. Both Niphne and I had also talked on multiple occasions with her. We had no reason to worry, as she was an applicant for the exchange program we're associated with."

"Saydi?" Maeve asked. "Is that the name of the person he was meeting?"

Imreth nodded. "Yes, Saydi Dalrosh. She's a young Nazhral who wants to become a xenobotanist. Our family business grows rare plants as well as a lot of organic produce, local and foreign. We've been involved in the exchange program for decades."

Although she did a great job of hiding it, I had felt Maeve stiffen upon hearing the species of Strasa's friend. The Nazhrals—a feline species—were famous for piracy and illegal trades. While it would be unfair to label the entire species as criminals, their culture and society condoned and even encouraged behaviors and practices deemed illegal or severely frowned upon by other cultures.

"Were they romantically involved?" I asked in a gentle voice.

"Oh no! Not at all," Niphne interjected while wiping the tears from her face with the back of her hand. "They were just friends."

"Are you certain, or was that merely what he said?" I insisted. "He is extremely handsome. And judging by his interactions with his friends, he seems very popular and charismatic."

"He is," Niphne replied. "Everybody adores him. But I can assure you that there was no romantic involvement between them. They were simply supposed to meet yesterday to establish a first contact in person. And tomorrow, Saydi and her parents were going to come here and have dinner with us so that we could show them what we could offer their daughter and the accommodations we provide the exchange students who stay with us."

"And you had spoken to her parents directly?" I asked.

"Yes," Imreth replied.

"At the same time?" I insisted again.

He hesitated and glanced at his wife with a questioning expression. She frowned, clearly searching her memory before she shook her head.

"No. Now that you mention it, we never spoke with more than one of them at a time, although we spoke with all three of them on various occasions," Imreth said.

By the commiserating expression on Maeve's face, she undoubtedly shared my opinion that the same con artist had impersonated all three characters to fool them and their son. Nowadays, technology made it extremely easy to modify one's appearance through vidcoms. And now, Strasa's parents were realizing how they had been played. Niphne sobbed, and her husband wrapped an arm around her, trying to console her even as he looked at us with despair.

"For as long as I can remember, my family has welcomed foreign interns for a few months and sometimes for an entire year. Nothing like this ever happened. We had no reason to suspect this kind of betrayal," Imreth said, his voice breaking with sorrow.

"Those people are good at what they do," Maeve said in a sympathetic tone. "They take advantage of kind-hearted people and come up with the most devious schemes to abuse the generosity and trust of others. You had no reason to suspect this because only a monster could plot and enact such a terrible plan."

"So we realize," Imreth replied, defeated. "Captain Ethra gave us a recording of Strasa entering that ship, if you want to see it."

"Yes, please," I said.

He turned on the giant vidscreen on the wall to our right and tapped a few instructions on his datapad on the table. Moments later, the footage of the docking bay replaced the news show playing on the vidscreen.

On it, we could clearly see Strasa walking alongside an attractive young Nazhral female. She had ivory fur interspersed with golden brown streaks. As per the short communication Captain Ethra had sent me, the young sapling didn't appear to have been coerced into getting on board. Nothing in the way he walked indicated he was inebriated or under the influence of any drugs beyond the natural high Edocits of his age fell under. While we couldn't hear their words, they appeared to be chatting amiably on their way to the vessel. Seeing him voluntarily climb on board with a big smile once again made me wonder if he had truly been abducted.

My thoughts must have shown on my face as Imreth took on an outraged expression.

"My son had no intention of eloping or running away," he said forcefully. "I don't care what this recording shows."

I nodded slowly, not wanting to hurt them any more than necessary. "Are there any recordings of her parents, or of anyone else who might have come in and out of the vessel during their stay?"

Imreth's shoulders slouched. "No. She was the only person seen coming in and out of the ship."

"She was the bait," Niphne suddenly said in an angry tone. "She was sent out to lure him into the trap."

"You think she was trying to seduce him?" Maeve asked.

"I don't know if she was. But my Strasa would not have been interested. He was happy here, and he had begun courting a lovely Utzac girl called Idova. He had even asked her for suggestions in the shaping of his house."

"Wow! Okay," I said, slightly taken aback. Noticing Maeve's

confused expression at my reaction, I turned to her to briefly explain. “If an Edocit asks another for their input in the shaping of their house, it is usually our way of saying I see you as a potential spouse. Therefore, we want you to have a say in the dwelling that might become your home in the future. Strasa would have been extremely serious about that girl if he did so.”

“He did,” Imreth said. “She has been coming regularly to his house. She even proposed several modifications to his garden, which my son has done.”

“Then we can eliminate the possibility of a romantic involvement with Saydi,” I said pensively. “At least on his part...”

“Is there any way you could grant us access to his computer or whatever device he used to communicate with Saydi?” Maeve asked. “It could help us try to track the origin of her messages or detect any clues as to their whereabouts.”

“Of course,” Imreth said. “Whatever you need to help us find our boy is yours.”

“That means we will also need you to give us a right of representation so that we can have access to anything law enforcement has to share with us,” I added.

“It is already done,” Niphne said with a sniffle. “As soon as Captain Ethra recommended you, we provided her with our consent. She simply could not enact it until you had accepted the case.”

“Perfect. Is there anything more you can share with us to help us track him down?” Maeve asked.

The parents exchanged a glance, each looking for the other to jog their memory as to anything they might have omitted. Both coming up empty, they turned back to us and shook their heads.

“No problem. If you can think of anything else, let us know. In the meantime, we would require Idova’s address, as well as those of his friends who were with him last night,” I said.

“Of course. My Niphne will give you their coordinates while I go fetch his computer,” Imreth said.

After they had provided us with all that we requested, the couple escorted us back out to our skiff.

"Please find my baby. Please," Niphne pleaded as she battled the tears welling up in her eyes.

"We will do everything in our power to bring him back to you," Maeve said.

My chest warmed when my mate hugged Niphne. The heart-broken mother hugged her back with the energy of despair. And yet, when they released each other, hope glimmered again in Niphne's eyes despite the tears that still drenched her face.

With a last farewell, Maeve and I boarded our shuttle and took flight towards Idova's village.

CHAPTER 9
MAEVE

My blood boiled with the familiar rage abduction cases systematically stirred within me. I always held a special hatred for those who believed themselves entitled to destroying the lives of the innocents just for profit. Beyond that brief meeting by the fountain, I didn't know Strasa. And yet, this kidnapping was personal.

I kept replaying in my mind the security feed of the young sapling entering that vessel. Nothing in his demeanor or body language remotely hinted at someone on the run. Even when they tried to appear nonchalant, fugitives and runaways always exuded some kind of tension, their eyes tended to flick around looking for anyone that might notice them, and they were either excessively stoic or over-the-top jovial to throw off any suspicion. Strasa had been none of the above—only a relaxed teenager chatting with a friend as they boarded the vessel.

My instincts told me he hadn't expected to stay there long.

But why did he go there at all?

My fingers burned with the urge to open up Strasa's laptop and datapad to dig through his communications with Saydi. But it was too short a ride to Idova's village. Once I started working and got in the zone, you had best not break my concentration. I could get quite rabid when disturbed.

Less than ten minutes after leaving Strasa's house, Helio began his descent towards one of the villages with flower-shaped buildings. I hated that my first visit to one of those traditional hamlets would be under such dark clouds. But I fully intended for my next trip here to be with Strasa playing tour guide for us once we'd rescued him.

Helio settled the shuttle down on one of the landing pads at the edge of the village.

"Isn't this a little far from Idova's house?" I asked as we disembarked.

"Unlike Strasa's village, the Utzac have not designed their hamlets with personal shuttles in mind as those vessels had not even existed at the time," Helio explained. "The trees that shape some of these houses are over a thousand years old."

"Right, that makes sense."

I wished I could feast my eyes on the beauty of the village and of its inhabitants. But I had already gone into investigator mode, and my mind was busy going over what few facts we had, listing the questions I wanted to ask Idova, and prioritizing the tasks I would tackle once we were done with this interview.

It didn't take long for us to reach the giant lotus-shaped dwelling where she resided. By the number of people gathered outside, I guessed the news of her boyfriend's abduction had already spread through the village. There were almost as many people as those who had been hanging out outside of Strasa's home to support the family.

Once more, the crowd parted as soon as we approached. A stunning young Utzac girl, her blue eyes slightly puffy, likely from crying, gave us a trembling smile. Her skin was as dark as ebony, the large leaves of her skirt had the beautiful gradient of bright greens and blues, the same color as her blue hair intertwined with vines.

"You must be Helio and Maeve, the bounty hunters?" she asked.

"We are," I replied.

"Thank you for coming so quickly. Please come in," she added, gesturing at the highly ornate wooden door that closed the entrance.

We returned the grateful, welcoming nods of a few of the villagers as we entered the dwelling. She let us into the living area and introduced us to her parents, who were already there. Although they clearly wanted to attend, probably more to support their child, they did not interfere as we began questioning Idova.

"We understand that you and Strasa were romantically involved?" I asked.

She nodded, a timid expression descending on her beautiful face. "Yes. Strasa has been courting me for the past year. We officially began dating three months ago. He has been seeking my advice on the shaping of his dwelling."

She appeared even more timid when she pronounced that last sentence, as a blushing bride would when revealing her boyfriend had just proposed. A heartbreaking mix of pleasure and sorrow settled upon her features as she likely reminisced about their time together.

"So you were planning a future together," Helio said as a statement, not a question.

Idova nonetheless responded. "Yes. We were making very specific plans, as it was going to impact the designs I have been working on for my own dwelling right here in Anehela. Strasa was excited about our future. He never would have left Zailia of his own free will, and especially not to follow *her*."

The sudden contempt that seeped into Idova's voice when she said 'her' didn't escape my notice.

"You are referring to that exchange student, Saydi?" I asked, already knowing the answer but wanting to let her expand without trying to guide her response with too pointed questions.

"I don't believe she was an exchange student," Idova said with conviction and an underlying anger. "There were too many signs that she was up to something. I should have accepted Strasa's invitation to join them last night. Maybe my presence could have prevented him from getting abducted."

Helio and I both perked up at those statements. He leaned forward, his gaze intense.

"What signs were those?" Helio asked.

"She supposedly wanted to come here to learn about our flora and agriculture," Idova said with a shrug. "And yet, she would spend more than half of their conversations asking him if he'd ever wanted to move away or explore the galaxy. She would go on and on about the wonders she'd seen and experienced on other planets. She even mentioned once that, should he ever want to go sightseeing, she would be happy to play tour guide for him and show him some of the coolest hangouts and space stations in the tourist networks."

"Hmmm," I said with a frown. "That *is* a strange conversation to have when you're trying to convince someone to let you come stay with them for your studies. But then why did you decline to go with him? I would have wanted to know what exactly that other female wanted with my boyfriend."

Idova shrugged again. "Although I was curious as to what she really wanted, I trust him. I *know* Strasa is very serious about us. He had already expressed some major reservations about her. Based on their previous conversations, I believe she was attracted to him, or at least was trying to make him think she was. She had made a few moves, but her species is reputed to be quite flirtatious naturally. I didn't want to appear territorial by showing up. And I also believed that, in my presence, she wouldn't reveal her true intentions."

"How flirty exactly?" Helio insisted.

"She was a little too clingy and too available. When she would suggest that they should go on an intergalactic tourist trip, he would tell her no. And yet, she would find different ways of bringing it back up. Finally, he told her he had absolutely no intention of going off-world, whether for tourism or otherwise, because he was happy here. She then replied *playfully* that maybe she would end up settling down here... with him."

"Wow, the nerve," I said, unable to resist.

"The nerve, indeed," Idova replied, her voice laced with anger. "Strasa politely told her he was not interested and that he was already in a committed relationship. She laughed it off, saying that she was just joking. But a week after that, she asked to come visit for the on-site internship interview. By then, Strasa was pretty convinced he didn't want her here. Yesterday was supposed to be a test to assess how problematic or not she might be."

"If he felt such strong reservations about her, why didn't he share his concerns with his parents?" Helio asked, echoing the thoughts crossing my mind.

"He knew that if he mentioned anything, they would automatically cross her off the list. Internships at his family's garden are highly sought after. She seemed quite knowledgeable about botany, and her school records were stellar. He didn't want to ruin her chances just because he thought she was too flirty. What if he was misinterpreting her true intentions? But my Strasa has always been too kind-hearted."

"What do you mean by that?" Helio asked.

"He always wants to see the best in people," Idova replied. "He's not naïve, but he gives people too many chances, and gives them the benefit of the doubt where others would have already drawn the line. For example, she sent him a few pictures of herself that I personally considered to be out of line. Obviously, with her being a Nazhral, she doesn't wear clothes. That didn't bother me. However, the poses were just borderline suggestive enough to raise an eyebrow, but not enough to be deemed risqué."

I shifted in my seat, the same unease resurfacing as I couldn't help but wonder just how indifferent Strasa had truly been about the young Nazhral's advances. Idova pushed a few prints in front of us, which turned out to be some of the images Saydi had sent her boyfriend. She was right in saying they were flirty enough to titillate but fell just short of giving grounds for her to be called out. Nazhrals were a feline species. Everything about them screamed both sensuality and danger—relics of their predatory ancestors.

A quick glance at my mate gave me reasons to think the same doubt had seeped into his mind. When I looked back at Idova, she lifted her chin defiantly and held my gaze unwaveringly.

"I know what you're thinking, but you are wrong. And no, I am not in denial or refusing to face an unpleasant reality," she said with conviction. "Like I said, Strasa wanted me to go with him. If he had any betrayal in mind, he wouldn't have done that. His plan was for that meeting to be a test. If she came on to him, or if her behavior in any way confirmed his unease or suspicions about her, he would have told his parents he no longer supported granting her an internship."

"Okay, but can you think of any reasons why he voluntarily boarded her vessel?" I asked in a kind voice.

"According to our friends, she apparently wanted to show him some exotic hybrid plants that she had growing aboard her parents' vessel," Idova explained. "This sprout was apparently extremely fragile and had to be kept in a very controlled environment."

"That sounds a little weak," I said gently, surprised that, after everything Strasa had told her, he would fall for such a generic trap.

"I would agree," Idova conceded. "However, she had not just

invited him to come see her sprouts, but all of our friends who were with him in town."

My eyebrows shot up upon hearing those words. Helio and I exchanged a look, the same thought apparently crossing our minds.

"I do not recall seeing anyone else with them in the security footage when they boarded the vessel," Helio said.

"Correct. That's because Strasa told them not to come. He wanted to see exactly how she would behave when they were alone," Idova replied. "He also didn't want her to use our friends to corner him into doing something he didn't want to. According to the message he sent me before he parted with them, he was only supposed to be there for thirty minutes to see the sprouts and meet her parents. He had promised to message me back as soon as he left her vessel. But I never heard back."

"I'm so sorry," I said, my heart breaking at the way her voice cracked on the last words and her beautiful eyes welled with tears.

"You've got to find him, please… before they…"

Idova never finished her sentence. The stoicism she had bravely displayed since our arrival finally shattered, and she broke down into tears. Her mother pulled her into her embrace and gently caressed her hair while whispering soothing words in Edocit. I couldn't understand them, but I didn't need to.

After promising to forward us all the conversations between Strasa and his daughter, regarding the Nazhral, her father escorted us out. There was still a considerable crowd outside their dwelling. Two males and a female were holding what I believed to be meals they had prepared for the family. My heart warmed at this display of support.

We walked silently to our shuttle, not wanting the locals to overhear our discussions. Moments later, Helio's com chimed, the notification informing him he had received new documents.

Without a word, he showed me the interface of his device.

"Perfect!" I said under my breath as I recognized an official report transmission from their law enforcement.

Strasa's parents had visibly informed Captain Ethra that we had accepted the mandate.

"Do you think Saydi was trying to kidnap multiple kids?" I asked as soon as we settled inside our shuttle.

"Yes," Helio said grimly. "There's no question in my mind that she could see him slipping through her fingers, so she sped up the process before he cut all communications with her."

"Agreed. Let's go home. I want to start digging into the data and find out what I can about this Saydi. If she truly is a top botany student—which I doubt—there will be records somewhere allowing us to narrow down her whereabouts."

"Excellent," Helio said with gratitude. "That will let me focus on tracking down the vessel."

The trip back home took an eternity and a day. A part of me felt guilty to be so ready and eager to jump on this mission only a day after our wedding. I had no qualms with my need to look for Strasa. It wasn't just the right thing to do; I *wanted* to do it. But I had not even shown the slightest dismay at our honeymoon getting cut short after it had barely started. As was my wont, I'd gone straight into Enforcer mode.

For all my griping about the poor quality of males in the dating pool, I had lost a few potential good partners because they'd grown fed up with me always putting career and missions first. What they took for ambition was merely my need to help those in dire situations. Between enjoying some quality leisure time and rescuing kidnapping victims, the choice was obvious.

Still, I didn't want Helio to think that our bonding time didn't matter to me. I definitely cared about having some alone time with him. We'd been off to an amazing start. And this mission together could bring us even closer, assuming we worked well together. What better way to assess if we were also compatible on that front? After all, the success of our union partially relied on the fact that I would become his partner. If I remained an Enforcer, we'd only have a part-time relationship.

I gave him a sideways glance. He appeared lost in thought as he silently piloted the shuttle. No doubt sensing my gaze on him, he turned his forest green eyes on me with a gentle but inquisitive expression.

"I didn't mean to stare," I said sheepishly. "Although I greatly enjoy the view."

Right on cue, his brown skin darkened, and his handsome face took on that adorable, embarrassed expression he always got whenever I complimented him. The buds in his hair flowering only made me melt even further inside.

"I'm happy you like what you see," he said in a soft voice. "I like you a lot, my mate."

"I like you a lot, too," I replied in a similar tone. "Today was… This morning with you was absolutely perfect," I added, choosing my words carefully. "I could have spent an eternity over there, just the two of us. But rescuing Strasa is really important. That's the only reason I was so eager for us to take on this mission. I wouldn't be able to give you all the attention you deserve while worrying about the boy. So please know it doesn't mean I don't want us to spend romantic time together and get to know each other."

Once I finished speaking those words, I realized just how stiff my spine was, and how I was all but holding my breath. His shocked expression threw me.

"Maeve, surely you're not apologizing to me about this?" Helio asked, incredulous. "Do you not understand what it means to me that you would so selflessly put aside a time that I know humans greatly value, just so that you could help a complete stranger? Since we left the cove, I've been wondering how I would make this up to you. The abduction of young Edocits is a very sore topic for us, and one of the principal causes I devoted my career to. I thought I was going to have to beg you to let me go look for him."

"About saving an innocent? That's one thing that will never happen," I said with a nervous laugh as relief flooded through me. "Chances are, you'll be the one begging me to stop trying to save everyone and their brother," I added, only partially joking.

"Then I guess we'll get along famously," he replied. "I will never resent you wanting to help someone in need. Knowing me, I'll be the one cheering you on and demanding to come with."

I laughed at the adorable boyish look he gave me as he spoke those words. "I'm sure I will insist that you do."

Helio extended his free hand towards me, and I took it. He gently squeezed it, his tender gaze wrapping me in a warm blanket.

As soon as we landed, we immediately went to work. We settled in his office. Ever the gentlemen, Helio offered to let me share his desk, but I declined, happy to crash on the comfortable couch near his desk. I was used to working with a tablet or portable computer in my lap. Legs crossed under me, my visors acting as a secondary monitor, I first reviewed the police report, the conversations Idova had forwarded me, and then spent a couple of hours going through all the exchanges between Strasa and Saydi.

This put to rest whatever lingering doubts I might have had regarding an involvement between the two of them. Saydi clearly knew what she was doing. Her advances had begun in a subtle fashion. Initially, it had been innocent enough compliments about Edocits, his parents' gardens, and his own talent and knowledge in xenobotany. Then the compliments took a more personal nature, about his appearance, voice, and personality. While flattered, the boy had still seemed clueless about her play until she became more openly flirty.

His unease was occasionally almost palpable in the way he responded or simply pretended not to have understood her underlying meaning. When she would get bolder, he would bluntly tell her he was involved, to which she would systematically respond with some dismissive comment, such as she was merely joking, or that she was simply teasing him because it was too funny to see him blush.

But the Enforcer in me recognized the pattern in her behavior. She was testing different approaches until he started resisting. Then she would slightly retreat, regroup, and attack from a different angle. Idova had been right. Very few of their conversations related to botany. Most revolved around Saydi praising the wonders of other planets to tempt him into leaving Zailia.

Fucking predators…

Sadly, she'd been extremely good at not giving away anything in their conversations that would help me narrow down a location she might have taken him to. Therefore, I shifted my focus to digging into her background.

My Enforcer credential gave me access to a wealth of information that I shamelessly leveraged. Before taking this sabbatical for my wedding, I had discussed my situation with Tedrick, our team leader. Or rather, *he* had sat me down for 'the talk' as he suspected that my union to Helio would likely result in me leaving the force.

To my relief, he had granted me the permission to continue using some of our tools with my logins, so long as it was for ethical reasons—not that he believed I would use it otherwise. However, there were some restrictions on what I could access. I had a strong hunch that Tedrick viewed this sabbatical period as a trial phase to assess what kind of privileges I could maintain the day we parted ways. Like me, our leader strongly supported any endeavor to protect the members of our galactic alliance, whoever they may be. So long as my intentions remained altruistic, he would help me achieve my goals.

I accessed the school records of the academy Saydi attended. Everything checked out. She was a top student, recipient of the most prestigious scholarships, multiple internships offers, and the picture of the person on file matched the photos Idova had shown me as well as the images from the security recording. As the Academy didn't provide remote learning for that program, it meant she had to be who she claimed. But then why jeopardize a promising future just to kidnap an Edocit teen?

Did she act under duress?

While that had happened in a few cases, this plot to lure Strasa had gone on for too long. People being coerced into doing these kinds of things against their conscience only lasted so long before cracks started appearing. My gut told me she was a willing participant.

Could she have a twin or a look-alike?

That thought gave me pause. Although I didn't fully dismiss it, I doubted it was the case. There were a few shapeshifter species with mind-blowing mimicking abilities. However, Strasa's parents would have communicated with the Academy during the early stages of screening the internship candidates. Had Saydi actually been an imposter impersonating a botany student, it would have been discovered long ago during that process.

The possibility of the real Saydi being her twin also felt weak to me. Why would the real Saydi accept having her future and name ruined for this type of ploy? Even if it had been the doings of an evil twin behind her back, it had gone on for far too long for her not to have discovered everything.

But that train of thoughts gave me a new idea.

If Saydi was truly a student at the Academy, she wouldn't blow her cover over a single Edocit. This abduction felt like a last-minute dash and grab before ending an operation. Someone at her school was either on to her, or she had already milked everything they wanted from this role.

A quick search took me down the most insane rabbit hole.

CHAPTER 10
HELIO

My efforts to trace the whereabouts of Saydi's ship were hitting one wall after another. A vessel didn't so perfectly vanish unless the pilot was deliberately attempting to remain hidden. She had made no contact with any of the communication relays in any of the neighboring areas she could have traveled through. If she did, she somehow managed to hide her ship's signature.

Assuming she'd left Zailia with a fully fueled and stocked ship, and depending at which speed she traveled, Saydi would either need to refuel within the next hour or would still have enough power for another couple of days. The Nazhral ship didn't boast the highest technology—at least in appearance—which could play in our favor. But it could also hide the finest power core in its belly.

I had already reached out to all of my contacts and sent out an APB to every bounty, rescue, and watcher channels for any sighting of her vessel. However, judging by how well she had executed this kidnapping, I had reason to believe she'd swapped vessels shortly after leaving Zailia. Worse still, her ship had been small enough to rendezvous with a bigger vessel. For all we knew, she could be safely sitting inside the hangar of a transport ship we'd had no reason to investigate.

With the odds of Saydi returning to her school being nearly nonexistent, my next best chance of narrowing down her possible location would be trying to infiltrate the next big illegal substance auction. I'd just started lurking in the underground market channels when my mate dropped a string of curses under her breath.

I lifted my head to look at her. She was still sitting on my couch located slightly to the right of my desk. Maeve looked beautiful with her hair mussed up from the countless times she'd run her hand through it or absentmindedly twisted a lock around her index finger. My mate constantly fidgeted and mumbled to herself in the most adorable fashion when deeply focused on a task.

A wave of tenderness flooded through me as I gazed upon her. Considering her rank and status as an Enforcer, I shouldn't be surprised by her dedication to her work. But we'd been at this for hours, and not once had she faltered or shown any signs of wanting to give up or just go relax. Maeve had mentioned in passing that once she was on a case, she became like a dog with a bone. I could now see it. It would fall to me to ensure she didn't overwork herself. Yet, having her by my side was not only a great help, it also galvanized me.

I couldn't repress a smile when she cursed again.

"You bitch!" Maeve whispered at her screen.

"I'm guessing those sweet words are not meant for your computer, but for the Nazhral?" I asked in a teasing tone.

Maeve jerked her head up and looked at me first with surprise before taking on a sheepish expression. "Yeah, sorry. I'm incorrigible when it comes to mumbling and muttering."

I smiled. "Don't apologize, my mate. It's beyond adorable. But it sounds like you found something of interest about our elusive abductor?" I asked, gesturing at her laptop with my chin.

An air of pure contempt descended over Maeve's pretty face. "Did I ever. Saydi isn't at all who she pretends to be. Her talent in botany? Her being a straight-A student? It's all thanks to a microchip implanted in her brain," Maeve hissed angrily. "That 'girl' isn't eighteen. She's thirty-four. Saydi is only one of her many aliases."

"Maker!" I whispered in shock.

After years of working as a bounty hunter, it shouldn't surprise me. But I had not expected this one. Based on the photos and security videos, Saydi genuinely looked like she was in her late teens, early twenties.

"She transferred to the academy just a year ago. At first, everything looked legit. Any regular person checking her background would think everything was fine. But I dug a little deeper. And lo-and-behold, Saydi Dalrosh materialized into this world at seventeen, exactly one month before her admission at the academy. She didn't exist in any galactic record before that instant."

"How convenient," I replied, my voice oozing with sarcasm. "I always try to give people the benefit of the doubt—it's an Edocit thing—but I doubt she created that new identity to hide from an abusive partner, or as part of the protection program."

"That, she did not," Maeve said with the same angry disbelief. "I've been able to identify at least four of her previous aliases. Every time, she made a play on the letters of her given name. First, she was Aydis, then Ysadis, Daisy, and the latest one, Saydi. Her last name completely changed. That's when I lost her trace. She likely used a completely different name before then. I just need more time to crack it."

"That's already a great start," I said, my voice filled with admiration as I rose to my feet to come sit next to her. "This should help us find out more about what shady business she's involved in."

"It has!" Maeve said smugly. "Little Saydi has been quite

busy. Since her arrival at the Academy, over twenty students have gone missing, all of them with unique anatomical traits that would make them valuable on the slavers' bloc, but especially on the organs market."

"What?!" I exclaimed, horrified.

"Yes," Maeve said grimly. "It seems she alternates between focusing on flesh trade under one persona, then drug dealing—both medicinal and recreational—and with narcotics in general with her next alias. Despite the few disappearances at her school, it appears she centered her efforts on botanical drugs. Previously, as Daisy, she was a modeling agent, scouting the galaxy for the most attractive or unique-looking people. You can guess how that turned out for many of her victims. Prior to that, under her Ysadis pseudonym, she was a galactic pharmaceutical broker. She brokered major deals, while offering turnkey services."

"Meaning she didn't just get the parties to agree on a sale, but also ensured shipment and delivery?" I instantly guessed.

Maeve nodded. "Yes. At first, she was just skimming on some of the merchandise. When she came close to discovery, Saydi just went all out and absconded with multiple shipments. Then she went underground."

"But surely her face would feature in the most wanted lists. Pharmaceutical companies do not play," I argued.

"They did. By then, she had already changed her name and her appearance."

I stiffened at that comment and stared intently at my woman. "Her appearance? She's getting surgery?"

"That's what I thought at first. But I stumbled on a medical report from when she worked for Chemix under the name Aydis."

"Isn't that the global organization responsible for cleaning toxic wastes, environmental disasters, and safely relocating the affected population?" I asked, confused by how this would benefit the Nazhral female.

Maeve nodded. "Yes. I had the same reaction at first. I couldn't find anything on the public news networks about a criminal with that name. But the Enforcer database reported the massive disappearance of the displaced, usually on primitive planets. Few people would hear about it or care."

"Maker. What kind of monster is she?!" I whispered, shock and anger boiling within me. "But how does that help you with determining whether she's getting surgery?"

She smiled apologetically. "Sorry, I'm getting to it. Because of the nature of their work and the risk the employees potentially expose themselves to when going to those disaster areas, a full medical exam is required for every new employee who wishes to go out in the field to handle these catastrophes."

"Which Saydi—or whatever her name was at the time—would have had to undergo," I said, understanding dawning on me.

"Exactly," Maeve said with approval. "Her blood works revealed that she's not a pureblood Nazhral, but a hybrid. One of her parents is indeed a Nazhral, but the other is a Qazak."

My jaw dropped. "The shapeshifters?! How the hell did a Nazhral come into contact with one of them? Isn't their planet completely off-limits?"

Maeve nodded. "It is, both for their protection *and* ours. But when has a galactic edict ever stopped a greedy Nazhral from doing what they wanted?"

I snorted. "Good point. So, Saydi is a shapeshifter?"

My mate shook her head. "Doubtful. From what I could find in the Enforcer database, the rare known hybrids didn't possess their Qazak parent's full shifting abilities. For example, a pureblood Qazak could go from looking like a human, to a Nazhral, then to an Edocit," she added, waving at me, "and no one would suspect they weren't truly a member of that species. But a hybrid could not change species. They could shift the color of their skin, scales, or fur, but not their shape or texture.

They can shift their facial features for short periods, from a few hours to up to a couple of days for the longest cases recorded."

I grimaced in disgust. "So *that's* how she avoided capture after each time she fled. No scan can detect shapeshifting."

My shoulders slumped, and the flame of hope and excitement my mate's findings had awakened in me dimmed. We couldn't interrogate every single Nazhral female of her general size, height, and age. As interesting as all this was, we needed something more, something unique to her that could help us pin her down.

Maeve gently caressed my cheek with an encouraging smile. "I know what you're thinking, and I felt the same way. How the hell do we find someone who can change names and appearance so easily? By using the wonderful tools available to Enforcers."

I perked up again at the sight of the spark in her eyes.

"I don't want to give you false hopes yet, because I hit a wall when you heard me cursing minutes ago," Maeve warned preemptively. "But I think I've narrowed down a possible location… or rather sector that she might call home. So we're still talking needle in a haystack."

"True, but it's a start. With a couple more parameters, we could pin down her position," I said, my voice filling with excitement. "Which sector? And how did you find it?"

"I ran a trace on the communications between Saydi and both the Academy and Strasa," Maeve explained. "Most of her calls with Strasa originated from the Academy, except a handful that were clearly routed through too many relays to get to the point of origin before it fizzled. The same thing was happening with all communications between Saydi and the Academy."

"Blast… That's at least twenty relays," I said, discouraged. "She really covered her trail."

Maeve nodded. "She certainly tried hard. But when I compared the relays she used between the Academy and Strasa, I discovered she was going through some of the same relays in both cases."

"Which allowed you to trace a path!" I exclaimed, my heart soaring.

"If you triangulate their coordinates, the approximate axis of each line would intersect here," Maeve said, pointing at the Odiom Sector on the star chart displayed on her holographic screen. "But that's not possible. A call from such a great distance would require her to go through at least a hundred relays. The signal would have degraded to unacceptable levels, not to mention that real-time conversations wouldn't have been possible."

"The quality of the vidcoms was too good for that," I said in understanding, while looking at my mate with admiration. "Which means she made those calls in a much closer area, but beyond twenty relays."

"Exactly. Based on the quality level of their vidcoms, it cannot have gone through more than thirty relays," Maeve continued. "Which brings us to this general area. But the radius is much too wide. It includes the entire Otein Sector. There are at least a thousand planets there, not to mention the moons and space stations. Thus my cursing."

"Wait a minute…" I said, further excitement bubbling within me. "Otein came up on my list during my search."

"What?" Maeve asked, her eyes widening with curiosity laced with hope.

I hopped to my feet and hurried back to my desk. Maeve put her laptop down on the cushion next to her, then came to join me. I could feel her vibrate with anticipation as she stared at my screen. Flicking through the windows, I brought up the chart I had calculated for Saydi's possible current position.

"Considering her ship model, and assuming that it was fully fueled, I calculated that she could reach one of the following sectors if she traveled at warp speed without pause before she needed to refuel," I explained. "Of the ten most likely sectors, Otein was one of them."

"Here!" Maeve exclaimed, spotting it on my screen at the same time I did. "Otein Sector, Navuks System, and the Hagiel region. She would be there now?"

I shook my head. "If she is indeed traveling at maximum warp, she should arrive there early tomorrow morning. She would need to refuel at one of these four locations," I added while typing a few instructions to zoom in on the region.

"Nilzin!" Maeve said. "That's where she will fuel, if she indeed goes there."

I frowned and looked at my mate with confusion. "What makes you so sure?"

"There's some major political unrest happening on Nilzin. When his rival nearly deposed him, the planet's current ruler entered into some desperate deals with one of the cartels in the region. He'll turn a blind eye to some of their dealings so long as they keep them out of their main cities."

"I never heard that," I exclaimed.

Maeve smiled smugly. "As it should be. The UPO is keeping that information as quiet as possible while monitoring the situation. If the news spread, other cartels would rush in to get their share of the pie before the first one gets too comfortably settled in. Nilzin has enough to deal with without also getting caught in the middle of a turf war."

"You think Saydi's base of operation would be there?" I asked, although with little hope.

"No, I highly doubt it. This would be a safe pit stop for her, whereas the other three locations would likely scrutinize her credentials and cargo more closely," Maeve explained. "If we are correct, we'll be able to track her arrival, and we might be able to get a tracker on her. Let me pull a few strings."

"You're amazing!" I whispered with awe.

"So I've been told, once or twice," Maeve said playfully, while flicking her hair over her shoulder with a flourish.

I laughed while rising from my chair, then pulled her into my embrace. Maeve wrapped her arms around my neck and lifted her face to receive my kiss.

Maker, everything about my mate was perfection, even the way she fit in my arms. What started off as a kiss of gratitude and admiration, soon took on a much different edge. My tongue teased the seam of her mouth, and Maeve immediately parted her lips, welcoming me in. I would never tire of her sweet taste and of the way our tongues mingled in a passionate caress that had my loins ablaze.

To my dismay, as soon as I tightened my embrace, Maeve slipped her hands from behind my neck down to my chest and gently pushed back. I broke the kiss to look at her questioningly. The smoldering look in her eyes had another surge of desire flare in my nether region.

"Hold that thought, handsome," she whispered in a voice full of promise. "Let me set my trap in motion, and then we can pick up where we left off."

With much reluctance—and a sliver of shame that I should have so easily become distracted—I released my mate. Maeve returned to the couch to start working on her laptop. As I had no idea how long it would take her, I seized the opportunity to refocus on my search about upcoming flesh trades and drug markets in the Hagiel region.

Even as the first results started appearing on my screen, Maeve audibly closed the lid of her laptop, drawing my attention. My blood rushed to my groin in response to the provocative look she leveled on me. My mate tossed her computer onto the couch next to her and rose from her seat with the slow and sensuous movements of an exotic dancer.

"Where were we, dear husband?" Maeve asked in a husky voice.

"We were at the part where I was itching to do some inappropriate things to you," I replied in a rumbling tone.

"Oh… By all means. Do your worst."

With a predatory grin, I closed the distance between us, picked her up, and reclaimed her mouth even as I carried her back to our room.

CHAPTER 11
HELIO

I loved the feel of my woman's hands on me. They were gentle but determined, delightfully taunting, yet eager. And so was her mouth. Maeve enjoyed kissing as much as she did touching. The softness of her lips on me had me shivering all over as they explored my face. They wandered to my neck, then parted for her tongue to lick at the *veris* next to my carotid. She couldn't begin to understand how sensitive it was and how good it felt whenever she did that.

My abdominal muscles constricted with anticipation. Aside from touching and kissing, my female also really liked tasting, and especially biting. I loooved a biter. Right on cue, her teeth closed on my *veris*, giving it a nice nip. A needy grunt escaped me as blood rushed to my groin. Maker help me.

I wanted to bite her too and fill her with my bonding hormone. I wanted to see my *veris* growing under her skin, to see them extrude and intertwine with mine as we coupled. Someday, soon I hoped, this physical and spiritual bond would consecrate our union and truly make us one.

But it was too soon for this.

Instead, I willed my sweat glands to release my aphrodisiac

pheromones. The thought of using Strasa's down leaf to enhance even more the pleasure I was about to give Maeve crossed my mind. I discarded it immediately. Under the circumstances, it would feel too insensitive, not to say disrespectful.

I carefully placed Maeve on our bed. Instead of remaining lying on her back, she immediately got onto her knees and removed her shirt. I grinned, feasting my eyes on her beauty as she stripped for me. The throbbing between my thighs intensified as I did the same. The swiftness with which my mate got rid of her clothes was impressive. Then again, her career likely had her well-trained in getting ready quickly for an urgent mission.

By the time I finished discarding my shirt, kicking off my footwear, and unclasping my pants, Maeve was already kneeling on the bed in all her glorious beauty. My mouth watered at the sight of the dark brown areolas around the hardening buds of her nipples.

Impatient to feel the warmth of her body all around mine, I pushed down my pants. To my shock, before I could finish stepping out of them, Maeve had crawled forward on the bed and was reaching for my cock. Hissing through my teeth, I threw my head back when the inferno of my woman's mouth engulfed my length.

Maeve immediately bobbed in front of me, taking me deep. Her right hand worked the base of my cock, squeezing and stroking it in counterpoint to the movement of her mouth. She swirled her tongue around the head before drawing me in, then her teeth gently grazed the ridges wrapped around my length, right below my bulb.

It was so insanely good!

When it came to what she wanted, my woman didn't play. I'd thought she'd be one to wish for long foreplays and abundant teasing and denying in the most exquisite torture. I couldn't have been more wrong. Maeve went straight for it. She wasn't a control freak but occasionally liked being the one in charge.

While I considered myself fairly dominant in the bedroom, I didn't mind letting go from time to time. And right this minute, I more than welcomed it.

Maeve was swallowing me with a greed that had fire burning in my loins, swirling in the pit of my stomach, and rushing down my legs. I breathed loudly, my fingers slipping through the silky strands of her hair. Watching my cock vanishing in and out between her plump lips was further fanning the flames raging within. I closed my eyes and moaned almost painfully as I battled the urge to rock back and forth into her mouth. She was already deep-throating me, and I didn't want to risk choking her.

A strangled cry escaped me when Maeve suddenly stopped sucking me to tease my bulb—the head of my cock. She'd wrapped her fingers around the base of my glans, shaped almost like a closed tulip. While I did open and close it to enhance my mate's sensation when I was buried inside of her, the thought of opening it now in front of her made me extremely self-conscious.

It was another of our traits that off-worlders tended to find creepy. When previously making love to Maeve, I'd only partially opened my bulb. She hadn't felt my ovipositor inside. I hadn't used it on her yet, as we had absolutely no chances of conceiving until we were fully bonded. Furthermore, assuming my ovipositor didn't freak her out, it was so extremely sensitive that she'd have me spilling my seed the minute she touched or licked it.

As much as I loved the pleasure she was giving me, I wanted to see her fall apart for me a few times before I indulged in my own climax. Anyway, despite the impossibility of her getting pregnant by me for now, I only wanted to release my seed with my cock buried deep inside her.

I pulled out of her grasp and, ignoring her gasp of protest, I pushed her onto her back before burying my face between her thighs. Maeve arched her back, one of her hands fisting in my hair. Once again, I mourned that she didn't possess *veris* just yet. They would have tangled with the vines in my hair. Then we could feel each other's emotions. I wouldn't feel my tongue on her like she did, but I'd share the pleasure she derived from my attentions, and the one she gave me would flow right back through her in an endless circle of bliss.

Maker, how I loved the taste of her on my tongue and the sound of her voluptuous moans in my ears. Maeve's hips gently gyrated as I licked and sucked on her little nub. My already stiff cock hardened some more when I slipped two fingers inside her. The slick warmth surrounding them reminded me how her inner walls squeezed my length from all sides in the most exquisite caress. The memory of how she writhed and trembled beneath me, of how her nails dug into my back had me burning with the need to slam myself inside her and ride her with unbridled fury.

And I would… But first, I needed Maeve to fall apart for me.

I accelerated the movement of my tongue on her clit and of my fingers making love to her, crooking them to rub on the tight bundle of nerves within. Blast, the way her body jerked each time I did, as if lightning was striking her, resonated directly in my cock. Maeve's legs began to tremble on each side of my face, and her hands fisting my hair tightened their grip, heralding her imminent climax.

Without slowing my ministrations, I lifted my eyes to admire her face. She was so beautiful. Her lips parted, her eyes narrowed down to slits, she looked at me with an almost pained expression. Her labored breath came out increasingly louder and in shorter bursts as she prepared to topple over. And then she did. Maeve's body seized. Throwing her head back against the mattress, she cried out. I tightened my hold around her right leg over my shoulder and pressed my right palm on her stomach to restrain the spasms of bliss coursing through her. I pursued my attentions until she started coming back down to reality.

Normally, I would give my female another orgasm before I

took her. Not tonight… My abdominal muscles were contracting painfully from the searing desire Maeve always awakened in me. I slid her further up the bed and claimed her mouth as I settled on top of her. She closed her arms around me, raking her nails along my spine the way she'd quickly discovered I loved. I moaned against her lips, my tongue diving in even as I pressed my bulb against her opening.

Maeve spread her legs wider, and her hands settled on my behind. Fingers digging into my cheeks, she eagerly lifted her pelvis to meet me halfway. I carefully inserted myself, reining in the passion I wanted to unleash. Although I could sheath myself a lot faster now, her body was still offering some initial slight resistance at my invasion.

Maker, she felt so damn good…

I began moving in and out of her, quickly picking up the pace. We kissed and caressed each other with a heated fervor. As waves upon waves of pleasure crashed over me, I gave free rein to my passion. I pounded into her, occasionally grinding my pelvis against hers to stimulate her clit. Liquid fire rushed through my veins, each stroke driving me mad with pleasure. When I felt Maeve once more nearing the edge, I slipped a hand between us to massage her little nub. In seconds, she shouted my name as she once more surrendered to bliss.

A savage cry escaped me when her inner walls clamped down on my cock. I pumped in and out of her a few more times, fighting the urge to climax. Pulling out of her, I flipped Maeve onto her stomach. With a swipe of my knee, I parted her legs open and lay down on her back. With one powerful thrust, I rammed myself in before immediately resuming a punishing pace.

Maeve cried out but didn't push back. Instead, she lifted her behind, meeting me thrust for thrust. Her moans mingled with my grunts and the slapping sound of our flesh colliding in a frenzy. I kissed and nipped at her neck and nape while a powerful wave grew deep within, building into an impending tsunami that would soon crash over me.

My nerve endings tingled, and my skin felt on the verge of combusting as I began to crest. Not wanting to leave my mate behind, I slipped my hands in front of her, one palm fondling her breasts while the other rubbed her little nub.

So focused on not yielding to bliss, I never saw Maeve's climax coming. She shouted my name, a violent spasm shaking her body before she collapsed onto the mattress. My orgasm crashed over me with such force, I thought my spine would snap in two. I roared and slammed myself deep inside my mate. I felt faint as my seed shot out of me in the purest form of liquid ecstasy. My body shook so much, my last few thrusts were erratic as I spilled every drop into my mate.

Wrecked, I let myself fall onto the mattress next to Maeve before gathering her in my arms. Lying on my back, I pulled her on top of me, and she rested her head on my chest. I gently caressed her hair and her back while we caught our breath.

When I started extruding the *veris* in my forearms and wrapping them around us, Maeve jerked her head up to look at me questioningly.

I gave her a mischievous smile. "Making sure you won't be able to escape before round two," I whispered.

Maeve laughed and gently kissed my lips. "Ready when you are, husband."

The next morning, finding my mate already gone from our bed took me aback. I always took great pride in being a light sleeper and for my impeccable environmental awareness. In my line of work, letting your guard down even for a minute could have lethal consequences. Granted, I felt safe in my home and with my mate, but it still bothered me.

It shamed me to admit that I wanted to impress Maeve and make her feel like I was a worthy mate for her. But she was a senior ranking Enforcer. What she'd accomplished in just a few hours yesterday would have taken me days… assuming I even managed to find out that much. Obviously, I was extremely grateful for her impressive skills. I just feared she would find me as lacking and inferior as I felt compared to her. It would kill me if Maeve ever believed she was carrying me instead of us pulling our weight equally.

I immediately chastised myself for these self-deprecating thoughts. Maeve had given me no reason to think she was an elitist. I couldn't even explain where such insecurities stemmed from. Based on Kayog's unwavering assessment of Maeve and I being soulmates, I should instead feel overconfident.

I just really… really like her.

Maker, you'd think I was a bumbling juvenile terrified at the thought of approaching the prettiest girl in school. She'd chosen me freely. And last night, just like our first night, Maeve's passion had clearly broadcast that she liked me, too.

Or at least that she wants me.

I hopped out of bed, took a quick shower, and hurried out of our room. Instinctively, I headed for my office, knowing my workaholic of a wife would already be there, tracking the Nazhral.

Although her fingers continued to type on her laptop, Maeve was already looking in the door's direction when I opened it. That stung. Was I this loud that she heard my approach, or was she just this talented? I chased those silly thoughts and let the warmth of her welcome wash over me.

Braless in a white tank top and what she called her comfy black boy shorts, she looked beautiful. Her tousled hair hinted at the focused work she'd been doing since she got up.

"There he is," Maeve said, echoing the words I greeted her with yesterday morning.

"Here I am," I replied with a smile as I walked towards her and took the hand she was extending to me.

I kissed the back of her hand before settling on the couch next to her. Our lips met. Despite the fire that instantly lit in the pit of my stomach, it was the tenderness of the exchange that messed me up.

I had a massive crush on my wife…

"I'm afraid I didn't prepare you as fancy a breakfast as you did for me," Maeve said sheepishly when we broke the kiss.

She cast a glance towards my desk. Following her gaze, I finally noticed the temperature-controlled tray of cut fruits, a few slices of toasted bread, and my favorite berry jam.

I smiled as I looked back at her. "Thank you, my mate. That's more than plenty, and you didn't have to prepare anything. You've been up long?"

Maeve shrugged, a sliver of guilt flashing over her face. "Not sure, to be honest. I was dying to know if we had properly identified her destination, and if I'd managed to tag her ship."

My brow creased as I once more wondered at the 'trap' she had set up for Saydi. "How would you tag her ship from here?"

Maeve opened her mouth, hesitated, then chewed her bottom lip. My frown immediately deepened. She shifted in her seat and tucked a strand of hair behind her ear.

"Why don't you grab something to eat while I give you a quick update?" my mate asked with a bit of a nervous smile.

My unease cranked up another notch, but I nodded and placed a couple of slices of toast with jam on a plate and some fruit next to them. Maeve quickly tapped a few more instructions on her laptop, finishing whatever she was doing just as I was joining her on the couch.

I braced for what would follow when she took in a deep breath before locking gazes with me.

"As an Enforcer, I have access to certain tools and technologies that most people have either never heard of or will never be allowed to use," Maeve explained carefully. "As you can imagine, the UPO has agreements with the various governments of the member planets within our organization. These governments allow us to have certain… Let's just call them surveillance and intervention tools in specific areas of their territories."

I slowly nodded, understanding dawning on me, accompanied by a hefty dose of relief. "Tools and systems that you are not at liberty to discuss, just like your parents could not discuss the sensitive projects they were working on," I said in a gentle voice.

Maeve exhaled audibly, the tension stiffening her shoulders lessening as she nodded with relief. "Exactly. I do not know how long I will continue to have access to these tools the day I resign from the Enforcers. But Tedrick allowed me to use some of them, should you require my assistance during our honeymoon for cases that would qualify as valid for our organization. Sadly, I cannot discuss some of the things that I will do to help us. Please know that it's not that I don't trust you. It's just—"

"You don't have to explain, my mate," I interrupted in a soft tone. "I perfectly understand. I'm just grateful they are allowing you to do this. Whenever something like this arises, don't feel bad about simply telling me you are bound by professional secrecy, and I'll back off."

"Thank you for understanding," she said with a grateful smile.

"No need to thank me. It's rather the other way around. However, is there anything you can share about where we stand with this tracking?"

Maeve beamed at me. "We caught her. She did change ships, but not before arriving on Nilzin. There was a lot of cargo on her vessel. It required a machine to transfer the container into the new vessel. As it is a ventilated container, I'm convinced Strasa and anyone else she has abducted are trapped within it. Based on the size, I suspect it holds at least ten people or more."

I whistled through my teeth, then immediately frowned as a thought crossed my mind. "If you were able to see all of that, why didn't you alert the Enforcers? If she indeed has ten people in there, that would be deemed a large scale enough operation to justify the UPO's involvement, no?"

Another air of guilt flitted over her features, and she gave me an apologetic look. "Unfortunately, ten isn't enough. There would need to be at least four or five times that for the Enforcers to even consider taking on the case. Usually, we only get involved when a hundred people or more are at risk of being affected by whatever is happening."

I clenched my teeth, a familiar anger rising within me. Each life, any life, deserved to be protected, especially when it was children. And yet, I understood that their mission was to focus on the welfare of people on a large scale. If they had to answer every single missing person call in the galaxy, there would never be enough agents throughout the entire organization to meet the needs of a single solar system.

"For what it's worth, I have sent a heads up to the Enforcers, just so that they can be ready to act should we find something big where we're headed," Maeve said in a soothing voice. "I have considered having the local authorities apprehend her but decided against it."

"Why?" I asked.

"Because I want her to lead us to her base of operation," Maeve replied, matter-of-factly.

I stiffened, torn between outrage on behalf of the victims and understanding as to her logic. Ultimately, outrage won.

"Every hour and every day in captivity, her prisoners are tortured," I said.

Maeve winced, that air of guilt crossing her features once more. But she cast it aside and held my gaze unwaveringly.

"You are correct, and I hate it every bit as much as you do. But we have to be careful and strategic about this," she said in a reasonable voice. "We don't know for a fact that the abductees are indeed inside that container. For all we know, it could be some exotic plants. She might have rendezvoused with someone, somewhere else along the way. We cannot risk being wrong. If the authorities tap her and do not find Strasa or any other missing person on her vessel, she will stay away from her organization to avoid luring us to them. And then we truly will have lost him."

"But surely, all those fancy tools you referred to earlier would allow you to check the contents, or you could have alerted the authorities to perform a discreet scan," I argued.

Maeve heaved a sigh. "I cannot tell you what we can or cannot assess. And you are correct again. I could have alerted the local authorities to perform a scan. But we do not know what kind of technology she possesses. Considering all the hacking she had to do to successfully falsify her records, she might have something strong enough to detect any unauthorized scan. Assuming she manages to fool their scanners, she will go underground because she'll know we're on to her. But if they find someone, they will be forced to act. However, it doesn't guarantee that it would save the people in that container. And I'm not ready to condemn all the others that are certainly being held wherever she's bringing these ones."

"That's not *your* choice to make!" I exclaimed. "What if she leads us to the middle of nowhere, and we allowed Strasa to pointlessly suffer this entire time?"

"At least we will have tried to save as many people as possible," Maeve countered with a stubborn expression. "I am *not* alerting the authorities."

I stared at her in disbelief, not recognizing the gentle and affectionate woman that I had been falling hard for over the past couple of days. She had seemed so genuinely concerned for Strasa. And now, she appeared to be considering him nothing more than an expendable statistic if he allowed her to score a bigger catch.

By the hurt expression on her face, I could guess as to how I was looking at her. Teeth clenched, I rose from the couch, tossed my plate of uneaten food onto the cushion next to me, and stormed out of the room. I vaguely heard Maeve call my name in a pleading fashion, but I ignored her.

CHAPTER 12
MAEVE

Shit. Shit. Shit. Shit. Shit! I couldn't have handled that one more poorly. Fuck! He certainly believed I was some heartless bitch, more interested in the fame of bringing down a big organization than in the welfare of the victims held captive. The worst part was that I could totally relate to how he felt because I'd gone through the same type of outrage when I'd first joined the Enforcers.

I needed to make him understand that this was the best course of action for everyone involved, and especially for Strasa. For the first time, I fully grasped how difficult it must have been for my parents to keep secrets from me, and why they resorted to lying. Lying would be so much easier and would make me look like the heroine instead of the villain. But this wasn't the type of relationship I wanted with my husband.

Things had been so perfect until now. A first fight had been inevitable. However, this went beyond a mere disagreement. The disappointed—not to say disgusted—way he'd looked at me before he stormed out cut me deep. I wanted to chase after him and explain, make him see reason, but my hands were tied.

I'd gotten up way early this morning so that I could verify if my suspicions were right without having to lie to him about anything. And they were indeed right. Yes, I could remotely scan the vessel. I had set up a subroutine that had done nothing but that all night. It captured a lot of questionable cargo, none of which I could do anything about because it would constitute an illegal search.

The UPO's scan was specifically designed to be perceived as the standard basic scan any vessel underwent whenever they docked or entered a ship hangar on any planet or space station. Standard scans basically sought to detect any sign of contamination, camouflage, a wanted or stolen vessel, or excess weight or dimensions that could bring on a fine, among other things. But ours actually assessed a variety of things, mainly the weapons systems and booby-traps.

Trying to scan the contents of the ships had too high a risk of triggering the ship's defense systems and alerting the crew. So, while I genuinely did not know if Strasa was onboard, I had recognized the booby-traps on Saydi's vessel. I had learned the hard way the horror that ensued should we trip it.

Mercenaries called it The Juicer, because once activated, the trap released a series of enzymes and acid that liquified any bio tissue, bones, teeth, hair, nails, fur, you name it. From the resulting sludge, we couldn't recover any identifiable DNA. Pirates had sacrificed nearly two hundred slaves to this heinous deathtrap rather than be caught with them in their hold.

The worst part was that we had not even been able to arrest them, as a similar sludge could result from the oxidation of a rare plant exposed to light and oxygen during a critical state of its development. Even though we all knew what had gone down, it never would have held up in court.

But I couldn't tell Helio all that I had discovered. Although I trusted him not to repeat anything, we kept secrets for a reason. Under torture, even the most loyal person eventually broke. Plus, I had given my word and sworn an oath. I had to make him understand without betraying the trust Tedrick and the UPO had given me. If only we'd had more time to get to know each other better…

Despite the burning need to hunt down my husband to discuss this mess, I forced myself to wait a short while longer to give him a chance to calm down. It took every bit of my willpower to focus on finishing my task to avoid losing my trace on Saydi while I patched things up with him.

Ten minutes later, I started looking for Helio. Everything was too damn quiet. Even the garden appeared to be holding its breath. Myma's branches seemed a little droopy, as if to express her sadness. Surely I was imagining things, but considering this garden, this land, even the freaking house were DNA bound with my husband, it wouldn't surprise me if they could feel his emotions. For the first time, I truly felt isolated and like an intruder here.

For a second, I feared Helio might have actually left the house. Since the skiff was still sitting on its landing pad in the garden, could he have called a harstag to go on a ride? Fuck, had I taken too long to search for him? I went back inside the house to check the armory. Maybe he was packing his weapons to go chase after Saydi?

No luck.

He wasn't in our bedroom. But the full travel bag on the bed indicated he was indeed preparing for departure. That it still lay open reassured me that Helio hadn't left yet. It then dawned on me that the healing room served not only as an infirmary but also to meditate. Could he be seeking inner peace there after our argument?

I made a beeline for that room. A wave of relief crashed over me while tears pricked my eyes when I spotted him in the meditation alcove across from the giant plants that served as healing pods. He was sitting on the bench with his legs crossed in something very close to the lotus position. But instead of his hands resting palms up on his knees, they were flat on the bench on each side of him. The *veris* from both his hands and feet, as well as the vines from his hair, were intertwined with the vines wrapped around the bench and which stemmed from the ground and the walls.

His closed eyelids slowly opened as I carefully approached. The absence of irises in his fully dark green eyes made it difficult to know for sure where he was looking. But I knew he was staring at me. His eyes were glazed over, like when he'd been projecting his consciousness before or had rooted with the land. Although his body and face looked relaxed, like when someone was just emerging from slumber, I could feel the tension emanating from him.

The vines on the ground and around the bench parting with a will of their own as I came near him freaked me out a bit. Myma had shifted her thick roots to open a path near her for us. That had been strange, but she was semi-sentient. Those vines shouldn't be this aware. I'd never considered myself the paranoid type, but would they try to strangle me if I ever made him mad enough?

As Helio's *veris* detached from the vines and slowly resorbed under his skin, his gaze lost its haziness as he continued to focus on me. I swallowed hard and nervously tucked my hair behind my ear, and I warily sat next to him. We were close enough that I could feel the heat from his body, but not enough to touch. To my relief, he didn't scoot away from me. Still, the coldness in his eyes cut deep.

I licked my lips, shifted in my seat, and took in a fortifying breath before launching into the little speech I'd mentally rehearsed while looking for him.

"I know you're angry with me. Had our positions been reversed, I would probably feel the same. But I promise you it's not what you think. If you give me a chance, I will try to explain."

He said nothing, but the way his gaze remained focused on me gave me the signal to proceed. I took that as a good sign.

"Whatever you may think, do not doubt that I want nothing more than to bring Strasa back home," I continued. "Despite what I said, I didn't keep from informing the authorities because I'm so hungry for fame that I'd be willing to sacrifice an innocent for a bigger catch."

The way Helio narrowed his eyes at me stung. Once again, he didn't have to speak for me to understand what his expression implied.

"What I said earlier was true. If we send the local authorities to search her vessel, we will alert Saydi to the fact that we're aware of her location," I explained. "But we don't know if Strasa is still onboard her ship. I did not scan for that."

His anger immediately flared again, and he bared his teeth, his fangs descending while he looked at me with an air of betrayal.

"There's an excellent reason I didn't," I exclaimed, raising my palms in an appeasing gesture. "Ships can detect when they're being scanned, and what type of scan is being performed. Even the Xurgen—who are the most advanced species in the galaxy—haven't managed to design a detection-proof scanner. Saydi's security system would have alerted her the minute I tried anything beyond the standard docking scans."

Some of his anger dimmed when I spoke those words. I continued quickly, pressing my advantage.

"You know I am bound to secrecy about many of the tools that I have access to. But what I can tell you is that from what I could gather about her ship, I am certain, beyond any reasonable doubt, that she will kill anyone onboard her ship if she gets detected."

Helio recoiled, disbelief giving way to a sliver of doubt as his eyes flicked between mine, assessing whether I was trying to pull a fast one on him. I held his gaze unwaveringly.

"That makes no sense. Killing them would only aggravate her situation," Helio countered.

My heart soared at that response, but I schooled my features not to let him see the sense of triumph this small victory had stirred within me. So long as we were talking, we could fix this.

"It won't if what remains cannot be identified as having been a person's body, not even through DNA," I said.

"What?" Helio asked with an air of pure confusion and disbelief.

"There are… technologies out there that can do terrible things. You cannot begin to imagine some of the horrors I've witnessed in my line of work," I said in a pleading tone. "What I found out about her ship would allow her to do it, and I'm certain she will. Saydi is a *monster*. The more I dig into her past, and the more I find out about the people that have gone missing around her, the more certain I am that what we will find is way bigger than either of us imagined."

I placed my hand on top of his. Helio stiffened but thankfully didn't pull away from me. He was still unsure about how he felt about the whole situation. What mattered was that he was listening and, more importantly, that he seemed to want me to convince him. Had he been closed off, things would have been much harder.

"I've told you how I hate lies. Therefore, I will never lie to you. I wish we would have had more time together for you to get to know me better. Under the circumstances, I realize it's a lot to ask, but I really need you to trust me. Right now, I'd give anything for you to be an Enforcer so that I could share everything openly. I don't want to keep secrets from you. What I can promise is that everything I can share, I will."

"But you have shared very little," Helio said in a calm voice laced with a hint of challenge. "Would that be enough for you if our roles were reversed?"

I pursed my lips as I reflected on his words. I was indeed

asking him to make a major leap of faith while remaining cryptic.

"In truth, I don't know if it would have been enough. But I want to believe I would have been able to give you the benefit of the doubt. What I *can* say about this specific case is that Saydi getting tapped by the authorities is almost guaranteed to get Strasa killed. I'm also convinced—but have no proof—that there are more captives inside that container that she transferred into a new ship. And I would bet almost anything that once we track Saydi to her next destination, we will need major backup to deal with what we will find there."

"What makes you think that?" Helio insisted.

I took a moment to carefully choose my words before answering. "Since I cannot go into specific details, I will say that criminals who deal in narcotics are constantly looking for the next big thing that will give people the most potent high while also being the most addictive. They want them hooked for life. Edocit down is so popular because it's not addictive and has no negative side effects while being extremely potent."

"Surely you don't mean that drug dealers are trying to turn our down into something addictive?" Helio asked with a horrified expression.

Once more, I hesitated, wondering how much I could share without betraying my oath. "If you were a ruthless drug dealer and your income was dwindling because people were not selling the shirts off their backs just to get their next fix, would you not want to tweak their favorite recreational drugs so that they became completely dependent on it and started bleeding their accounts just to get more?"

"Our down is what it is," Helio argued. "Anyone who purchases something other than the very recognizable leaves is making a choice. They are not being conned into anything."

"Half the people who went missing from the Academy are Raitheans. The drug dealers use the insulin their species naturally produces as a base in the majority of the most addictive drugs. Do I know that Saydi is making an addictive version of Edocit down? I don't. However, I do not believe in this type of coincidence. If she injects Strasa with that insulin…"

My voice trailed off. Helio didn't need me to finish my sentence to understand.

"She might be doing it as we speak!" he whispered in horror.

"She might, but I doubt it," I said, relieved that he seemed to side with my assessment. "Saydi would want to be in a safe and controlled environment to perform these experiments. Frankly, I doubt she runs them herself. From my understanding, she's the bait and the transporter. I need more than suspicions to get the Enforcers involved, but I have tipped them as to what I believe we've stumbled upon. If you're willing to trust me, I would like us to leave as soon as possible, immediately even."

"Let's go," Helio said, jumping to his feet.

To my delight, he grabbed my hand, leading me after him. I followed, giving his hand a gentle squeeze. He gave me a sideways glance, and I smiled, letting my emotions shine through.

"Thank you," I whispered, my stupid throat tightening.

His face softened in the most wondrous way. "Thank you for taking the time to explain. This is… difficult. I'm not used to walking in the dark. But I believe you meant every word you said."

"I do," I confirmed with a nod.

As soon as we entered our bedroom, I grabbed a couple of bags and swiftly threw some clothes inside, while Helio finished packing the one he had already started working on.

I gestured at his bag with my chin. "Would you have left without me?"

He locked gazes with me. "I was calming myself down while trying to rationalize your actions. I intended to come reason with you after, but you beat me to it. Had your response not swayed me, then yes, I would have left without you. I am determined to bring this sapling home."

I smiled and nodded, grateful for his honesty. "You do not know how I wish you were an Enforcer so that we could openly discuss everything."

Helio snorted. "I'm too much of a free spirit to follow the stringent rules of that type of organization."

"I hear you. Maybe we should tell them to set up a special division for people like us, who could be free agents. I hate the thought that I might someday lose access to these tools. But being able to do our own thing, and occasionally tip them off when applicable, would be perfect," I said wistfully as I finished packing my bags.

As I turned to retrieve the badass bracer and set of stones Kaida and Cedros had given us as wedding gifts, I noticed Helio staring strangely at me.

"What? Why are you looking at me like that?"

"Could they be considering just that?" he asked.

"Considering what?" I echoed, confused.

"Making you a special free agent," Helio replied. "It baffled me that they would allow you access their tools during your sabbatical, especially when you say that you're pretty sure Tedrick expects you to resign at the end of our trial period. Could this be a test run?"

I chewed my bottom lip, reflecting on the matter before answering. "Honestly, I don't know. That thought crossed my mind. The Enforcers are pretty controlling, so your guess is as good as mine if they would be willing to grant me this much freedom. I don't really think they would keep me on their payroll, but they would welcome any tip I give them. By now, they know me enough to trust I won't betray them."

"But they don't know *me*…" he countered.

I stiffened, and my eyes widened at a sudden realization. "A test run…? Not for *me*, but for *you*?"

Helio nodded slowly. "I'm sure they performed a complete background check on me the minute you announced our impending marriage."

He gave me an indulgent smile when my face heated with guilt. They absolutely had done a complete—and probably highly invasive, borderline illegal—investigation into his past, connections, and activities.

"It would make sense for them to see if I will attempt to abuse the powerful tools you have access to, if I'll try to influence you negatively, or if I will betray anything you may confide in me," he said, matter-of-factly.

I shifted on my feet, my brow creasing as I further reflected on the situation. "You are correct. They would want to assess a security risk. But now I wonder. We have special... collaborators. No one really knows much about them. They don't have an official designation. I always thought they were informants, but it seems to go beyond that. Maybe they are free agents. That would be amazing! Would you be open to that?" I asked, hope seeping into my voice.

Helio smiled. "If it would allow you and I to have open conversations about everything, I'd certainly consider it. But no promises until I read the fine print. You know that's where they always screw you over."

I chuckled and nodded. "Agreed."

My heart filled with affection, and I walked up to him. Helio drew me into his arms even as I slipped mine around his waist.

"Thank you for giving me a chance to explain. I never want you to be disappointed with me," I said, hating the trembling in my voice.

An air of guilt flashed over his handsome face. He smiled and gently caressed my cheek. "We will have other arguments and disagreements, Maeve. It is inevitable. If I get really angry, I will walk away to gather myself. But I promise that I will *always* come back so that we can discuss it. Even if I don't want to hear it, I *will* listen with as open a mind as I possibly can. And I will expect the same from you in return."

"Deal," I whispered, my eyes prickling again.

I lifted my face to demand a kiss, which he gladly gave me. I melted against him, feeling safe in his strong arms. Yeah, I would fall hard for this male. Come hell or high water, I would fight to make us work.

"Come on, let's go get our boy," Helio whispered after we ended the kiss.

"Lead the way, husband."

CHAPTER 13
HELIO

Eager to depart, we only updated Strasa's parents and Idova after we were airborne. Choosing what information to share proved challenging. We didn't want to worry them more than they already were, but we also didn't want to create unrealistic expectations.

It upset me that we had to leave before I could introduce Maeve to my parents. I had informed them of our urgent mission, and they had obviously given me their blessing. Knowing that my mate—an Enforcer at that—was coming along for the ride made them feel better about it. As much as my parents trusted in my ability to take care of myself in dangerous situations, they always hated that I worked alone, without backup, if things got uncertain.

I actually would have wanted a partner. I had discussed such possibilities with a handful of bounty hunters whose ethics aligned with mine. The problem was more a question of finances and the prioritization of contracts. I did not need wealth, and always picked a lower-paying contract that stirred me emotionally over a highly paid one for a corporation to settle some scores.

We had not even discussed compensation with Strasa's parents. I didn't plan to either. This was definitely an emotional contract, even though his family was quite comfortable. As was often the case with sapling abductions, the family gave the bounty hunters what they could afford, either in credits, goods, or services. It wasn't uncommon for parents to encourage their younglings to sell some of their down not only as a starting fund for their future but also as a stash to pay for a potential bounty should the worst come to pass. It infuriated me that this should even be a possibility.

I cast an affectionate glance at my female. Maeve hadn't been kidding when she had called herself a workaholic. We'd been traveling for two days now, and she'd only stopped digging into whatever information she could gather about Saydi to eat, sleep, or when I dragged her away to have my way with her.

My mate was so perfect. Not once had she brought up compensation either. It shamed me that I had doubted her when she first mentioned not alerting the authorities after locating Saydi on Nilzin. Both in words and interactions, Maeve was demonstrating how dedicated she was to this case. Without her, I'd still be back home trying to figure out where the Nazhral could be. Yet the Maker knew that speed in those first few days was critical in rescue missions such as this one.

However, what Maeve suspected about Saydi's operations tremendously worried me. Beyond the fact that it rang far too true for comfort, it also implied we were likely headed into a very dangerous situation.

I didn't doubt Maeve's combat skills. She'd likely partaken in battles I couldn't even begin to imagine. What she'd told me about the shadow beasts they'd fought when they first met Cedros confirmed it. But she'd been wearing top-of-the-line armor with high end weapons and battled with an elite team by her side. I was a good fighter and felt confident in my ability to be an excellent partner for her in a reasonably even skirmish.

However, I was an Edocit. So long as I had a way to connect with the soil, I could speed up my regeneration in case of serious injury, and even shelter my soul from death if I could connect with a tree. But Maeve?

We were still in the early stages of getting to know each other. Although I wasn't in love with her, I could see myself getting there sooner than later. And yet, I felt devastated at the thought she could come to harm. Humans had too few natural defenses. A part of me wished we'd already bonded. Then I would have passed on some of my rooting and regenerative abilities to her. It wouldn't make Maeve invincible, but it would be an additional layer of protection.

"I think I know where they're going," Maeve suddenly said, her eyes still glued to the holographic screen of her computer.

While I made it a point not to look over her shoulder in case her screen displayed sensitive information, I loved that my mate seemed to trust me enough to work next to me instead of hiding in a separate room. I wanted her to know that I would never deliberately put her in a difficult position when it came to honoring her word. Despite being a loner, I enjoyed her mere presence next to me, even with each of us focused on our own tasks.

"Where?" I asked, my curiosity piqued.

"Based on their current speed and trajectory, and the relays their recent communications have gone through, it all seems to point to Lipnas or Shimli," Maeve said, semi-absentmindedly, while still typing.

"Recent communications?" I exclaimed in disbelief. "You're able to tap into their coms? I'm sorry, forget I asked," I quickly added when the familiar uneasy air flitted over Maeve's face.

"I'm not listening in on their conversation. I'm merely looking at which relays their outgoing and incoming coms go through," Maeve said carefully.

I nodded. However, I had not missed how she had not denied

being *able to* tap into their coms. She'd merely stated that she *was not* doing it. Obviously, that didn't imply that the UPO actually possessed the ability to eavesdrop on vessels flying at warp speed without actual spying devices onboard.

But it also doesn't exclude that possibility.

"Whatever helps, I welcome it," I said with a gentle smile. "I'm not familiar with either of the places you named. Are they planets or space stations?"

Maeve beamed at me and waved at the navigation map charted on her screen. "Both are planets. I traced most of her communications back to Lipnas, and only a handful to Shimli. And yet, I believe the latter is her destination."

I raised an eyebrow, eager to hear more. "What makes you think that?"

"Lipnas is an old refugee colony where lots of shady business turned into a lucrative manufacturing haven," Maeve explained. "The refugees were horribly exploited and basically used as slave labor until the UPO cracked down on the abuse. We relocated many of the refugees to give them a new, better start. However, the corporations who had been thriving there didn't want to lose their established market, so they had to hire actual employees under proper working conditions."

"Now that you mention it, I vaguely remember hearing about it. Didn't it turn into a very prosperous society?" I asked.

"Yes," Maeve said. "With the UPO keeping a close eye on them, and the scandal that had threatened to destroy what they had, they offered some very enticing packages to people who would come work for them. The population has very comfortable wages, great living conditions, and low taxes. There is still shady business happening there, but they are very careful about not shitting in their own backyard, if you see what I mean?"

"I… uh… think I do?" I said with a sheepish expression. "You mean they avoid doing anything so bad it would mess up the good thing they otherwise have going?"

"Correct. They know we won't intervene unless it's something that could have major negative galactic repercussions," Maeve explained. "The kind of questionable activities happening there should be handled by the local authorities."

"Who, let me guess, conveniently turn a blind eye to most of it," I replied.

She snorted. "Exactly. Which then brings us to Shimli. That place hosted one of the biggest scams in the sector. It was supposed to be a high end, exclusive, luxury colony for only the wealthiest. The conglomerate behind the project had promised it would be like a VIP club at the scale of an entire planet. No one but the richest and most powerful people could reside there, aside from the servants and personnel, of course."

I laughed at the contemptuous way in which she spoke the last sentence and the very telling eye roll that accompanied it.

"Aside from this sounding more like a nest of high maintenance idiots instead of a fancy paradise, it mostly screams to me like an endless treasure trove for kidnappers. Even if they didn't perform their abductions directly on that planet, pirates and slavers would certainly lurk around the areas their patrons would travel to get there," I said.

"And you, my dear, are right on the money," Maeve said approvingly. "We never found out if some employees of the conglomerate were in on the whole scam, but this entire experience was very short-lived. The patrons paid millions of credits for a house or apartment on Shimli."

"The conglomerate ran with the money?" I asked.

Maeve shook her head. "No, they actually started construction. They completed Phase I, with over two hundred and fifty single luxury houses and an apartment complex for another two hundred families. Below that complex, they'd built a huge underground 'city' for the staff to live out of sight."

"Charming," I said with as much sarcasm as I could muster.

"Tell me about it," Maeve replied in a similar tone. "Naturally, they had a high-tech medical facility that could also provide every type of plastic surgery and enhancements rich folks are so fond of."

It was my turn to eye roll. "I can think of a billion different ways they could have put those credits to better use. But I'm confused. It sounds like the conglomerate was holding its end of the deal. Why did you call it a scam?"

"Because as soon as that phase was completed, they opened it to their patrons. Barely two weeks after their arrival, a general power outage took the security and defense systems offline. Moments later, pirates raided the planet," Maeve said.

"What? That doesn't make sense!" I exclaimed, incredulous. "If it was such a luxury colony, they would have had solar energy, crystal generators, and backup systems! There is no reason in this day and age for anyone to ever go without power, especially not the wealthy."

"Exactly. So how did that happen unless it was an inside job?" Maeve asked.

"It had to be," I concurred. "What happened?"

"Pirates kidnapped hundreds of people. They ransomed most of them, but some were executed by rivals or enemies. And then others we never saw again, mainly young females," Maeve said with disgust.

I muttered a few curses under my breath. Unscrupulous collectors often paid a high price to acquire the beautiful young daughters of the ultra-rich and powerful as trophies. Some of the bounties that occasionally came up on the hunters' channels made my blood curdle.

"A lucky few managed to flee the planet. But even among them, at least a third got intercepted by pirates," Maeve continued. "Needless to say, the colony never recovered from that tragedy. The conglomerate went bankrupt from all the lawsuits. But the founders didn't come off too hurt by the project's failure. They had other ventures. We suspected that they more than made up for the loss with the ransoms and bounties that were paid—assuming they were indeed in on it."

I whistled through my teeth, helpless anger simmering within me. While I held little affection for elitists and the excessively wealthy who believed themselves above others, no one deserved this kind of fate simply because someone else coveted what you had.

"Are you saying that, since the project went under, the facilities fell into shady hands? Like Saydi's hands?" I asked.

"I have no official knowledge of it," Maeve said cautiously. "The planet was abandoned. Nobody would touch it for another project, even though it has a truly wonderful climate. People deem it cursed. There have been reports of some minor activity to and from the planet. But nothing to warrant an investigation. It is an uninhabited planet, aside from the local fauna. Ballsier prospectors could be visiting it to see if they could set up a new venture there. But the Phase I installations provide everything slavers could need."

"Including an entire underground city to hold the slaves in, and a high-tech medical facility to run the experiments you believe them to be up to," I said, understanding dawning on me.

"Exactly," Maeve said. "What better place to run their activities with no one bothering them on top of great accommodations already provided?"

I tapped a few instructions on my navigation board. "At our current speed, we should reach Shimli in four days. If your tracker is correct, we may need to slow down a little to remain behind them."

"How long before we catch up?" Maeve asked, perking up.

"We should be within firing range in about thirty-eight hours. By my calculations, they are going at this slower pace to save their power and avoid another stop before reaching their destination."

"Perfect. Although we're not planning on shooting them, right?" she asked, giving me the side eye.

I burst out laughing. "No, my love. As much as I want to blow them up, I shall behave."

"Good! I'm the only person you should misbehave with," she said in a provocative fashion.

I snorted and smiled tenderly at her. "Have no fear. I fully intend to," I replied in a voice full of promises. "But work first, pleasure next. That luxury colony should have had tons of blueprints, photos, and other documents and specs made available to the would-be buyers. Surely, we can get our hands on some copies. It would be good to get an idea of what we're walking into."

"Agreed," Maeve said with enthusiasm.

We both got back to work. But in my mind, a single thought replayed.

Hang on, Strasa. Hang on for four more days.

CHAPTER 14
MAEVE

I stared at the dusty blue silhouette of Shimli as Helio began our descent through the planet's atmosphere. Over the past two days, I'd been constantly on edge, my husband's calm demeanor helping me keep my wits about me.

Despite knowing Helio's ship was state-of-the art, I had constantly feared discovery. We'd been following Saydi's vessel at a reasonable distance while in stealth mode. Each time they performed the routine long-range scans every vessel did to check for potential trouble, my heart skipped a beat. I was always nervous with the Enforcers as well, but the even more insane equipment at our disposal helped significantly dampen my unease.

More than once, I contemplated hacking into their ship's artificial intelligence. However, even with the Enforcers, I would have abstained because of the booby traps the scans had detected on Nilzin. Taking over their vessel before they landed would have made things a lot easier for us, not only to rescue Strasa, but also to make an undetected approach to the colony.

To my relief, they had not upgraded the security system of the luxury complex. The only visible modifications were tall energy fields fencing off a large section of the colony. It didn't seem to serve as a way to keep people trapped inside, but more like some kind of enclosure. Aside from Saydi's ship flying over the sprawling little city, still looking unexpectedly pristine despite being abandoned, there wasn't a single soul in sight.

"What the fuck?" I whispered.

Instead of heading for the massive ship hangar a short distance from the apartment complex, Saydi's vessel continued on towards the forest beyond. In the colony's promotional brochure, they had boasted that it provided a safe hunting ground at a walking distance from home. Back then, there were only small mammals, most of them herbivores. For bigger predator hunting, the patrons would have had to take a shuttle for a half-hour flight to reach the savage grounds.

"The greenhouse!" Helio said, an odd mix of excitement and dread slipping into his voice. "They had planned on building a giant greenhouse at an equal distance between Phase I and Phase II. It was supposed to have various sections supporting multiple ecosystems so that you could experience the most beautiful gardens of the galaxy in a single place, and not through a holodeck."

I frowned. "Right. I remember reading that, but they had not started it at the time all hell broke loose. They—"

I never finished my sentence. The silhouette of a massive building made of giant interconnected glass domes appearing in the distance silenced me. No visible roads led to the structure erected in the middle of the forest. The couple of shuttles parked on a large landing pad next to the greenhouse appeared to be the primary method of transportation to and from this place. To my surprise, there was another tall energy field. But this one fenced off all access to the greenhouse and the landing pad.

"They've been busy," Helio said in a grim tone. "At a glance, they only built half of the structure originally planned. But unlike the Phase I complex, they clearly want to control who can come in and out."

"And I bet you it's to keep them in," I muttered.

"Agreed."

Even as we spoke, Saydi's vessel landed close to the shuttles occupying a small section of the landing pad. We hovered at a safe distance, to avoid getting heard, and Helio zoomed the camera in to give us a better view of what was happening.

The hold of the vessel opened, and a Nazhral female disembarked first, followed closely by a Nazhral male. Although she had yet another distinct face than the one she'd been luring Strasa with, or the one she had on Nilzin before changing ship, I recognized the female as Saydi.

"I bet you this is her real appearance," Helio said, making me nod in agreement. "Judging by the red lights above the main entrance, I suspect they use some kind of facial recognition as a locking mechanism."

"My thoughts exactly," I replied, tension stiffening my back as Saydi waved with an abrupt gesture for one or more people I couldn't see yet to come out of the ship.

My heart seized when at least twenty captives walked out, a pain collar attached around their necks. More than half were Edocits, Strasa among them. However, it struck me that many of the other Edocits were well past their teens. Their down leaves wouldn't be potent enough to justify this abduction. The other captives, four Raitheans, one human, and two Prometheans, followed with the same defeated expression. An icy shiver ran down my spine as my fertile imagination began forming one horrible hypothesis after the other as to what Saydi planned on doing to them.

At least, they look unharmed for now.

The Raitheans, a kraken-like species with tentacles for legs, were a reasonably advanced species. Although they had achieved enough interstellar travel capacities to be found in most main intergalactic hubs, they didn't travel that much. As amphibians, they preferred living close to large bodies of water. I recognized two of the four Raitheans as the students who had gone missing from the xenobotany program at Saydi's Academy. They'd been studying foreign aquatic plants that could help their people heal their aquatic ecosystem after a toxic spill had caused a catastrophic environmental disaster on their homeworld.

So while I could see how Saydi had gotten her claws into these two, how the fuck had she captured those Prometheans? The humanoid moth-like species was not only classified as primitive, but it had not achieved space travel yet, nor did its people particularly aspire to it. We'd had to clean up the mess some greedy prospectors had created by violating the Prime Directive to establish some trade and commerce with them. Most people weren't even aware of the existence of the Prometheans.

But if someone knew of some of their unique abilities...

My stomach twisted further with apprehension. Silencing my misgivings, I whipped out my reader to try to get a lock on the collars. We were too far from them for me to latch onto their signal and take over control, but I'd at least be able to get the model and start working on a backdoor. Once we figured out a way to get the prisoners out, we couldn't risk their captors thwarting our efforts by inflicting the type of debilitating pain that would have the abductees writhing on the floor, screaming for mercy.

Helio's own hands were flying over the controls of our ship's navigation board. He was running low-level scans, akin to a GPS, that wouldn't trigger any security system.

"There's a wide enough clearing for us to land safely about one kilometer northwest from here. It's where they were going to build Phase II," Helio explained. "I'm not detecting any advanced security surveillance system. These guys are either overconfident that they won't be discovered, or they're royally fooling my equipment."

"I'm also not detecting anything," I replied at the same time my reader beeped, confirming it had identified the model of the pain collars.

It immediately went to work, pulling up the algorithms necessary to override the controls. But I focused my attention on the ship's giant screen, giving us a close-up view of what was happening outside the greenhouse.

The red lights above the large doors of the greenhouse turned green as soon as Saydi came within range. She stood in the line of sight of the camera while the prisoners filed inside. The Nazhral male followed behind them with a large hover platform loaded with several crates bearing biohazard labels on them.

"I'm guessing this isn't enough evidence yet to call in your friends?" Helio asked with a sliver of hope.

I shook my head. "No, not enough for an Enforcer raid. They would dispatch whatever galactic peacekeepers are patrolling this area. The problem is we don't know how much they would look the other way, since the corporations on Lipnas mostly fund them. Considering how many communications Saydi had with Lipnas…"

"Right," Helio replied with disgust as the security doors closed behind the hovercart following the Nazhral. "Then let's give your friends a reason to get here. I'm going to land the ship."

A few minutes later, we were settling down in a clearing that had been artificially leveled in preparation of the construction that never took place. Dressed in my generic Enforcer armor—one without logos or signs that could link me back to the galactic organization—I eyed Helio with a bit of worry. His leather armor was of excellent quality, designed to convert some of the damage from blaster shots into energy to further power its deflectors and stealth shield. But once again, I wished he had Enforcer grade equipment.

He caught me eyeing him, and I smiled, hiding my thoughts.

Bemoaning the situation wouldn't change a thing about it. After so many years working as an Enforcer, I had to remind myself that things were different now. I was no longer surrounded by my team, and I would no longer have the best of every technology available. This was my new partner. I trusted him and didn't doubt his ability to pull his weight in keeping our team safe. But I was a creature of habit who now needed to adapt to my new reality, just like Helio had been bending over backwards to adjust to working with someone else.

"Let's do this," Helio said with an encouraging smile.

He leaned forward to kiss me. I returned it then activated my personal stealth shield. Helio did the same. With them synced on the same frequency, we could still see each other, although his colors appeared a little dimmed. We disembarked from our cloaked vessel and headed towards the forest.

Short-range scanners showed very few lifeforms, small mammals, birds, and insects. There didn't appear to be any of the bigger game the brochure boasted the residents could hunt here. However, it was the expression on Helio's face that retained my attention.

"What's wrong?" I asked.

"The land is distressed," he said with a grim expression. "Terrible things are happening here."

"Are you able to get any kind of insight from the local flora?" I asked, feeling a little clueless. "They don't seem to have the vines that plants on your world do."

He nodded, his eyes flicking in every direction. "Yes, I can, but it is harder with certain plants than with others. I'm looking for the best candidate."

We walked for a few minutes, Helio looking almost nauseous. I couldn't see or perceive whatever was affecting him. He wasn't even rooting, which made it all the stranger that he should feel so strongly whatever distress emanated from the local flora.

"This one," Helio suddenly said, pointing at a thick tree with a dark greenish-brown bark and ropy limbs.

I couldn't figure out what made it a better candidate than the dozen other more-or-less similar trees around us. But I didn't argue. To my shock, the soles of Helio's boots retracted, folding over to expose his feet to the ground. His *veris* extruded from his feet and forearms, the vine-like tendrils peeking out from under his sleeves and boots. Then the vines in his hair lengthened.

Fascinated, I watched him sit on the ground, partially on the large roots of the tree, and rest his back against the trunk. He leveled his dark green eyes on me, a tender and reassuring expression on his handsome face.

"I will go as deep as I can," he said in a calm voice. "I may become unaware of my surroundings. If you need me to come back sooner, step or pull on one of my *veris*, and I will return. Just be aware that it may take a few minutes."

"I'll watch over you," I pledged.

"I know you will," he replied affectionately.

My throat tightened with growing apprehension as his *veris* sank into the ground, some appearing to pierce through the thick roots and bark of the tree, as did the vines in his hair. Helio's eyes glazed over, and his face became slack as he sank deeper and deeper in this ethereal world I couldn't even begin to imagine. After a couple of minutes, his eyelids grew heavy, then slowly closed.

And thus started the most uncomfortable and longest watch of my life.

CHAPTER 15
HELIO

I didn't like rooting with the flora outside of Zailia. They didn't have *veris* to connect with, which forced me to pierce their outer shells. It hurt both of us. Projecting my consciousness through them also required more effort, and their communications skills were even more basic from their obvious lack of training.

To my shock, my intrusion didn't confuse this tree as it should have. It had experienced a similar spiritual connection before. Judging by the ease with which I flowed through it, the tree had had many months, if not years, of experience. My innards twisted at that thought. How many of our younglings might have been wasting away here all this time?

The same nauseous sensation I'd been feeling ever since stepping inside the forest came back with a vengeance. These trees had experienced pain and extreme anguish. Their colors were off, their bark had dried up as if they had wept too much for our kin, and both their limbs and leaves drooped from the unbearable burden of sorrow.

I wanted to pause and spread my consciousness far and wide to soothe the land, but now wasn't the time. Saydi wouldn't delay before putting her evil plans into motion. If Maeve was right, and she had been on pretty much every point so far, Saydi's experiments would inflict irreversible damage on her prisoners. We hadn't come all the way here only to fail them now.

Normally, when I hunted on my own, I would take a good half-hour just scouting the premises for any lurking danger. But with Maeve watching over me and our short-range scanners having detected no nearby threat, I projected my consciousness directly towards the greenhouse.

With the smaller plants resisting me, I had to jump bigger gaps from tree to tree, which both slowed me down and drained my energy. It should have gotten easier the closer I got to the greenhouse, not harder. The flora appeared to be shielding itself, the way an abused pet instinctively flinched whenever someone extended a hand towards them, expecting a slap instead of a caress. They resisted me the same way at first, before timidly yielding.

But for all that, the more I advanced, the more my heart soared. This level of distress meant the Edocit prisoners had direct contact with the land. That would mean direct contact with me. If they welcomed me, I could know exactly what was going on inside. Even if they didn't, whatever plants they were rooting with would provide a window for me to get a good sense of what we would walk into. However, I needed to be careful. If the prisoners were drugged or otherwise sick in reaction to whatever was being done to them, it could negatively affect me and even make me ill if I connected to their minds.

As I reached the last tree before the clearing where they had built the greenhouse, I descended to its root in search of the next conductor I could ride. This would slow me down even more. There were very few plants, mostly grass, random weeds, and the occasional bush. Projecting oneself through grass and weeds was like trying to empty a pool with a drain the size of a straw.

I literally crawled my way into the greenhouse. Built directly over the ground, no floor blocked my path, only the scarcity of roots, forcing me to circle around the building until I reached an area where a series of almost mature bushes were spreading their roots, far and wide. I did not recognize those plants. There was something familiar about them, and yet not. It wasn't until I latched onto their roots that I finally understood.

Horror washed over me as I recognized the feel of a boquila. That plant mimicked the leaves of other nearby plants to blend in its environment. It didn't even have to be in contact with that other plant, only be in its vicinity. And the leaves were shaped like Edocit down. Worse still, while I didn't feel any toxin that could harm me, everything about this plant was wrong. They had tampered with its DNA. The plant was fighting with itself, trying to assimilate its conflicting nature.

I couldn't tell how long it had taken my consciousness to trickle in all the way here. It felt like a long time. Hopefully, not so long that Maeve would be in distress. But she hadn't tapped for me to return. With luck, she wouldn't need to, as it would take me a while to get back. Once more, I thanked the Maker for my mate. This would have been an impossible mission to tackle alone.

Having infused myself in the plant, I opened my mind's eye to observe our surroundings. Even with the slightly blurred, monochromatic way the world displayed when viewed through mental projection, helpless anger filled with horror surged through me.

The twelve Edocits who had disembarked from Saydi's vessel represented but a fraction of those she had abducted. Even with my limited vision, I recognized a few faces of people reported missing for years. They were not saplings, but mature adults. They were sitting directly on the ground. Their overly bloated *veris* buried in the soil looked like ancient roots. Even the vines in their hair now resembled thick tree limbs that had fused with those of the bushes surrounding them.

For a split second, a terrifying thought flashed through my mind. What if the bush I had projected myself into was a similar growth from whatever experiment they were performing on my people? But then the leaves on their bushes were different, and I couldn't feel another consciousness sharing this plant with me.

Despite the fury and devastation that threatened to rob me of rational thoughts, I forced myself to focus. I needed to gather as much information as possible to free them. We were their only chance. Another look at their hardened *veris* strengthened my belief that they would never be able to retract them back into their skin. If those poor souls were ever to be freed, their *veris* would have to be cut off. The Maker only knew if that would forever sever their link to the land. But that was a problem for later.

The section I was in appeared to hold the long-time prisoners. At least twenty Edocits, all males, sat in a similar fashion around the outer edges of the circular room. While it took a little longer for me to perceive sound when projected outside of my body, there was none to be heard here. The males appeared to either be unconscious or to have projected out so they wouldn't feel what had to be torture. No wonder the land was distressed.

I moved on to other rooms, my movements greatly sped up by the abundance of plants here. The only thing slowing me down was avoiding connecting with the captives. I wanted to get a good view of the global situation before I attempted to speak with one of them. After so much trauma, there was no telling how they would react. I couldn't risk them giving away my presence just yet.

The next three large rooms were essentially hydroponic greenhouses, with rows upon rows of altered narcotic plants. Even just breezing through them, I could feel their incredible potency. Thankfully, it wouldn't affect me. The plants were healthy thanks to the well-hydrated soil rich in nutrients, the perfect room temperature, and the abundance of sunlight. This would sell for billions of credits on the black market.

To my dismay, I couldn't get into the next couple of rooms as they were completely sealed off from the ground. They likely served as office space, storage, or laboratories. I had to backtrack to access a different wing. This time, voices greeted me. Even after I finished projecting myself into the room, the voices remained muffled, as if I was hearing them underwater.

"Why the fuck did you blow your cover?" asked a human male, with a thick drawling accent. "You were supposed to grab a bunch of them flower heads during that internship. The boss ain't gonna be happy."

"You let me deal with him," Saydi replied in a clipped voice completely different from the youthful and playful voice she'd used in her recordings with Strasa. "Things were getting too hot. The brat was getting suspicious, and you idiots bungled the abduction of the Raitheans. I had the perfect cover at the Academy. Now, I have to start all over. Anyway, we have everything we need to finish the project."

"Everything we need?" the human exclaimed, incredulous. "You brought a bunch of old trees. We needed the young ones who bloom the potent shit."

Saydi rolled her eyes. "First off, leaves don't *bloom.* They sprout or blossom, you ignorant toad. Second, we won't need the young ones anymore. The enhancement will have the adult Edocits sprouting hundreds of the most addictive, most potent down leaves anyone could have ever imagined."

"What your furry ass ain't getting is that the fucking enhancement doesn't work!" the human snapped.

"It will!" she snapped back, looking mightily annoyed. "Remember that hot little human I brought? She's not for your entertainment. She is ranked among the top ten best xenochemists in the galaxy, and she also has more degrees in xenobotany than your uneducated ass can count. The projects she's been working on are extremely close to ours, though she had very different goals. She will fix the stability issues. Before the month is over, we will dominate the galactic market, and the boss will lick my *furry ass*… As will you."

The human muttered something under his breath, but Saydi was no longer paying attention to him. She quickly tapped some instructions on the interface of her datapad before glancing back up at the man.

"Urthan has finished assembling the pool. Get the Raitheans soaking in there and drain their insulin every hour, on the hour. They received a glycemic implant that will keep their pancreas working overtime. When you're done, prepare the pretty Dryad for his phlebotomy. His blood is saturated with that damn hormone. One sip will give you as big a high as his down leaves. Speaking of which, pluck those while you're at it. And remember not to help yourself to any of his stuff. I know exactly how many leaves there are."

Without another word, Saydi walked out of the room while the human uttered a string of foul swear words aimed at her. Despite his hushed voice, she had undoubtedly heard him, and I believed it had been intentional on his part. While the dysfunction within the team could serve us, we needed to get moving before they really hurt Strasa.

I should have returned to Maeve at once, but first, I wanted to give the boy a heads up and have him prepared for when we raided. However, as I began to push my consciousness further into a new room, I felt a powerful tug. Someone had struck one of my *veris.* The second, even stronger tug erased any doubt I might have had. Something bad was happening, and Maeve needed me to come back immediately.

CHAPTER 16
MAEVE

This waiting had me on the verge of climbing one of those damn trees. I hated feeling this useless, and especially of being this blind. During infiltration missions, we always had our short-range scans and coms to keep tabs on each other. But how did you track the progress of someone's consciousness literally leaving their body through a network of roots and plants?

To distract myself, I used my reader to try and connect with the pain collars of the captives. I felt insulted by the ease with which I succeeded. These assholes were far too confident and complacent. Sure, it played in our favor, but such arrogance only further fueled my hatred for them.

Despite my urge to disable the collars, I merely reduced the amount of pain they would inflict. Should they attempt to punish the captives before we could free them, I didn't want their captors to know I had tampered with it.

Next, I checked their biometric lock. That one, too, would be a breeze to override. It wasn't a cheap model, but also not a fancy one that would have required me to painstakingly bypass each security lock within the system. This was the type of locking mechanism you used when the only thing you feared was a bunch of weaponless people trying to leave without your blessing.

As much as I loved a good challenge, I welcomed its absence this time. I wouldn't mess with the lock just yet, either. Hopefully, Helio could find us a backdoor entrance instead. If not, I would wait until we were close enough to remotely disable it, and we would enter still cloaked.

My stomach knotted when I cast another glance at my husband. He'd gone frighteningly still, the heaving of his chest as he breathed almost imperceptible. The color of his skin had dulled, making him look almost like a corpse. But it was the additional *veris* extruding from him and binding him further to the tree and the ground that freaked me out the most. I'd seen a lot of Dryad art growing up. As much as I'd found them beautiful back then, seeing my husband looking half-fused with the tree was creeping me out.

My bracer quietly vibrating startled the living daylights out of me. A quick glance at its interface showed me Tedrick's response to the message I had sent him earlier. As we had begun our descent into the planet's atmosphere, I had informed him of our arrival. It had been both to let him know that a call for the Enforcers' urgent intervention could come any minute, but also for me to get a sense of how long it would take for them to receive it.

With the great distance between us, even moving at lightning speed through various relays, it took time for the signal to travel. It had been just shy of forty-two minutes since I sent that message. This meant it took about twenty-one minutes for him to receive any communication from me. And then God only knew how long they would take to arrive.

Feeling once more helpless, now that I was idle again, I heaved a sigh and glanced back at my husband. Despite his disturbing appearance right now, my fingers itched with the desire to caress his hair. A part of me wanted to touch him to confirm he was still fine, regardless of his comatose state. As I didn't know how physical contact would affect him, and not wanting to risk him perceiving this as an urgent call for him to return, I silenced the urge and instead ran another short-range scan of the area.

Like with the billion prior scans I'd performed, there was nothing to report. No threat and not a single living soul in sight. Even the scurrying little critters that had strutted about while going on their merry business had vanished. At least, eyeing the unusual fauna of the planet had been entertaining. Maybe I should…

I froze, my heart skipping a beat as the underlying meaning of my thoughts sank in. Another quick look at the scanner on my armband confirmed what I had seen; nothing. Not a single small rodent or mammal displayed on my device in a wide radius. I jerked my head up to glance around us. Nothing but vegetation as far as the eye could see.

I finally noticed the deafening silence. Gone were the chirping of the birds and the joyful buzzing of the insects flying by. The plants and trees appeared to be holding their breaths, even their leaves remaining unnaturally still despite the soft breeze, as if they feared their rustling would draw unwanted attention to themselves.

One look at Helio reassured me that his stealth shield continued to hide him from view. I had kept mine active in the highly improbable case Saydi's crew would have some kind of aerial surveillance scouting through the forest. Pulling my blaster from its holster, I set it to the highest stun, then moved closer to the tree to get out of the path of whatever might be approaching. I held my breath as I strained my ear, hoping to catch a hint of what might have frightened the fauna, my hearing enhanced by my earpiece.

The answer came shortly thereafter. My heart nearly leapt out of my chest when a blood-curdling cry rose from about five hundred meters away… a human cry. Although muffled by the distance, if not for my earpiece, I never would have heard it. I once again glanced in confusion at my scanner. It showed no approaching lifeform. Nothing but plants and me. Even the thermal detector only identified me, and that was because I was inside the stealth shield. Unless they had the frequency of my shield, anyone else scanning the area would not pick up my heat signature.

If the person—the male—who had emitted that cry was hiding behind a stealth shield, why reveal his presence with this scream? Anyway, he couldn't be camouflaged. The fauna wouldn't have known to go into hiding otherwise, just like they'd been blissfully unaware of Helio's and my presence.

Helio!

He, too, was showing on my scanner as a plant. Could that male be…?

"Help! Help me!" the distant voice shouted, breaking the otherwise eerie silence.

Heart pounding, I adjusted the infrared settings of my scanner to match the body heat emitted by an Edocit and focused it on the direction whence the voice emanated. This time, a silhouette clearly stood out against the dense vegetation. The male was moving northwest, the zigzagging pattern of his movements akin to those of a drunk person failing miserably to run in a straight line.

A drunk or a severely injured or drugged victim who had escaped their captor.

Although I could leave Helio alone for a brief moment, I didn't know if the escapee's captors were on his trail. My scanner showed nothing, but then it hadn't shown the Edocit either at first. Not wanting to take any chances, I pressed the tip of my foot on one of Helio's *veris*. Just as I was doing so, another loud scream nearly had me jumping out of my skin.

Who screams like that?

I had never heard an Edocit scream before, but this was giving me the creeps. As if he had heard my thought, the escapee made a sudden shift from the northwest direction he'd been running in to head straight for us. Had he felt Helio through the land? Whatever the reason, he was coming at us fast.

This time, I all but stomped on Helio's *veris*, praying to all the powers that be that he'd felt it and was coming back to his body right the fuck now. I then moved away from him, standing directly in the path of whoever was approaching. The escapee was moving fast, and yet time stretched on forever as I waited.

And then I saw him emerge from the dense vegetation behind a tall tree.

My heart broke at his dreadful appearance, while anger soared within me. He seemed to be in his late teens, early twenties. If not for him being completely naked, his frail constitution might have made me believe he was a female. His skin had lost the smooth silkiness that gave young Edocits this glowing air of health and joy. It was as parched and cracked as his lips, as if he was covering himself in bark. Not a single down leaf remained in his hair, the vines entangled with his burgundy locks appearing withered and dried out. His gauntness made the *veris* in his arms and legs appear three times too thick.

"Help! Help me!" he cried out again.

His steps faltered, as if his run here had drained whatever energy he had left. Frankly, I didn't even know how he had mustered this much strength. He looked like he'd been starved and barely given enough water to keep him alive.

I deactivated my stealth shield and holstered my blaster before raising my palms in front of me in an appeasing gesture.

"Don't be afraid. I'm here to help," I said in a reassuring tone.

The male stopped dead in his tracks and stared at me with a stunned expression. I'd expected him to recoil in fear, maybe even take a few steps away from me while debating whether to flee or take the gamble to trust me. After all, he had no reason to believe anyone on this planet could have good intentions towards him. Instead, he appeared frozen, as if his mind was struggling to process what he was seeing.

"I came to rescue other Edocits who got abducted," I explained, forcing myself to stay where I stood so as not to frighten him.

To my shock, he stretched his neck to look over my shoulder, directly where Helio would be. I no longer doubted he had felt my husband through the land. Could he see him or even feel him through the stealth shield? A powerful wave of unease twisted my insides. I hated that Helio was sitting here, so vulnerable to factors outside of my control.

I opened my mouth to draw his attention back to me, but my scanner vibrating claimed my own. On the interface, another silhouette was moving away from the greenhouse and into the forest.

Did Helio find a way to help them escape?

I looked back up at the Edocit just as he was returning his focus on me. The strangest expression settled on his face. He no longer seemed terrified. He looked disturbingly as if any emotion had been drained out of him.

"Help! Help me!" he said, his voice almost conversational.

"Yes, I will help you. What's your name? How many others escaped with you?"

"Help me," he repeated while resuming his advance, this time at a walking pace towards me. "It hurts."

"What hurts?" I asked, taking a couple of steps towards him while trying to identify the source of his pain, beyond the obvious ravage captivity had inflicted on him.

"Help. Help me."

My spine stiffened when he once more said those words, a sense of dread washing over me as I watched him slowly approach. “My name is Maeve. What’s your name?” I asked, taking an involuntary step backward.

When he continued to advance, repeating his plea for help, my blood turned to ice. This couldn’t be happening. We weren’t on Zailia. Surely, Sayeefs couldn’t spawn here? Didn’t it require a specific type of tree for them to rise out of?

Even as those questions fired off in my mind, I whipped out my blaster while quickly backing away from him. Still refusing to accept the possibility he could be a doppelgänger born of the suffering of the Edocits captives, I lowered the setting from highest stun to medium level. If he truly was an escapee whose mind was addled by the abuse he’d sustained, shooting him at the highest stun level in his weakened state could kill him. But my ass was also not taking any chances, especially not with Helio depending on me to keep him safe.

“Don’t take another step,” I warned, my blaster trained on him. “I will shoot. Now tell me your fucking name!”

He looked at my weapon as one would an odd insect hovering in front of their face but didn’t stop his advance.

“Last warning,” I snapped, adrenaline pumping through my veins.

When he once more ignored my order, and with him barely ten meters away from me, I no longer hesitated. I aimed at his thigh and fired. The strength of the blast would make his leg temporarily go numb.

A sharp yelp escaped him, and his leg buckled. Although he doubled over, holding his thigh, he didn’t fall. He stared at his leg in disbelief, then he snapped his head up to look at me.

“Stay where you are, or I’ll shoot again,” I shouted.

Holding my blaster with both hands, I turned it towards his other thigh. A glimmer of understanding flashed through his eyes. My innards liquified when his helpless mask fell off. His face appeared to melt, his nose all but vanishing while his eyes grew bigger, and his lips disappeared into a thin, wide line.

Simultaneously, the texture of his skin thickened in a crackling sound reminiscent of fissuring ice. However, I recognized the phenomenon as the nearly bulletproof bark Edocits could cover their skin in when entering battle.

"Oh, shit!" I whispered under my breath.

I showered him with blaster shots that seemed to bounce off his hardened skin with no effect. As I switched the setting to lethal, the Sayeef opened his mouth impossibly wide, revealing two rows of sharp teeth pointing in every direction. He emitted a deafening sound that had me crying out in pain. For a split second, I believed he'd busted my eardrums. I yanked out my earpiece, which had enhanced his banshee screech, and stumbled back, both disoriented and in pain. My vision blurred from my eyes watering, I almost didn't see him launching his attack.

In the distance, I heard a second screech echoing his. Despite the terror this awakened in me, I had to focus on the threat in front of me before worrying about the incoming one.

On instinct, I threw myself to the ground, barely dodging something long and dark that had speared towards my face. I rolled left, just to hear a loud clapping sound, as if a bullet had been shot right behind me. Using my momentum, I jumped back to my feet while raising my left wrist in front of me. The energy shield of my bracer immediately formed, just in time to stop another 'spear' that would have stabbed me right in the chest. I grunted and stumbled back under the force of the impact.

Blinking away the tears the Sayeef's screech had provoked, I stared in horror at the creature. The spears were in fact the oversized *veris* along his forearms—three on each side—which he used like harpoons. Fists raised before him, like a boxer in a defensive stance, the Sayeef rushed me at the same time he launched his harpoons. Shield raised facing him, I ran away at an angle while shooting at him. A couple of harpoons struck my shield in glancing blows, almost making me lose my footing.

The damn creature was moving too fast. If its strength even

remotely matched the power with which its *veris* harpoons hammered me, I would never survive a close encounter. Arms and legs pumping to lure him as far away as possible from Helio, I whipped out a concussion grenade from my weapons belt and threw it at the Sayeef. My heart leapt when he instinctively caught it. It detonated seconds later, knocking him to the ground with an ear-piercing shriek.

I deactivated my energy shield and turned on my stealth shield instead. Although it wouldn't fully mute the sounds of my steps, I hoped the wailing of the doppelgänger, still writhing on the ground in pain, would cover my approach. If the Sayeefs were anything like Edocits, you had to repeatedly batter the same spot to weaken and eventually shatter their protective bark to access the vital organs below.

I was taking a huge gamble, but time wasn't on my side. With the second Sayeef rapidly closing in, Helio and I would both be dead if I didn't take at least the first one out. Guns blazing, I ran towards the creature while trying to focus my shots on its torso. Although it couldn't see me, the blaster shots striking him gave away the general direction they were coming from. Pushing himself up onto his knees, he opened his terrifying mouth wide to scream again, but I made him swallow my blaster shot first.

The Sayeef's head jerked back so hard, it looked like his neck had snapped. He emitted a slightly wet raspy sigh, then his entire body appeared to collapse in on itself. This time, his skin didn't make the crackling sound of his bark thickening. It was something akin to a thick, simmering stew, bubbling at a low heat. He withered before my very eyes, his body deflating and darkening into a twisted pile of desiccated, gnarly roots. The smell of mold and rotten leaves rose from its remains.

I could have wept with relief, but another of those nightmarish things was coming in hot and fast. To my dismay, my radar showed it making a beeline for Helio.

"No!" I whispered, horrified.

I thought the ruckus would have lured it our way. I dropped my stealth shield and ran back as fast as I could towards Helio. The war cry that rose from my throat might as well have been the roar of a beast. For a few terrifying moments, I thought he would reach my husband first. Thankfully, I beat him by mere seconds. I lobbed a concussion grenade at him, hoping he would catch it like his predecessor, but he swatted it away with the back of his hand.

This one had not even attempted to fool me by impersonating a captive. I could only presume the screams of the first Sayeef had warned him the gig was up. Intending to repeat my previous stunt, I raised my energy shield in front of me and fired my blaster at the monster. But this son of a bitch acted nothing like the first one. I never had time to attempt luring him away from Helio.

The Sayeef didn't raise his fist in front of him to harpoon me. He flung his right arm in a swiping motion in my direction. His *veris* extruded at the same time, coming at me like the strings of a giant cat-o-nine tail whip. Although I blocked them with my shield, the force of the blow sent me flying backward.

I landed a few meters back with a loud thud. Pain radiated through my arm holding the shield. Stunned and winded, I blindly aimed my blaster at the Sayeef. Before I could get a single shot off, a stinging pain slashed at my right lower leg. I first thought he had whipped my leg with his *veris*, but they actually wrapped around my ankle, tightening painfully.

A terrified scream tore out of my throat when I suddenly began sliding forward as he yanked me towards him by my ankle. Panicked, I tried to shoot at the vines, but couldn't get a proper aim. In desperation, I dropped my blaster and drew out my sword to hack at them. The Sayeef screamed and yanked so hard, lifting my leg up, that I banged the back of my head against the ground. My teeth rattled, and my vision blurred for a second.

I tried to slash at the vines again, but his harpoons struck my shield, slamming it against me. It knocked the wind out of me. He pulled me once more, and then my foot touched his. Petrified, I watched my death lunge at me, the energy shield between us my only protection.

But the next blow never came.

Sharp wooden spikes shot out of the ground, impaling the Sayeef from below. I gaped at the creature, too stunned to move. His *veris* released my ankle, and both his hands clawed at the spikes protruding through his body. The tips that had pierced through his chest and right thigh glistened with a semi-translucent substance that almost looked like sap.

Snapping out of my daze, I scrambled backward on the ground while fumbling to retrieve my second blaster from its holster. I fired away at its face, one shot finding its mark inside his mouth, silencing his screeching wails.

Just like with the first Sayeef, his body withered into a gnarly pile while the spikes that had impaled him resorbed into the ground. Only then did I notice that they were actually linked to thick roots that receded away from the creature's corpse. The ground above the roots collapsed as they retreated to their origin… back to Helio.

"HELIO!" I shouted when I found him staring at me, looking groggy. "Oh, my God, Helio! You're back!"

Ignoring the pins and needles stabbing at my right foot as blood rushed back in, I got up and ran to my husband. I all but threw myself at him. I examined him to make sure he was unharmed, then cupped his cheeks to lock eyes with him.

"I'm so fucking happy to see you," I said with a nervous laugh laced with the tears that wanted to choke me. "I was getting my ass kicked. You saved me!"

He gave me a slow, tired smile, like someone heavily sedated. "You saved me first, my mate," he said in a slurred voice. "We saved each other."

"As it should be," I replied with a teary laugh.

I crushed his lips with a kiss. Although he responded, I could feel him still struggling to regain control of his body. At least, the thick, root-like *veris* that had spread all around him—making him look half-melded with the tree—were quickly resorbing.

"Can you stand?" I asked.

"Not yet. I will need a few minutes," Helio replied, sounding weak. "Call your friends. They'll want everything that's in there."

CHAPTER 17
HELIO

It took a solid ten minutes for me to fully recover from the drunken state I felt from having projected so deeply through the foreign flora. Explaining what I had seen and heard to Maeve kept me from losing my mind over the fact that she'd faced two Sayeefs alone. I should have prepared her better, taught her the best techniques to take them down. But I never imagined they could spawn off-world.

In my years of rescuing abducted Edocits, I'd never experienced cases where the captors gave the abductees direct contact with the land. However, it explained the fencing around the greenhouse. It wasn't to keep their prisoners inside, but to prevent any Sayeef that spawned from attacking their little base of operation. As the captives projected their consciousness away from the origin of the pain, the Sayeefs would form in the woods.

"Does it mean that this experiment Saydi's team is running killed two more Edocits?" Maeve asked with a devastated expression, as we started heading towards the greenhouse.

I shook my head. "Not necessarily. A Sayeef can spawn without someone dying. There just needs to be sufficient pain and anguish. The Edocits I saw were in a terrible shape, but none struck me as being at death's door."

"Thank God! They're too close to freedom to die now," Maeve said with relief. "So there was no other way in?"

"I didn't see one," I replied in an apologetic tone. "But I didn't get to explore every area. We can check as we approach, but we should be fine even if we enter through the front door. I saw a limited number of staff. Granted, I couldn't see inside at least a couple of rooms. But everywhere else only had a couple of people per room, if anyone at all. I didn't see any weapons, except the ones on Saydi's belt and on the human male she was talking to. However, it doesn't mean they don't have any stashed somewhere."

"Agreed," Maeve replied with a frown. "But what of the scientists? Any species with particularly lethal abilities?"

I shook my head with a sheepish expression. "I couldn't get a good look, but it seemed to be humans, a couple of Nazhrals, and an Obosian male."

"An Obosian?!" Maeve exclaimed, looking shocked. "What the heck would he be doing here? These guys are the biggest sticklers for rule in the universe. There's a reason the most savage prison planet in the galaxy is under their control."

I nodded. "It shocked me to see him there, but I believe he's also here against his will, like that human xenochemist Saydi just brought with the other captives."

"That would make sense," Maeve replied pensively. "Did he have a collar?"

"He was facing away from me. His massive wings were blocking his neck… and pretty much all the rest of him," I said with a shrug.

"Oh wow! So he's a full-on Hell Lord?" Maeve asked.

I blinked, unsure what she meant. "Hell Lord?" I repeated.

She chuckled and waved a dismissive hand. "To us humans, Obosians look like a mix between dark elves on steroids and demons. As you probably know, the size of their wings determines their caste. If his wings are as big as you imply, he's likely a mature warrior. They are usually granted full control of a sector of the prison planet Molvi. That place is so atrocious, we call it Hell."

"Aaah, that makes sense," I said. "Judging by who Saydi was able to abduct, she and her people clearly have been scouring the most remote and improbable corners of the galaxy to get what they wanted."

"Clearly. And now it's time for us to free them all," Maeve said with a determined look as we closed in on the greenhouse.

There were no visible secondary entrances. Our scans showed that certain sections of the dome could open to allow large cargo to be flown down directly inside one of the rooms I had not been able to visit. We assumed it served as storage.

"Take this," Maeve said, extending a thin black stone to me. "It's one of the shadow stones Cedros and Kaida gave us as a wedding present. If things get ugly in there, crack it. It will open a portal directly inside the Enforcers' HQ."

I recoiled. "Why are you giving this to me? We're not separating in there. If this needs to be used—"

"I know, silly male," Maeve said with a laugh, interrupting me. "We're not separating, but I could have my hands full when the shit hits the fan. I also have one in case you're the one getting overwhelmed. Tedrick is aware a portal could open any minute."

My eyes widened. "So why don't we summon them now?" I exclaimed.

"Because they do not have a warrant to go in yet. Tedrick is undoubtedly trying to obtain one based on the information you gathered and which I sent him. But it will take a bit of time for him to get it and confirm that I can bring them over. However, if one of their agents in an undercover mission gets into a sticky situation that would require a rescue, then they would be expected to come by whatever means necessary. We do have a 'leave no man behind' policy."

I snorted, both amused and annoyed. "You Enforcers have too many rules impeding doing what needs to be done."

"You're right. But those rules protect both the rights of the public and the Enforcers. That Saydi bitch is *not* getting off on some technicality. I'll be sitting in the front row when her ass gets sent to Molvi."

The vicious glare in Maeve's eyes did funny things to me. "You're hot when you're savage," I blurted out.

Maeve's stunned expression reflected my own. Then her shock gave way to a smoldering gaze. "Hold that thought for when we celebrate later."

"Deal," I said with a grin.

I tucked the stone into my weapons belt for easy access. Despite the dampening effect of our stealth shields, we kept the noise to a minimum as we headed to the front of the greenhouse. The birds were chirping again, providing the only sound in the otherwise seemingly deserted area.

We stopped next to the entrance, out of the way if anyone would come out, and I rooted again. This time, thanks to the extremely short distance to travel, I did a light projection, the type that kept me aware of my body's surroundings. It allowed me to quickly verify that no one awaited us near the entrance.

I returned to my body and indicated that the coast was clear with a sharp nod. Maeve smiled and tapped a few instructions on the portable device she called a reader. The red lights above the entrance turned green, and the front doors swished open.

We hurried inside, the door closing immediately behind us. To my relief, Maeve didn't reactivate the locking mechanism. At this point, we were committed. If we got discovered, it would likely be because a new ship arrived, which meant they'd overwhelm us either way. With a will of its own, my hand settled over the shadow stone. I could never put into words the relief I felt knowing there would be an easy exit for my mate if things got bad.

The 'reception' area, if it could be called that, only had a few rows of long, empty potting tables. I presumed they'd moved the seedlings it once contained or planted them elsewhere. The reflective glass wall behind them kept us from seeing what was happening on the other side, without blocking sunlight from going through. I already knew what nightmarish spectacle awaited us there.

Taking point, I headed left, the only direction we could go. The large door separating the second connecting dome of the greenhouse lay wide open. We entered one of the two gardens I had visited. With it being still empty, we moved to the third room, yet another hydroponic garden. A closed door on the other side would open on the hallway which had led to the room where I'd observed Saydi talking with the human male. To our right was yet another closed door, but this time to one of the rooms I hadn't been able to enter.

As if summoned by that thought, the door opened, and the Obosian I'd spotted earlier walked into the room. Nearly seven feet tall, with bulging muscles rolling under his charcoal skin, and massive black horns surrounded by long, silver-white hair, he looked like a vengeful god.

My stomach dropped when he immediately turned to look in our direction. His gaze locked with mine as if my stealth shield didn't exist. I held my breath and silenced a gasp when his icy-blue eyes flicked towards Maeve. To my shock, my mate raised her left palm and made a gesture that I didn't know with her fingers.

Showing no emotion whatsoever, the imposing male turned away from us and stretched in the oddest fashion. For a beat, I wondered if my mind had played tricks on me. Maybe the Obosian hadn't seen through our shield. And then I saw it. He was stretching with his right arm pointing at the top left corner of the room. A discreet camera, easily missed, spied on us.

"Thank you," Maeve whispered, her voice so low I barely heard her.

With an almost evil grin, she aimed her device at the camera while typing some instructions. The speed with which she had it replaying a segment of a prior recording where nothing was happening in the room left me reeling.

The Obosian immediately turned back to face us. "I felt your disincarnated presence earlier, Edocit. Your soul wasn't familiar to me. But I didn't expect you to show up again in the flesh."

Speechless, I barely kept myself from gaping at him.

"So, you are indeed a Hell Lord," Maeve asked while deactivating his collar, totally unfazed that he could see us, despite our stealth shields still being active.

The Obosian waved a disdainful hand. "Obviously not at the moment. But I thank you for this," he added, removing the collar from his neck. "There are only four here. Three Nazhrals and a human male with a scar. You will have no problem apprehending them. *DO NOT* kill them. They are mine. I will make them the stars of my playground on Molvi."

The icy way in which he spoke those words had a shiver running down my spine. I almost felt sorry for them. The Molvi prison planet was unforgiving. Being sent there was worse than a death sentence.

"Everyone else here is a prisoner. You must hurry if you want to save the new Edocits that were brought in earlier. They're being prepared for their first injections." He looked over our shoulders. "Where's the rest of your team?"

"Acquiring a warrant," Maeve replied.

"Tharmok takes your warrant!" the Obosian hissed. "I invoke Clause 286. Get them here now! Then go save your saplings. I'll free the Raitheans."

Without waiting for our response, the Obosian stormed out of the room, back to the previous one he'd been in.

I stared at the door closing behind him in disbelief. "What the…?"

Maeve snorted. "Hell Lords have the best bedside manners. We don't just compare them to demons because of their appearance, but also because they can feel and see souls. You can't sneak past one of them. Which is one of the traits that makes them the best guards in the universe."

"What's 286?" I asked, still stunned by the Obosian's dominant, if not flat-out rude behavior.

"A treaty by which the UPO pledges its unconditional support to allies in case of dire need. That Obosian must be very high-ranking among his people to not only know of the clause but also feel entitled to invoke it. Who am I to deny an Obosian Lord?" Maeve asked in a singsong voice.

Just as she was breaking her shadow stone, a scream of agony resonated in the distance. I instantly broke into a run towards the closed door on the other side of the garden at the same time the portal formed with a thunderclap sound.

"Helio!" Maeve called out, but I didn't stop.

I whipped out my blaster as I brutally opened the door. The screams having stopped, I ran down the wide corridor before all but breaking down the first of three doors I encountered. Scared gasps greeted my irruption inside what turned out to be a lab. A Nazhral male turned to look at who had so unceremoniously barged into the room, only to stare down the barrel of my blaster. He never got a chance to grab his weapon. I fired twice at the highest stun setting. A single shot would have been enough to knock him out, but I wasn't taking chances and had no time to waste.

Two humans in the room, both wearing pain collars, screamed and took cover. I didn't take the time to reassure them as the agonized shouts had resumed two doors down. Spinning around, I glimpsed Maeve running towards me, blaster in hand, while a sea of Enforcers appeared to be pouring out of the portal.

Just as I was reaching the door whence the screams were emanating, I heard the now too familiar voice of Saydi.

"Get on the fucking table or I will—"

The screaming stopped a split second before Saydi went quiet. I nearly bashed the door in, finding an adult Edocit lying on the floor, his hands holding on to the collar around his neck. Standing a couple of meters in front of him, Saydi was pressing the buttons of a remote with a confused expression. I realized then that Maeve had deactivated the collar.

It took me a split second to take in the rest of the room. Along the back wall, six Edocits huddled together fearfully. They had already strapped four others to a table, some kind of drip being administered to them intravenously. In the opposite corner, Strasa sat in a chair, looking devastated, as the scarred human male was removing the last of his down leaves.

Every head turned towards me, each person displaying the same stunned expression. Time appeared to stand still for a beat, and then everything happened at once.

"You!" Strasa whispered, shock, disbelief, and hope mixing on his face.

I raised my blaster towards Saydi. Moving at lightning speed, she dove behind an examination table to take cover. The human male yanked Strasa out of his chair to use him as a shield and pressed the tip of his blaster under the boy's chin.

"Everyone out!" I shouted in Edocit to my brothers while simultaneously raising my energy shield in front of me.

Not waiting to be asked twice, they stampeded towards the exit. One of them only paused long enough to extend a hand to the male on the floor who'd been tortured for refusing to get on a table. He pulled him to his feet, and they ran after the others.

"Fucking zap them, you stupid cunt!" the man holding Strasa shouted at Saydi, his voice filled with panic.

The fool hadn't realized yet that the Nazhral no longer controlled the collars. The commanding voices of the Enforcers ordering the captives to approach with their hands up reached us from the hallway.

"She can't. We control everything in here now," Maeve said in a fierce voice that I found incredibly sexy.

Horror descended over the man's features as it finally dawned on him that there would be no escaping this one.

"Come out of hiding, Saydi, there's no more running for you," I hissed, before turning my attention to the human. "And you, release the boy at once."

"Like fuck I am!" the man shouted. "You're gonna let us the hell out of here, or I'm blowing his pretty head right off."

I looked at Strasa straight in the eye while forcing myself to ignore his terrified expression. The sapling was trying to be brave, but he was trembling with fear. Hatred burned in my gut. They would pay dearly for traumatizing and torturing such a pure and innocent soul, only because they coveted what he had, what he was.

"You're going to be okay, son," I said in a reassuring tone. "The human messed with the wrong people. And it's time for him to pay. They can't hurt you anymore."

"SHUT UP, you fucking flower head!"

Ignoring him, I continued to talk to Strasa, while Maeve carefully circled around the empty examination table behind which Saydi had taken cover. The Nazhral was desperate enough to potentially be working on some last-minute move to get out of this bind.

"Strasa, the human has forgotten that every rose has its thorns," I said, my gaze intense in the hopes he would get my underlying meaning.

The sapling's eyes widened both in fear and understanding. He slightly shook his head, while looking at me with a pleading expression.

I felt more than I heard a few Enforcers walk into the room. But I ignored them, too.

"It's fine, Strasa. You will be fine," I insisted, hoping he would comply.

"I said shut the hell up, or I'll blow your fucking head off," the human yelled.

As he spoke, he brutally tightened his hold around Strasa's neck, visibly constricting the boy's airways while shifting the aim of his blaster towards me. The sapling instinctively stretched his neck and pulled with both hands at the man's arm… in vain. He'd done exactly the opposite of what he should have. By stretching his neck instead of bowing his chin down, he'd made it even easier for his captor to strangle him. In his distress, I doubted the human even knew that he was slowly killing his hostage.

"DO IT!" I shouted, my eyes still locked with Strasa's.

Thinking I was calling his bluff and daring him to shoot me, the human blinked, an air of confusion laced with panic settling over his face. He knew very well he'd never touch me with my energy shield raised before me. He also couldn't see me rooting, thanks to the examination table hiding my legs and feet.

But Strasa spared me from using my backup plan. Suffocating, he closed his eyes even as the red dots from the Enforcer's aiming lasers began appearing over his captor's forehead.

"Lower your fucking weapons! I'll kill him! I'll kill them all!" the human added, pointing his weapon at the four Edocits still strapped to the tables. "I'm gonna—"

He finished his sentence with a loud shriek when Strasa finally summoned his thorns. The thick and sharp, five-centimeters-long needles erupted all over his body, including his face, stabbing the human everywhere they touched.

The man pulled away from the boy, further shredding his own skin in the process. Blood gushing everywhere, he screamed again while stumbling back.

"Strasa, to me!" Maeve shouted, one hand extended towards him and her blaster pointed at the human.

As soon as the sapling started darting forward, Maeve and I fired. Although we targeted his chest, the human's head snapped back, his body seizing violently before he collapsed to the ground.

In a brief instant of panic, I feared Strasa would slam into my mate with his thorns still out, but he resorbed them seconds before throwing himself into her arms.

"I've got you, sweetie. I've got you," Maeve said, holding him and caressing his hair while backing away from the area Saydi still hid in. "You're safe now."

My heart constricted seeing him desperately cling to my mate, his body rocked by sobs even as the buds in his hair flowered with gratitude. One day, this could happen to our son. Another wave of fury surged through me at that thought.

"Come out, Saydi," an Enforcer male said. "Your time is up. We've got this place on lockdown. There is no escape and no rescue for you. Make it easy on yourself and just surrender."

I didn't know him, but suspected he might be Tedrick, Maeve's unit leader.

"I don't think so," Saydi suddenly said from behind her cover.

The shimmering of an energy shield appeared, and she slowly rose to her feet. My stomach dropped upon recognizing the cylindrical shape of the grenade in her hand. Her clawed thumb hovered over the detonator. If it was the model I believed it to be, it possessed a fifty-meter blast radius that would wipe out the entire greenhouse and a short distance beyond.

"Suicidal? Really?" Tedrick asked, his voice dripping with contempt. "Put it down. You lost."

"I never lose. Even in death, I win against you self-righteous *Grovas*," Saydi said, her voice filled with hatred. "Nobody cages a Nazhral. As humans say, see you in Hell. And my regards to—"

Just like Strasa's thorns had turned the end of the human's last sentence into a scream of agony, my spears interrupted Saydi.

The scream came out like the high-pitched roar of a feral cat as three needle-thin spikes shot up from my roots, piercing through her legs and arms, one through her stomach. From shock and excruciating pain, she dropped the grenade. An Enforcer rushed to take it away, not realizing Saydi was effectively impaled and unable to move.

"Don't kill her!" Tedrick shouted at me. "Stand down, hunter," he added, his voice tense.

Eyes locked with Saydi, who was gasping in pain, I let an evil grin stretch my lips.

"Do not worry, Enforcer. I will not kill her," I said in a menacingly sweet voice. "There's an Obosian looking forward to giving her and that human an exclusive tour of Molvi. But before I hand her over to him, I'd like to give that vermin the payback she deserves."

"Helio," Maeve called out in a worried voice, Strasa still held in her arms.

"Our younglings aren't merchandise for you monsters to use and abuse for profit. I will hunt down and destroy every single one of you who dares steal their innocence, their freedom, and their youth out of greed. No sapling should ever live in the constant terror of being taken away by the likes of you simply for being what they are. This is but a taste of all the pain you have inflicted and that awaits you for the rest of your miserable existence."

Even as I spoke those words, I summoned fungi at the tips of the spears that protruded outside of her skin.

"Helio, stand down!" Tedrick shouted, panic seeping into his voice. “Your role is done. You saved the boy. She’s *our* prisoner now.”

“No! No!” Saydi cried out, her voice constricted by pain.

Her screech when the fungi popped and released their spores was the most delightful music to my ears. Everywhere the spores touched her, the lustrous fur in that area fell off while white sores bubbled over her skin.

“FEZIL!” Tedrick called out before raising his blaster towards me.

“Tedrick, no!” Maeve shouted, raising her palm in an arresting gesture towards her team leader.

But I was done. An Enforcer stormed into the room just as I was releasing Saydi from my spears. He stopped dead in his tracks, his mouth gaping before his head jerked towards me. Only then did I realize he was an Edocit. That took me aback. I hadn’t realized any of us had actually joined the Enforcers.

“A Warrior of Chalda?” he asked, looking at me in shock. “I thought these ancient battle techniques had been lost.”

“They’re not. I am trained in their ways,” I said matter-of-factly, before turning towards my mate and Strasa.

Maeve released the boy so that I could embrace him instead. I hated how he continued to tremble despite his visible efforts to regain control. I intertwined the vines in my hair with his, soothing him at a spiritual level. His arms tightened around my back as his gratitude flowed into me in waves through our connection.

“Fezil, can you help her?” Tedrick asked, annoyance filling his voice.

“Yeah, she’ll be fine. Well, not fine, but she will live. She’ll just *really* hate the next few hours,” Fezil said dismissively.

While some of his companions were freeing the four Edocits still strapped to the table, two others approached Saydi. Fezil gestured for them to back away.

“Nobody touches her until those sores become clear and start drying up. Unless you want to get a taste of what she's having," he said.

"Can't you stop it?" Tedrick asked.

"Even if I could, I wouldn't," Fezil said, his anger echoing the one I felt. "But I can't. So you can't slap me for insubordination. Those spores are unforgiving. As you humans say, karma is a bitch. And this monster just got an extra-large serving of it. As she deserves… For now, I'll go tend to her victims. I could use a Warrior of Chalda's assistance in this," he added, looking at me.

The deference with which he addressed me had my skin darkening from embarrassment. I never knew how to handle compliments and admiration. I was just Helio trying to do the right thing.

"Please, call me Helio. And of course, I will help, though I may need guidance," I said.

"Then I insist you call me Fezil," the male replied, his amber eyes—the same fiery color as his hair—gleaming with approval as he watched me soothe Strasa the way a parent would their sprout or young sapling.

I gently released the boy. He looked at me with bright eyes, full of trust. With two fingers, I wiped the tears still wetting his face, although he no longer cried.

"I'm going to help our brothers now," I said with a reassuring smile. "As soon as we're done here, Maeve and I will take all of you home."

"My parents! Idova!" Strasa said with a crestfallen expression.

"They helped us look for you," I replied. "They will be ecstatic to know you are safe. Your young lady is lovely and very fond of you."

"She's everything. She's my soulmate," Strasa replied with an unshakeable conviction that warmed my heart.

"Then let's send them a message to let them know you're

coming home soon while Helio helps Fezil," Maeve said with a maternal smile, further melting my heart.

Fezil—who turned out to be a Chief Medical Officer with the Enforcers—did quick work of assessing the state of the four males on the table. I could have cried with relief when he informed us that the drip contained nothing that would modify their DNA just yet. It had merely been a first step to cleanse their system and prepare it to better assimilate the treatment Saydi had planned for them.

We walked out of the room to head towards the areas where the other Edocits had all but fused with the bushes lining the walls. To my surprise, we found the Obosian in an intense conversation with Tedrick and a female I immediately recognized as Kaida. Of course, I should have guessed she would be here as a member of my wife's team.

"We'll head there immediately," Tedrick said in a commanding tone. "Kaida, you're in charge here. Secure all the research data and get the captives out of here."

"Acknowledged," Kaida replied.

We watched Tedrick and most of the Enforcers walk out with the Obosian as we approached Kaida. She briefly embraced my mate before smiling warmly at me.

"What's going on?" Maeve asked.

"According to Kronos—the Obosian—there are a couple of hundred slaves in the undercity of the main complex. Some of them work in the clandestine drug lab, while the other slaves are just held there until the next auction," Kaida explained.

"Fuck me," Maeve whispered.

"Saydi was trying to call them for help when she was hiding in that room, but we had already blocked all outgoing signals," Kaida said smugly.

Maeve frowned, as did I.

"Didn't you just send a message to Strasa's parents?" I asked.

"I did," Maeve said, looking questioningly at Kaida.

"We blocked everyone *but* Enforcer frequencies. You are still an Enforcer *and* our primary contact here," Kaida said teasingly. "Even though you're technically on a sabbatical, I'm sure Alec won't mind if you help him scrape all of their files for us while we take care of these poor folks."

"Try and stop me," Maeve said in a similar tone.

She kissed me then went into the labs where one of the two human Enforcers who had stayed behind had gone in, probably the Alec Kaira referred to.

"We're getting the captives aboard our shuttles. Fezil, let us know if you need any help with the others," Kaida added with a commiserating expression.

"We will," Fezil replied with a friendly smile before leading the way to that dreadful room.

A familiar anger rose through me at finding my brothers in such a state. Fezil immediately began to scan them.

"Please, tell me they can unroot," I asked in a tensed voice.

"I'm not sure," Fezil replied, looking dejected. "They've gone extremely deep to escape this nightmare. We can try to bring them out, but I have to make sure that linking with them will not infect us."

I gave him a sharp nod and waited restlessly while he performed a series of tests. After what felt like an eternity, he finally turned to me with a mildly positive expression.

"These roots aren't their *veris*. They are parasites latching on to them," Fezil explained. "We'll have to chop them off. But first, we need to bring their souls back."

"A ring?" I asked.

He nodded.

We went outside to round up the other Edocits but froze in shock the minute we exited the building. A massive black vortex swirled in the sky whence Enforcer vessels were emerging, most heading straight for the Phase I complex, the smaller shuttles settling on the landing pad of the greenhouse.

It took me a moment to notice the giant black and gold dragon flying near the portal.

Cedros.

As far as I knew, he hadn't joined the Enforcers.

"Are you done?" Kaida asked, surprised to see Fezil and I, interrupting my musings.

We quickly explained the situation and, as I had expected, every Edocit agreed to form a circle with us. After I warned of the possibility of another Sayeef spawning, Kaida commandeered one of the troop's vessels heading to the complex so that they would come protect us instead.

We walked a short distance inside the woods and formed a circle holding each other's hands. We simultaneously rooted, the *veris* of our forearms intertwining over our hands, and those of our ankles diving deep into the ground to connect to each other, like the roots of a giant tree. With one voice, we called out to our wandering brothers through the land, through the trees, through every plant and grass blade, enjoining them to return.

On Zailia, such a powerful call would have had every tree shaking their leaves with such strength it would sound like rolling thunder. Here, it sounded like the distant hum of the wings of a thousand alibelles. But it didn't matter. One by one, the lost souls of our brothers timidly responded to our call, their presence strengthening as they slowly flowed back to their roots.

Once they had reintegrated their bodies, Fezil heavily sedated them before severing the parasitic roots shackling them. They would have to spend the next few weeks, maybe even several months in healing pods. They wouldn't even be able to do it in their own homes but in isolated pods to avoid the risk of contaminating their lands.

Still, knowing they wouldn't lose their connection with the land was a major victory. Permanently severing that bond was akin to death for us. I just prayed to the Maker the healing pods could revert most if not all that had been done to them. It was unlikely, but at least they were free and would regain some quality of life.

"Ready to go home?" Maeve asked after we had loaded the last unconscious Edocit in the special medical vessel the Enforcers had brought.

"Definitely," I said.

"Good," she replied. "We're traveling first class."

I raised an eyebrow. "Oh?"

"Mmhmm," she said smugly. "Kaida is going to fly us back to our vessel in the clearing. And then Cedros—your favorite buddy—will portal us all back to Zailia. We'll be home in ten minutes."

My eyes nearly popped out of my head. "He can really cross such great distances?"

"No distance is too far for a Shadow Lord," Maeve replied with a grin. "Let's go."

We flew aboard the shuttle piloted by Kaida, with Cedros flying overhead in his battle form. He measured at least three meters tall that way, his body a dark shadowy color, and his features even more draconic than in his normal, golden form.

"Did he join the Enforcers?" I asked as we approached the location of our ship.

Maeve snorted. "We all wish. He just takes his wife home from work every evening. Him taxiing us around just means he gets her back sooner."

I chuckled and shook my head. "I approve of the kind of friends you hang out with."

She burst out laughing and kissed me as the shuttle began its descent. Moments later, we boarded our vessel with Strasa in tow. As soon as we were airborne, Cedros opened another massive portal. We flew in, and my jaw dropped when we found ourselves over Strasa's hamlet. Kaida came out of the portal behind us and immediately veered towards the city, shadowed by Cedros.

The villagers came running out of their dwellings, every single person gaping at the spectacle of this giant vortex in the sky from whence two ships and a dragon had emerged. People would talk about it for years to come. As we began our descent, I recognized Idova and her parents standing next to Strasa's mother and father.

We had barely touched down than Strasa was opening the shuttle's door and storming out.

"Strasa!!" his mother shouted.

The boy sprinted towards his family, who also came running towards him. Like a tidal wave, the buds in the hair vines of every villager bloomed. My throat tightened when Niphne collided so violently with her son, she nearly knocked him off his feet. He managed to remain upright, and they held onto each other as if they were drowning. His father joined them, embracing them both while they laughed and cried.

Maeve reached for my hand. I took hers before giving her a sideways glance. Eyes brimming with tears of joy, a quivering smile on her lips, my mate was staring at the reunited family. My heart melted, and I drew her against me.

"We brought our boy home. Thank you for everything. I couldn't have done it without you," I said, my voice thick with emotion.

She turned to look at me, her gaze filled with affection. "We did it together. I couldn't have done it without you either."

I lowered my head, and our lips met in the most tender kiss. The sudden whistling of the tree leaves interrupted us. I looked up to see Idova and Strasa walking towards each other. Her beautiful young face was drenched in tears. He extended a hand towards her. She took it and caressed his hair with the other. Although we were too far to hear what he said to her, I suspected he was reassuring her that his down leaves would grow back.

Idova slipped a hand behind Strasa's nape and lowered his face towards hers. I thought they were going to kiss, but they merely pressed their foreheads against each other. Their hair vines intertwined, as did the *veris* on their forearms, binding their hands together.

"They truly are soulmates, aren't they?" Maeve whispered.

"They are," I confirmed, feeling blessed to witness such pure and innocent love. "As are we," I added, forcing my gaze away from the lovely tableau to look at my mate.

"As are we," she echoed before we kissed again.

CHAPTER 18
MAEVE

In the days following our return, we did everything but resume our honeymoon. My husband and I became something of an overnight sensation. The visits of gratitude from Strasa's parents and his future in-laws, we'd expected. Random parents introducing us to their saplings in the hopes we'd form a bond that would motivate us to search for them like we had searched for Strasa took me aback. But people wanting to see and touch the friends of a dimension-traveling dragon had left me speechless.

Although I was technically on a sabbatical, Tedrick had made me write a complete report of the events and of the research we'd performed to track Saydi down. By opening a portal to bring in the Enforcers right at the start of the raid, we'd locked them out of their own systems before they could delete anything. We hadn't found any obvious names we could pin down as accomplices. However, the treasure trove of recovered data provided countless easy trails to follow to some mega big wigs.

Many big heads were falling, and the UPO wanted to make sure nobody would get off on technicalities. Their lawyers were trying hard to argue that it had been an illegal raid. But considering we freed over four hundred slaves of various species, confiscated billions of credits worth of illegal drugs and substances, and foiled a plot to introduce a devastatingly addictive new drug, many allied planets were more than happy to turn a blind eye to us skirting the laws.

However, we had not.

Beyond the fact that Kronos had given us legal grounds for the raid by invoking Clause 286, this had not been an Enforcer raid. It had been a bounty hunter's mission. Bounty hunters were held to far fewer rules than law enforcement. The Enforcers and the UPO repeated it to anyone who would listen. While it had indeed been Helio's mission, they made a massive showing of rewarding him for it.

There had been a ridiculous amount of bounties pending over Saydi's head and hefty rewards for her capture. Tips to drug busts of the magnitude we performed on Shimli were also generously rewarded. As I was still officially an Enforcer, I didn't qualify for any recognition as they deemed it a part of my job. Therefore, Helio received the totality of the credit, including the monetary ones. The sums awarded to him verged on the obscene. He could retire today and still live in luxury for the rest of his days.

Or rather, I should say that *we* could retire for life.

As soon as he received the money, Helio evenly split it, sending half to my personal account. I hadn't asked or expected him to do so. Wealth had never been important to me. But it said a lot about him that he insisted I accept half and that he made sure to remind everyone that he'd only succeeded because I had helped. I loved his humility, his generosity, his kindness, and selflessness.

Even before we'd known we'd get such a mind-blowing reward, we had declined any financial compensation from Strasa's parents. But this money turned out to be a game-changer for us. Not only did it allow us to acquire the finest equipment available in the galaxy, it also gave us the power to focus on emotional missions instead of corporate ones to pay the bills.

A part of me suspected the UPO's excessive generosity had been for that very purpose. I no longer doubted Tedrick was using our trial period as a test.

In the three months since my marriage to Helio, we'd had plenty of interactions with the Enforcers. There hadn't been another huge bust where we'd worked side-by-side in a raid, but we'd been able to tip them about shady stuff we encountered and that warranted further investigation.

But today, I had better things to do than to worry about work. The alibelles would start emerging from their chrysalises any minute now. Helio had hyped that event so much that he had gotten me super excited about it. In turn, I'd gotten Kaida just as curious.

Our families had remained very close, despite the great distance. Thanks to Cedros, we took turns visiting each other every other weekend. Once they would port here, the next one, we'd go visit them on Dramnach.

The initial awkwardness between Cedros and Helio belonged to ancient history. They were quite the sight for sore eyes, walking side-by-side in the streets of Veloya, while we awaited the chrysalises hatching. They were having an animated conversation while keeping a close eye on Cedros's and Kaida's little hellions. Their firstborn twins weren't so bad, but their daughter was mischief personified. With the dense crowd swarming Zailia's capital city to witness the new alibelles' first flight, it would be too easy getting separated.

Kaida and I followed a short distance behind our husbands, my arm hooked around hers. Unlike on Dramnach, she didn't need to stay within range of Cedros in order to allow him to withstand being surrounded by other people. Edocits didn't have a phase shifting ability to travel through dimensions like the Derakeens did. Therefore, their presence didn't cause the physical discomfort Cedros felt around his own people, and which only Kaida's presence could dampen.

It always warmed my heart to see him take great pleasure in freely mingling with others and opening himself up more. He was like the big brother I never had.

"So… When are you planning on bonding with that Dryad of yours? My brats need a few cousins to play with," Kaida said teasingly.

I snorted. "Fire and wood don't sound like a good mix. Your kids will light my future ones like a bonfire!"

Kaida burst out laughing. "Nah. They rarely use true fire. They mostly spit shadow flames, which don't burn the same way."

"And that's supposed to reassure me?" I asked, giving her the side eye.

"They've been at your house many times already, and still haven't burned it down," Kaida snickered. "Anyway, you're deflecting. When are you making things official?"

I made a face at her. "You're worse than my mother. By PMA standards, Helio and I still have two and a half months to decide—not that their rules actually apply to us. And I seem to recall you waited until the fifth month to decide."

Kaida waved a dismissive hand. "Our situations were completely different. I had more or less been coerced into that union. You *asked* Kayog to find you a hot husband. Are you still unsure?" she asked, this time with genuine curiosity.

I shook my head and replied without hesitation. "No, I *know* he's the one. I'm pretty damn crazy about him. Sure, we're still getting to know each other and have our occasional disagreements and differences of opinion, but he's definitely the one."

"So why aren't you bonding with him? I understand it will make you two even closer on top of giving you some very useful enhancements."

I bit my bottom lip while trying to figure out how to word

my feelings. "Well first, he hasn't offered or asked for us to bond. It's just something we have kind of hanging over our heads."

"Why don't *you* ask *him*? Maybe he's waiting for *you* to give *him* a sign that you're open to the idea or ready for it," Kaida challenged. "The way he's looking at you, that male is head over heels in love."

"That's what I think, too. But what if he's not there yet?" I asked. "What if he says he's not ready?"

"Then he'll just say as much! One thing I learned since marrying a Derakeen is that we waste way too much energy speculating on what someone else thinks and hoping they will guess what we want," Kaida said with conviction. "Just speak your mind. Open communication is a freaking blessing. Then you always know what time it is."

I scrunched my face. "I know. But rejection blows."

"I'm not a Temern, but I'd bet my left boob Helio will be on cloud nine and more than eager to accept," Kaida replied with an encouraging smile.

I heaved a sigh. "You're right. Deep down, I'm pretty sure he will happily say yes. I want to bond with him, but if I'm honest, it scares me a bit," I confessed with a sheepish expression.

Kaida's eyes widened in surprise. "Really? Why?"

My face heated with embarrassment. "It's the mutations and the weird baby gestation," I said, feeling ashamed for even thinking it. "I've read about it. I won't be the first woman to bond with an Edocit. But it freaks me out to know I won't be human anymore, if that makes sense?"

To my relief, instead of showing the disappointment I dreaded, Kaida smiled, her face melting into an air of pure sympathy.

"There's nothing to be ashamed about. It's a huge change. You *should* have concerns about it. You'd be completely irresponsible otherwise. *I* was afraid of the changes bonding with

Cedros would do to me. But it's the best thing that ever happened to me."

Kaida stopped walking to stand directly in front of me. Oblivious to the crowd moving ever closer to the edges of the city, she took both my hands in hers.

"Nothing will ever stop you from being human. Yeah, you'll be enhanced. You'll have vines shooting out of your forearms in a Dryad version of Spiderman," Kaida said, making me snort. "And your fetus will waltz out of your womb on two legs to finish maturing inside a tree. Okay, that's weird for us humans, but it's also a major blessing. Take it from a woman who had to push out three massive babies with wings and horns. I'm surprised I can still walk. The back pains, the hot flashes, the freaky cravings, getting your bladder kicked around the clock, especially when you finally found a comfortable enough position to fall asleep? You'll be spared all of that."

"Right, but that's part of the experience of maternity," I argued weakly.

Kaida waved a disdainful hand. "True, but maternity is only the tiniest part of motherhood. Being a mother is about raising and nurturing your child. Being there for the joyous moments, to wipe the tears, kiss the booboos, clean the poopy bums, feed the hungry mouths, manage the tantrums, and everything else that comes with it. How long you carried a child, or whether you or someone else pushed them out doesn't make you a mother. It's the unconditional love you give them while raising them into the future adults they will be that matters."

My heart melted with love for my friend. "If you're trying to make me feel stupid over my irrational fears, you're doing a bang-up job," I said, giving her a baleful glare.

Kaida beamed at me with a shit-eating grin. "Not trying to make you feel stupid, but definitely trying to get you knocked up! However, I'm happy to hear that my work here is done! Now bond with your man and get a bun in your oven. My youngest will want someone his age to play with."

I gaped at her with a questioning look.

She smiled, almost looking shy this time, as she released one of my hands to pat her flat stomach. "Yep, fourth kid, another boy, on the way."

"Oh, my God! Congrats! Sheesh, you guys just keep popping them out!" I exclaimed with a laugh before hugging her.

"If Cedros had his way, we'd have a full soccer team," Kaida said with a long-suffering sigh.

I released her, still laughing, then opened my mouth to reply. But the general gasps of the crowd interrupted me. All around the city, the luminous chrysalises dangling in the trees started cracking open as the first alibelles emerged, immediately taking flight. I had wrongly assumed they would need to let their wings dry a bit at first.

They glowed like tiny flying flames in the fading light of the early night sky. Children squealed in delight, brandishing long sticks with spiced honey puffs at their tips. The hungry alibelles rushed towards the treats, up to four of them eating at the same puff simultaneously. It made the sticks look like magic wands casting a light spell.

Mesmerized, I watched the buds in every Edocits' hair flower. To my shock, many of the alibelles went from eating the puffs to feeding on the nectar in the Edocits' hair. At least two dozen of them hovered in front of Helio's white flowers. Kaida and I approached him with the same awed expression plastered all over Cedros's face.

"They are bonding with me," Helio said happily. "In the next few days, they will join our land." He drew me into his arms, the warm glow of the little dragon fairies feeding from the flowers in his hair feeling like a gentle caress on my face. "And one day, soon I hope, they will bond with you as well."

My heart leapt in my chest. The way he was looking at me

left little interpretation as to his meaning. Kaida was right. I needed to tell him I was ready instead of both of us dancing around the issue, not knowing where the other stood.

"Sooner than later, I hope," I whispered back.

Shock settled over his features, followed by uncertainty. His eyes flicked between mine, questioning. I smiled to confirm he hadn't misunderstood me. The way his face melted into an air of pure adoration had a swarm of butterflies take flight in my stomach. Goosebumps erupted all over my skin as he leaned down to kiss me.

Before our lips could touch, the voice of Kaida's daughter rose in a shrill scream in the distance.

"Theka!" Kaida shouted, worry etched on her face.

Cedros immediately took flight while Kaida, Helio, and I started running in the scream's direction. Guilt gnawed at me. A single moment of distraction had potentially exposed the children to danger. But what danger? This city was safe! My mind immediately imagined some other freak like Saydi attempting to kidnap a Derakeen child. With their world constantly shifting between dimensions, no one could voluntarily fly to Dramnach. Meeting a Derakeen in the flesh was virtually impossible, which would make their child a valuable prize.

Up ahead, her older brothers—the twins, Kairzan and Kinshu—were flying in place and gesturing at their sister to come up. That alleviated part of my panic. As the crowd parted before us, I finally spotted the little girl. Like her father and brothers, she was covered in golden scales, with a long tail and dark dragon wings. Theka only possessed four golden horns for now, but if she ever became a Shadow Lady like her sire was a Shadow Lord, she would gain a pair of shadow horns and a shadow crest that would allow her to travel the galaxy in seconds.

To my utter confusion, she was doing angry shooing gestures at the vegetation.

"Theka! Come back here!" Cedros commanded his daughter in a stern voice.

She turned her four-year-old face towards her father with a mulish expression. "They're trying to hurt the labibells!" Theka exclaimed with her outraged baby voice while pointing an angry finger at the vegetation in the forest surrounding the city.

Relieved to find her unscathed, I couldn't decide if I was more baffled by her strange accusation or amused by the way she'd slaughtered the word alibelle. Then I nearly jumped out of my skin when a thick appendage shot out of the center of a gigantic plant, vaguely reminiscent of a lotus flower. It darted towards Theka's hand, appeared to stick to her skin, then yanked her towards the plant.

Theka shrieked while stumbling forward. Her parents called out her name, Cedros diving to her rescue. An even shriller shriek drowned their voices when Theka opened her mouth and spit a huge flow of purple flames at the plant. Instead of withering from the heat, the petals of the plant swelled up in what I presumed to be blisters. Had I not seen it before, I would have thought it was some giant cauliflower.

My stomach dropped, and my eyes nearly popped out of my head when the handful of other similar plants nearby of varying sizes suddenly got up onto two almost bird-like feet and hightailed it away from the little girl. Freaked out, Theka roasted a couple more of the fleeing plants before her father wrapped an arm around her waist and flew backward with her.

Arzigs! Freaking arzigs were crawling in the forest surrounding the city!

"Relax, it's okay. She's fine," Helio said in a reassuring tone to both Kaida and me.

I nearly panicked when the Edocit kids rushed towards the edge of the forest, their parents smiling as they tagged along.

"What the fuck are they doing?!" I exclaimed. "The children—?!"

"Will be fine," Helio interrupted in a soothing voice while Cedros landed next to us, his daughter still tucked in his arms, and the twins landed beside their father. "Arzigs often lurk around the city during hatching season to get an easy meal out of the alibelles. That specific arzig got greedy. Theka is much too big for those plants to eat. The bigger ones would struggle to swallow a newborn, so forget a child her size. None of the children here are in danger. They could easily free themselves with a few slaps or kicks at the arzigs."

"That still feels overly dangerous to me," I mumbled.

Helio smiled. "It's not. But on top of saving the alibelles, this little lady just provided everyone with a delicious treat."

"What?" Kaida exclaimed, her face reflecting the same disbelief I felt.

To my dismay, the children were tearing big chunks of what I'd assumed to be welts on the arzig. From where I stood, they appeared to have a spongy cake texture. The kids then walked back to their parents, while happily chewing on their 'treat' with blissful moans. A handful of adults picked up the 'roasted' plants, bringing them inside the square for all to delight in.

"See!" Theka exclaimed. "I saved the balibells! The big plants were trying to catch them like this!" she continued, flicking her reptilian tongue this way and that.

This time, I couldn't help laughing, both at the adorably ridiculous face she was making and at the way she continued to slaughter the word alibelle.

"You're not supposed to use your shadow flames in public, and especially not around non-Derakeens," Cedros said sternly. "You could have hurt someone. They do not have scales like us to protect them."

The mulish expression came back with a vengeance on the little girl's face. "I had to save the baby dragons."

"They're not dragons," Cedros argued.

"Yes, they are! They're dragon fairies! I saved them. I'm a

protector, too. Not just you. And I didn't hurt anyone. Just the bad plants. See? All the Dodocit people are happy! They're eating them! Uncle Alio said I made treats for everyone. I want some, too!"

Halfway through her self-righteous speech, I had to cover my mouth with my hand to hide my burning urge to laugh. Theka's parents looked at her like she was a hopeless case, and Helio was biting the inside of his cheeks not to stick his foot in his mouth.

"Me, too!" Kairzan exclaimed before running towards one of the roasted plants, closely followed by his twin.

Seeing her older brothers take off, Theka struggled to wiggle free of her father's hold. He released her, looking both amused and discouraged.

I gave Kaida a sideways glance. "So… What were you saying again about shadow flames not burning plants?"

She gave me a playfully baleful glare and elbowed me. I laughed.

CHAPTER 19
MAEVE

We returned home a couple of hours later, the kids exhausted but happy. Saying goodbye to Kaida was always bittersweet. I missed hanging out with her at work every day. With her new pregnancy, she'd soon be given a desk job as they couldn't put her in the line of fire in her condition. Once she got on maternity leave, I'd be able to kidnap her over here more often.

We parted with a final hug, my heart melting as I watched Helio kiss the scaly forehead of Theka sleeping in her father's arms, while the twins nodded and yawned while leaning against his legs. Their little draconic faces were beyond adorable. Helio came to stand next to me, his arm slipping around my waist as Cedros opened a portal back to his homeworld. We waved them goodbye as they walked through the giant vortex, which collapsed with a suction sound behind them.

I turned to face Helio, who was looking at me with a world of tenderness. I melted against him, my hands clasping behind his neck. He closed his arms around me, drawing me against his firm body.

"Thank you for a magical evening," I whispered, my fingers

fiddling with the vines in his hair. "It was every bit as enchanting as you promised."

He beamed at me. "I'm glad you enjoyed the hatching. It *is* a magical moment. But it's the younglings who make it even more special."

"Especially children named Theka who shadow roast creepy walking plants," I said with a shudder.

I'd wussed out of tasting the plant. Kaida had been ballsier than me. Apparently, it tasted like gingerbread popcorn. For now, I'd take her word for it.

Helio chuckled, his arms tightening around me while his face took on a wistful expression. "I want a couple just like her to make my leaves wither and my vines dry up from the stress of what fresh trouble she'll get herself into."

I snorted. "I didn't realize you were a masochist."

"Sometimes," he said in a purring voice, his gaze smoldering.

"Well, you married me. That definitely makes you a sucker for punishment," I replied teasingly.

Instead of laughing and replying with a clever quip, Helio took on a serious expression. He caressed my cheek, his palm continuing its journey upward to brush a rebellious lock of hair out of my face.

"If being your husband is a punishment, then I pray the Maker never forgives my trespasses, so that this may be everlasting. I've fallen quite madly in love with you, Maeve," he said, almost in a whisper.

My stomach did a couple of backflips, and a wave of emotions constricted my throat. I swallowed hard, my pulse picking up as I pressed myself more closely against him.

"I'm quite happy to hear that," I replied in the same hushed voice. "As I've kind of also fallen madly in love with you, I figured I'd keep you for good."

Right on cue, the white flowers in his hair blossomed. I smiled and brushed a finger against one of the petals.

"It also doesn't hurt that you really smell good when you flower like that," I added teasingly, although my voice was thick with emotion.

"For you. Only for you, my mate. Will you bond with me?"

"I thought you'd never ask," I said with a nervous laugh. "Yes, Helio. I want to bond with you, with your land, and with your world. I want us to be one forever."

"My love," Helio said, his eyes filled with adoration and a sliver of seriousness. "You understand that there will be no going back, right? The bond cannot be undone."

I smiled. "I know. The changes I will undergo scare me a bit, but I want this. I want *us.* Others have done it before, and it was fine. Kayog wouldn't have paired us if we weren't meant to be. I trust you and the land to take good care of me."

"That, I promise we will," he replied with fervor before reclaiming my lips.

After a few kisses and caresses, Helio plucked a leaf from the vines in his hair and brought it to my lips. I didn't hesitate and accepted his gift. I immediately began to chew, and he picked me up in his arms, carrying me like a bride inside the house.

He didn't take me to our bedroom, but to the healing room. That had my stomach fluttering with a mix of fear and anticipation. Once we bonded, I would fall into some kind of coma induced by the bonding fluids he would inject into me with his fangs. While my body assimilated it and transformed, the land would also bind me through the vines in the healing room.

I didn't want to think about that for now. All that mattered were the lips of my husband still kissing me and the warmth of his muscular body surrounding me. Helio put me down in the center of the room covered in short grass. We undressed each other with slow, tender caresses, interspersed with deep and languorous kisses.

As much as I loved the unbridled passion that inevitably unleashed itself whenever we were intimate, these affectionate preliminaries had really grown on me. I tended to go straight for gold, but Helio had taught me the virtues of foreplay.

It wasn't even for me, but for him. My husband was the most generous lover, always giving me multiple orgasms before he gave in to his own release. So foreplay for me was all about pleasuring him. His responses to my touch made me feel like a freaking sex goddess. The way he looked when I caressed him, sounded when I went down on him, and shivered under my touch turned me on beyond words.

As soon as he removed his shirt, my lips latched onto his nipple. I loved his spicy sweet taste, the strange texture of his skin, almost like polished wood, and yet supple and pliant. As was my wont, I nipped at his yevins—the embossed swirling tattoos on his chest. Yeah, I was a biter. At first, I feared it might hurt him as the marks—which still resembled scarification tattoos to me—were a little harder than the rest of his skin. But Helio's shivers and needy moans had more than reassured me on that front over the past three months. Even now, biting on the spiraling yevins on his chest had him taking a shuddering breath, followed by a rumbling sigh.

I licked a trail down his stomach, my hands lowering his pants at the same time. To my delight, Helio never denied me the pleasure of exploring his body as I saw fit or taking the lead for a while. A lot of males needed to be fully in charge in the bedroom. While plenty of females enjoyed that, I liked being in control from time to time without having to beg or fight for it.

Helio was undoubtedly dominant, but not a control freak. That he always made me feel equal in all things played a huge role in me falling so quickly and so hard for him.

I licked and teased his navel on my way down, making him chuckle. Edocits had relatively small navels as their gestation in their mother's womb was so brief, their *veris* and the vines in their hair taking over the role of umbilical cord once they settled inside their Myma's knot. Despite its small size, the cute little button that served as Helio's navel was very sensitive. I could have him in stitches just by flicking a finger over it a few times.

But there would be other times to tickle my husband.

For now, my prize called to me. Helio stepped out of his pants at the same time I kneeled before him. It pleased me tremendously that he no longer squirmed each time I looked at his cock. My mate had proven so irrationally self-conscious when we first met. It still boggled my mind that he could have even imagined I'd find him lacking or get turned off by any parts of him.

Sure, Edocits had some significant anatomical differences with humans, and their peens would have many off-worlders raise their eyebrows. But their species as a whole was freaking gorgeous. And my husband certainly ranked high up there… at least as far as I was concerned. Helio was perfection. I was so used to women struggling with their body image that I never really expected it from a fit and sexy male.

However, I'd come to realize his insecurities had not actually been a lack of self-confidence but worry that our differences might turn me off. Not everyone responded well to things that strayed too far from what they deemed the norm.

I smiled internally as I began stroking his length, the ridges draping the upper half of his shaft right below the head tickling my palm. And it was that head—his bulb—that had been his primary source of worry. If I were honest, I'd have to admit that the thought of the tip of a penis literally opening like a flower so that a long stamen could extrude and wiggle its way through my cervix and inside my uterus to drop his swimmers in, had initially messed with my head. I wouldn't have run for the hills, but in hindsight, I was grateful he'd gradually revealed himself to me.

I licked his bulb a few times, the spicy flavor of mulled wine exploding on my taste buds. Slightly paler than the golden-brown color of his shaft, his bulb looked a bit like a closed tulip. I continued teasing the seams for a few moments longer while continuing to stroke his cock. When I finally took the head inside my mouth, Helio hissed in that sexy way that systematically resonated between my thighs.

My tongue tingled, as did my skin. Part of it was attributable to his down leaf I'd eaten, which was making my nerve endings extra sensitive. Another came from the natural lubricant mostly contained inside his bulb, but that seeped around the seam. And the last part came from his pheromones. Where active humans' sweat glands had a way of sending people running for the hills, the Edocits' version had the exact opposite effect. They secreted the most enticing aroma, which also acted like an aphrodisiac. And right now, my husband was putting his to good use.

Soon, he'd have me so hot and bothered, I'd push him on the ground, impale myself on his cock, and ride him until it fell off. But I wanted to make him fall apart for me at least once before I lost control.

I accelerated the movement of my hand on his shaft, squeezing the ridges below his bulb on each upward motion. Bobbing faster before him, I grazed my teeth over his head, reveling in the throaty moans that were now pouring out of him. Helio's hand fisted in my hair, and he began rocking back and forth with shallow thrusts. This clear sign of him nearing the edge emboldened me.

Slipping my other hand between his thighs, I squeezed and fondled his testicles, my tongue working his bulb with a swirl before I took him again deep in my throat. At last, I felt the seams begin to part like a blooming flower, revealing my prize. The taste of clove and cinnamon was even stronger now, making my nipples painfully harder with need. Helio didn't extrude his stamen—he would instantly climax if I touched it. With the tip of my tongue, I reached for its tiny anther—the head of his stamen—glistening with lubricant.

Helio cried out, his fist tightening in my hair, giving it a serious sting that once more resonated in my nether region. The dull throbbing in my core went into overdrive, and I released his testicles to rub my clit. I flicked my tongue back and forth over the sensitive bud inside his open bulb, and Helio grunted, his body seizing with intermittent spasms.

I expected him to yank me off him any minute. My husband had always refused to release his seed anywhere other than between my thighs. But not this time. The urgent way in which he growled my name was the only warning I got. On instinct, I took him deep in my mouth half a second before he shouted his release.

The force with which his seed shot out into my mouth nearly choked me, but I wasn't so easily defeated. I continued to bob in front of him, swallowing every drop. Holding my hair with both hands, Helio was rocking in and out of my mouth, almost pained moans steadily flowing out of him. Judging by the way his abdominal muscles constricted and his biceps bulged, my husband was summoning every ounce of his willpower not to go wild and fuck my face into oblivion.

By the time he pulled out, the combined effects of his leaf, lubricant, pheromones, and now his seed had me on the verge of combusting. My skin was on fire, my clit so swollen and achy, you'd think my racing heartbeat was pulsating through it. My inner walls contracting so impatiently to be filled had me trying to push Helio onto his back so that I could ride him as if my life depended on it. But my man had plans of his own.

He pulled me to my feet and captured my mouth in a searing kiss. A desperate moan escaped me when my overly sensitive nipples pressed against his chest. Without interrupting the kiss, his tongue plundering my mouth, Helio picked me up. Chest against chest, I wrapped my arms around his neck and my legs around his waist. Feeling his shaft between us, already hardening again, had me whimpering. Starved for greater friction, I rubbed my pelvis against his.

With both hands resting on my bum, Helio pressed his cock against me. I bit his neck to silence the painful cry of unsated need that was rising in my throat. In response, he emitted a growling shout, which further fanned the fire raging inside me. I was so hot and bothered that I hadn't even noticed my mate had carried me closer to the wall.

More than any other areas in our dwelling, that section clearly showed the house had been shaped from a living tree. The original roots and vestiges of a trunk were still visible. Helio lay me down between the roots covered in spongy moss. Spreading my legs wide, I opened my arms, beckoning him. He settled over me and gave me a passionate kiss while dry humping me. Each motion of his cock rubbing against my clit was sending electric sparks throughout my body. With a strangled cry, I sank my nails into the plump flesh of his butt and lifted my pelvis to meet his, making my message ultra clear.

To my dismay, my mate didn't give me what I desperately needed. Instead, he kissed a path down my body.

"No!" I exclaimed, both distressed and incredulous.

I lifted my hand to pull him back up to me, but a series of vines from the wall and the ground bound my wrists and ankles. My attempts to free myself only resulted in more vines joining the fray, effectively shackling me. As much as I enjoyed a bit of bondage from time to time, if Helio didn't fuck me into next week right the hell now, I would combust and turn into ashes.

Throwing all pride to the wind, I pleaded and begged for him to take me. Helio silenced me with a kiss.

"Soon, my love, I promise. You're not ready yet," he whispered, his voice almost apologetic.

What the fuck did that mean "not ready yet"? I was so damn wet, I'd soon need a dam to avoid flooding the entire room!

However, my barely intelligible protests died in a stunned cry when Helio suddenly sank his fangs into my neck.

The purest form of liquid ecstasy flowed through me. A blinding light exploded before my eyes as a brutal orgasm swept me away. It was the oddest sensation. Although I'd gotten the release I ached for, my body felt cheated out of what it truly needed. As I continued to fly on the wings of bliss, Helio's hands and mouth were all over me, kissing, biting, caressing, sucking…

I never got a chance to fully get back down from my high. The minute Helio's lips finally settled on my engorged little nub, I went off again like a rocket. His fingers slipping inside me while he continued sucking on my clit had me screaming at the top of my lungs, my head rolling from side to side from pleasure almost too much to bear.

By the time my husband settled on top of me, I'd already had more orgasms than I could count. But him finally pushing himself inside of me gave me at long last what I'd truly been craving. Only then did I realize that the tips of the vines shackling me had actually sunk under my skin.

It hadn't hurt then, nor did it now. But I couldn't focus on it. My universe had narrowed down to Helio's cock pounding me, his bulb opening and closing inside me, sending lightning bolts through each of my nerve endings every time it grazed my sweet spot, the scorching feel of his skin against mine, and his weight pinning me to the land that was claiming me.

I drowned in an endless sea of pleasure as my husband wrested one orgasm after the other from me. In between, he would bite me again, injecting me with more of his bonding fluids. On a few occasions, I vaguely felt his stamen sinking deep inside me as he roared his release. And yet, he didn't stop.

By the time he relented, I was wrecked, utterly destroyed, my mind fractured by this excess of bliss.

My entire body tingled, and I felt light, as if my soul was

about to take flight, leaving my corporeal vessel behind. My eyes grew heavy as I struggled to stare at Helio's face. Still lying on top of me, he was looking at me with infinite adoration.

"I love you, Maeve. We belong to each other forever now. Sleep my beauty. When next you wake, we will be one."

I wanted to respond, to tell him that I loved him, too. But I felt both too heavy and too light. As he continued to whisper words of devotion, I stared at his beautiful face smiling at me until I finally lost the battle.

CHAPTER 20

HELIO

Kneeling on the grass in the healing room, I gazed lovingly at my mate while running a damp cloth over her naked body. My com going off startled me. I glanced at it only to roll my eyes in annoyance. Tedrick was once more asking to speak with Maeve, even though I'd told him repeatedly that she would be unavailable for a few days. Dismissing him, I returned my focus to my woman.

Four days had gone by since we'd bonded. It would take at least two or three more days before the greater part of her mutation was completed. At which point, she would finally emerge from this semi-comatose state.

Even halfway through the process, my Maeve looked stunning. She had been breathtaking in her original human appearance, but I couldn't deny loving the Edocit traits now visible on her. *My* Edocit traits…

Possessive pride filled my heart as I traced the yevins on her chest. I could see why she had initially believed them to be scarification tattoos when she'd seen mine. The swirling patterns marked her as now belonging to my family line, with new motifs showing her unique identity. A few of them had also appeared on her forehead.

However, as much as I loved her yevins, it was the delicate *veris* swelling around her wrists and ankles, as well as the couple of vines in her hair that had my heart filling to bursting. The vines from the house no longer had to dig into her skin to establish a connection. They now intertwined with the thin tendrils of her *veris* which timidly protruded from under her skin.

Although still tenuous, Maeve's bond with the land and me had already grown much stronger than I imagined it would, or even could. The house had changed and would continue to do so as more of her DNA became a part of it. Even the grass, the plants, and trees—both in the healing room and in my exterior garden—no longer felt the same. They felt richer, fuller, their colors more vivid, and their perfume more irresistible. They felt like *us*.

A swarm of alibelles flew inside the room through an open window, each finding a spot to settle on top of my mate. Although they didn't possess any *veris* to establish a direct connection, they were still bonding with my Maeve through their tail light, which they trailed over her as if attempting to draw light patterns on her skin.

My breath caught in my throat when a tiny bud in her hair vine bloomed. Had she felt the loving caresses of the alibelles? Unable to resist, I placed a hand over hers and extruded my *veris* to connect with hers. The vines from the house receded a bit to give me some space. It wasn't much, but they had precedence over me in this instance. In a few weeks, Maeve's *veris* would grow long and strong enough that this would no longer be an issue.

Still, it was enough for me to feel some of her emotions flowing through me. Maker! My mate was as beautiful inside as she was on the outside. Pure joy, wonder, and love crashed through me, wave after wave. I had no idea what was causing such powerful emotions in my woman. Was it her connection with the land? Dreams? A mix of various other things?

Without conscious communication, I couldn't see what she was thinking. And even then, Maeve would need to *choose* to share her thoughts with me. I couldn't simply plunder them without her consent. However, I could get a sense of how she felt, and I shamelessly basked in the wondrous emotions swirling inside her.

It dampened some of the terrible longing that gnawed at me since she'd closed her eyes after our bonding. I missed her. For someone who'd been a happy loner my entire life, you'd think I'd handle a few days by myself better. I missed her laughter, her shameless teasing, the way she'd go from snuggling with me to then bossing me around.

Above all, I just missed her holding me like I was the greatest treasure she'd ever beheld, like she feared I was an illusion that might vanish otherwise.

I love her so much...

I jerked my head up to look at the healing room's door. There wasn't anyone behind it, but the mood of the house had shifted. Knowing that I'd be neglecting myself while watching over my mate, my parents had dropped by a couple of times to bring me food. But the house rejoiced when they came over. It didn't brace like it was now. A stranger was approaching.

I passed a swift command to the house before disconnecting my *veris* from Maeve's. More vines crawled towards my mate, covering her modesty as I headed to the entrance. As I usually flew with the skiff parked in the garden, or rode Laros through the back gate, I rarely used the front door of my house. Since I didn't live in a hamlet like Strasa and Idova, there were no nearby neighbors likely to just drop by. Whoever it was, they were lost or wanting something.

As I opened the door, my jaw dropped at the sight of Tedrick standing by himself on my porch. He didn't even have a speeder or personal shuttle.

"Greetings, Helio. May I come in?" he asked, in a polite, if not forcefully jovial way.

I narrowed my eyes at him, concerned that the land continued to be tense. "What are you doing here?" I asked, ignoring his request.

"Coming to check in on Maeve, of course," he replied, as if that was self-evident.

My face hardened, and my voice took on an icy edge. "I've told you repeatedly that she's unavailable."

He also dropped any semblance of friendly demeanor, the tough Enforcer Senior Officer coming to the fore.

"You have," he conceded in a harsh tone. "For the past four days, at that. Maeve always returns her messages within minutes. At worst, within a couple of hours. How can she be 'unavailable' for four days straight? What's going on? Where is she?"

"There's nothing 'going on' the way you seem to imply," I retorted, trying to rein in my annoyance. "Maeve isn't available. That's all you need to know. She'll get back to you in a few days."

"I'm not going anywhere without seeing her," Tedrick hissed, taking a menacing step forward.

Although stunned by this unexpected display of aggression, I stood my ground. Anyway, he was no threat to me. White spheres immediately swelled on the branches of the bushes lining the pathway to the front porch. Tedrick blanched, recognizing the fungi I had used to punish Saydi during the raid. An almost evil smirk stretched my lips as I gave him a taunting look, daring him to make another threat.

I had not ordered the plants to do this. They were merely protecting me from a perceived threat.

"A team within the Enforcers is like a family," Tedrick suddenly said, his tone softening, almost taking a pleading edge. "In every mission, our survival depends on being able to rely on the fact that we have each other's back. As the team leader, it is my duty to make sure my crew is fine, wherever they are. Won't you at least reassure me that she's okay?"

"I've already told you she was fine, just unavailable," I replied, forcing myself to take on a less belligerent tone.

"Why so secretive?" he asked, looking utterly baffled. "Had our roles been reversed, and you worried about someone important to you, would this kind of answer be enough?"

I flinched. The eerie similarity to my question to Maeve when she wouldn't tell me what she'd discovered while tracking Saydi struck a nerve. In truth, I wasn't trying to be secretive. However, my mate was in a vulnerable state. The bonding process was sacred for us. And his constant meddling almost felt like a violation, if not a threat.

"She's in the process of bonding, is that it?" he asked in a soft voice.

My spine immediately stiffened, and I gave him a warning look, my protective instincts surging forward with a vengeance.

He raised his palms in an appeasing gesture. "I'm not here to interfere with the process. I knew it was only a matter of time. Maeve is crazy about you. I just want to see her."

"Yes, she's bonding with the land," I hissed. "You have your answer. There's no need for you to see anything. Now, please leave," I added, gesturing in the distance behind him.

To my utter annoyance, he stood his ground, taking on this reasonable expression parents took with a brat throwing a tantrum. I wanted to punch him in the throat.

"Tell me something, Helio. If Maeve was conscious right now or able to speak for herself, would she want me to come in or leave?"

That struck another nerve. My mate loved that wretch and her entire team like family… just like he had said. She would have welcomed him in a heartbeat.

"If you honestly think she would want me to leave, then I will do exactly that, without another argument," he continued, further rubbing it in.

I bared my fangs at him, the urge to drop kick him burning deep in my gut. Despite my anger, I knew myself defeated. Even the land felt it as the fungi from the bushes resorbed. Although he kept a neutral expression, I didn't miss both the glimmer of triumph in Tedrick's eyes and the subtle way his shoulders relaxed as the land stood down.

"You have five minutes," I said through my teeth before spinning on my heels.

He followed me inside quietly. My head knew that he'd never endanger Maeve. But when it came to the safety of my soulmate, rational thinking had a way of taking a leave of absence.

"Thank you," Tedrick suddenly said in a soft voice, as I opened the door to the healing room.

"Don't thank me. Thank her. I'm merely doing what she would want," I replied in a grumpy tone.

"No. Thank *you* for being this protective of her," he replied.

I gaped at him, robbed of words. He gave me an indulgent smile, then just pushed past me to enter the room.

The look of wonder mixed with fraternal tenderness that settled on his features when he saw Maeve instantly made me feel stupid for having been so difficult. She looked magical with the alibelles still gliding over her. They took flight when Tedrick came to kneel beside Maeve, but not in fear. They danced around, their tail lights blinking like tiny stars in the dim lighting of the room.

Circling around Maeve, I also settled by her side, my legs crossed under me. My throat tightened when Tedrick gently took a vine in her hair between two fingers, letting it glide out of his hand in a gentle caress. The instinctive jealous possessiveness I expected didn't rear its head. His gaze and demeanor were too—fraternal, almost paternal—for that.

"I will not accept her resignation," Tedrick said, his eyes still locked on Maeve's face. "I know that's the first thing she'll do when she awakens."

"I cannot speak as to her intentions," I said carefully, despite knowing for a fact that he was right. "All I can say is that she loves her team."

He snorted, finally turning his gaze towards me. "Diplomatic answer. Coming from you, it's a little surprising under the circumstances."

My brows shot up. "Surprising coming from me? How so?" I asked, genuinely surprised.

"You already know her decision. There is no question she discussed her plans with you. Seeing how you were dead set on keeping me out, I would have expected you to eagerly tell me tough shit."

This time, it was my turn to snort. "If that's the response you expected, either you don't know my mate as well as I believed you did, or you know me even less than I assumed," I replied mockingly.

"How so?" he echoed, in what I suddenly realized was a game leading to the real reason for his visit.

"Whatever my personal feelings, and however protective I may feel about my mate, nobody makes decisions for her. As you humans say, Maeve would kick my ass every which way from Sunday—not that this expression makes any sense—if I ever made that kind of statement on her behalf without her express permission," I replied matter-of-factly.

Tedrick chuckled while slowly nodding. "You do know your wife quite well."

"I do," I said smugly.

He smiled wistfully before giving me an assessing look. "I'm guessing you'll be relieved when she resigns. It must have put a great deal of pressure on your relationship that she had to keep secrets from you."

I shrugged, dodging his trap of trying to get me to admit she was indeed resigning. "Whatever Maeve decides, I will support her. Secrets are always unpleasant, but especially if they are born out of deception. Maeve swore an oath. We learned how to work around those restrictions. I can handle those kinds of secrets. It's my mate who suffers the most for it. She hates that she's doing to me what she endured as a child."

"Which confirms that she's going to resign," he insisted.

I snorted. "Stop, Tedrick. Confirmation, if there is any, will come from Maeve, and Maeve alone. You're focusing on the wrong thing if you assume her dislike of secrets would be her motivator for eventually resigning. Unlike Cedros, I cannot summon portals with a wave of my hand to bring her home every night. We're not so entitled as to expect him to be her chauffeur. And a long-distance relationship while she's on missions with the Enforcers isn't exactly the kind of marriage we want."

"You could join us," Tedrick retorted.

The speed with which he'd said it confirmed he'd been waiting for an opening to do so. I smiled and tilted my head to the side as I observed him.

"You have an impeccable past. You master an ancient form of combat believed long lost. As proven by the past few months, you can keep a secret and not try to take advantage or abuse your privileged access to sensitive tools and information," Tedrick said in a conversational tone, as if he was merely reading the headlines of a random newsletter. "Like us, you're devoted to justice and protecting the innocent. You clearly make a great team with Maeve. Not only would she get to keep her access to our finest technology, but so would you. *And* she'd no longer need to keep any secrets from you. Win all around."

I shook my head at his shameless sales pitch. "You know, I'd kill to get a glimpse of the file your organization put together on me. I bet you kicked every limit of legality in the teeth. You probably know everything, down to the color of my underwear."

"You never wear any," he deadpanned.

I burst out laughing, and he smiled. A comfortable but pensive silence settled between us for a few moments before Tedrick's stare weighed on me, serious and heavy.

"Once again, I will not speak for Maeve. She will miss your technology, but you've made us filthy rich with Saydi's capture. We can afford to buy equipment that nearly rivals or maybe even surpasses yours directly from the Xurgens," I said in a factual tone. "As for me, I'm a free spirit. The Enforcers have too many rules, and the missions you prioritize are not the ones I would. Innocent people like Strasa need people like me who will focus on the cases no one else can be bothered with or deem not important enough. Maeve and I love that we've been able to choose those types of cases."

"Done," Tedrick said in a firm tone.

I blinked. "Excuse me?"

"Join us, and you both get to pick the missions you want to do, even ones that the Enforcers would deem too small for us," Tedrick replied.

I stared at him, my wheels spinning while trying to make sense of his words. "I thought that wasn't possible. My understanding is that you have 'collaborations' with free agents and informers. But those individuals are not actual members of the Enforcers."

"So, you two have discussed it?" Tedrick asked, although it was more of a statement.

I smiled in a non-committal fashion.

He smiled back with a mocking expression that made it clear I did not fool him. "Do you have any idea how many intergalactic organizations spent years trying to get their hands on Saydi?" he asked, the sudden switch of topic giving me whiplash. "Maeve has a unique way of thinking and of tackling puzzles. She makes associations few people manage. And so do you, it seems. I've read her report on how you tracked down Saydi. Without your contribution narrowing it down to the Hagiel region, that wretch would have escaped again. Maeve is in awe of you."

My skin heated with pleasure. It was hard for me to comprehend that I could impress someone so amazing. Tedrick's face softened upon seeing my embarrassment.

"I cannot give access to our tools to anyone outside the Enforcers. I've already pushed things to their limits by allowing Maeve to use them during her 'sabbatical'. But beyond us needing Maeve's talent to crack open what no one else can, we need both of you to pursue what you have been doing. There are countless instances like the mess you found on Shimli that we suspect but do not have the standing to investigate. As bounty hunters, you can go wherever you want and do almost anything you please without bringing heat to the Enforcers or the UPO."

My heart soared. "So we *would* be free agents?"

"In practice, and as far as the entire galaxy knows, yes. You would be. But you will be secret agents."

I chose to ignore the cockiness with which he said we *will* be secret agents instead of we *would*.

"Maeve left her parents because she didn't want to be a secret agent," I countered.

He shook his head. "No, she hated constantly having to lie and live in the shadows. She won't be lying, and she will live openly as a bounty hunter. She'll just keep us informed of what she stumbles on and do some extra tasks for us on her computer. Call it a side gig."

"You think of everything, don't you?" I asked, unsure if I was more impressed than disturbed by all of this.

"It's my job," Tedrick said matter-of-factly. He turned to look at Maeve and gently caressed the back of her hand. "Take good care of our girl, and make sure to convince her once she wakes up. I'll expect to see you both in my office to sign your new contracts after your Edocit wedding."

With that, he got up and simply walked out.

CHAPTER 21
MAEVE

On a bright Saturday morning, I woke up from the most incredible dream. I'd traveled all over Zailia, first through its soil, then through the grass, flowers, and trees. Then Sera, the harstag, had extended her *veris* towards the tree I'd been visiting, drawing me into her before taking me on the wildest of rides. When she finally stopped for a sip of water at the river, a stunning sea creature—part seal, part betta fish—invited me to hop on for the most breathtaking underwater journey. A few more sea mammals hosted me before an amphibian one brought me back to the shore where a bird took me on a flight through the sky of Zailia.

I couldn't tell how much of it I'd imagined and how much had been real. But most of it felt much too vivid to have been a hallucination. If my transformation caused any pain, I dreamed right through it. I woke up to Helio watching over me, along with a swarm of alibelles cuddling with me. A handful were swiping their light tails over my skin in a sweeping caress. The soft heat instantly triggering a powerful sense of familiarity. They had done this while I'd been unconscious… or at least partially unconscious.

Helio leaned over me with a worried expression. "Maeve, you're awake! How are you feeling, my love?"

A billion responses pressed themselves on my tongue. I wanted to tell him about the wonderful 'dream' I made, how the air smelled incredibly pure, how the world looked different, and how even the soil beneath me felt alive against my skin. I wanted to say how happy I was to see him and to hear his voice again, and how I ached for him to hold and kiss me.

None of that came out. Instead, I blurted out two words.

"Feed me!"

The shock on his face reflected my own disbelief that these should have been my first words post metamorphosis. Helio burst out laughing before picking me up in his arms.

"As you command, my mate," he said affectionately, before nuzzling my neck.

It tickled, my giggle getting drowned by the powerful growling of my stomach. That made Helio laugh even harder. I had assumed that my very first act upon awakening would have been a beeline to the bathroom to check out my new look, but I was beyond famished.

Finding out I'd been unconscious for twelve days certainly explained my rabid hunger.

"Twelve days? How did I not keel over? Did you feed me with some drip?" I asked between two bites of the food Helio was steadily piling in front of me.

"No. You took enough nutrients and water from the soil, the sun, and the alibelles' lights," Helio explained.

"Wait, I can survive from sun and water like a plant now?" I asked, flabbergasted.

Helio nodded with a smug grin. "Yes, my love. As a pure-blood, I can survive almost up to three months from just sun and water. Almost twice as long if I can root with rich soil. But you should be able to last around three weeks to a month right now. With time, you could go up to two months."

"Wicked!" I whispered, before shoving another huge spoonful into my mouth.

Helio lifted me from my chair to settle me in his lap. He hugged me, nuzzling my nape and kissing my shoulders while I ate.

"I missed you so much," he whispered, his voice barely audible behind me.

My heart melted, and I turned to look at my husband over my shoulder. To my shock, a powerful tingling manifested itself in my scalp, followed by a pulling sensation. Stunned, I stopped chewing at the sight of a very thin, almost flimsy vine in my hair extending towards one of Helio's. They wrapped around each other, like one would twist two wires together.

A tsunami of emotions crashed into me—Helio's emotions. I couldn't define or isolate each one, only feel their combined effect. And the result was an overwhelming maelstrom of love, adoration, wonder, and infinite joy sweeping me away.

Tears flooded my eyes, blurring my vision as he smiled at me.

"I love you, Maeve. We are one, now and always."

In the week following my awakening, I practiced summoning my *veris*. I was driving my poor husband crazy with my restlessness. If it had a vine or something that even remotely looked like it had *veris*, I was all over it trying to connect. And if I couldn't find anything, he was my fallback plan. For all his playing martyr about needing a break, Helio was loving every bit of it. That physical and spiritual connection made it impossible for someone to lie about their feelings—not that he tried to.

Naturally, he had to caution me about not connecting with sick plants or creatures. While they were few and far between, considering how much Edocits protected the health of their land, it inevitably happened once or twice. Or rather, I got spanked for my eagerness. Could anyone really blame me, though? I was rediscovering the world I'd lived in for a few months, but this time by feeling it and seeing it through its own eyes.

And today, we would finalize our bond.

I turned this way and that, admiring myself in the mirror. The off-white dress I wore had a short embroidered bustier, and a layered skirt which stopped mid-thigh in the front, and to my calves in the back. The partially sheer fabric was a vegetal silk that Idova's family weaved from plants they acquired from Strasa's family gardens. She had designed the dress for me to make me look like a female of her tribe. It put on full display the lovely *veris* that now graced my shoulders down the sides of my arms to my wrists, and the sides of my calves to my ankles.

Barefoot, no makeup, and my hair twisted in an intricate updo, my only other adornments consisted of the handful of vines in my hair that fell loosely out of my bun, the buds having flowered with a will of their own from the joy I felt.

"It's time," my mother said in a sweet voice.

My stomach fluttered, and I gave her a nod, feeling nervous.

"You look beautiful, my darling. Your father and I are so very happy for you," she continued before gently kissing my forehead.

"Thank you, Mom," I said, my throat choked with emotion.

We exited the room to find my father waiting for us. He too embraced me, the pride and love in his eyes making me feel like daddy's little girl all over again. Standing on each side of me, they held their palms up, and I placed a hand on top of theirs. Walking ahead of us, Idova started shaking an instrument that vaguely reminded me of a tambourine.

My hands still resting on top of my parents' palms, I let them lead me outside into the garden. Edocit friends, Kaida and her family, a few of my Enforcer colleagues, and Helio's relatives formed two half circles on our left and right, in front of the

Mother Tree. Helio stood at Myma's feet, flanked by his parents. He wore nothing but embroidered off-white shorts, made of the same luxurious fabric as my dress. Like me, he was barefoot.

As soon as Idova started playing that instrument—which frankly sounded more like a cymbal roll—the Edocits outside had started singing a haunting hymn in their language. As per Edocit customs, an honored family member presided over the ceremony. In our case, Helio's illustrious Uncle Bron Kflen would do the honors.

My parents and I stopped right outside the door, waiting for our cue. Standing in the center of the garden, Hunt Master Bron gave me an affectionate smile before turning to my husband. Despite his age, Bron was looking mighty fine and like he was barely older than me. It tickled me pink knowing that, thanks to my bonding with Helio, I would also keep an insanely youthful appearance for decades, well into my nineties.

"Oddai, Thilgra, present your offspring," Bron said in a booming voice to Helio's parents.

My mate placed his hands on top of his parents' palms, and they led him towards the center of the garden. As they walked, Bron turned to us.

"Rowan, Ines, present your offspring," he told my parents, who proceeded to lead me to the center as well.

In Edocit culture, both parents gave their child away.

"Helio, Maeve, your parents have brought you here, under the light of the Maker and the benevolent gaze of your Myma to lay down the roots of your life together," Bron said. "Helio, do you wish to eternally bind your life, your home, and your land to this human female, Maria Maeve Riley?"

"I do," he said, eyes locked with mine, and his voice filled with emotion.

"Maria Maeve Riley, do you wish to bind your life to this Edocit male, Helio Breisa, and to become one with his home and his land?"

"I do," I said, my own voice shaky from emotion.

"Parents, give your offspring to each other," Bron commanded.

My throat further constricted when our fathers, standing on our right side, placed together our hands they held. Then our mothers, standing on our left, did the same. Helio's *veris* extruded to wrap around my hands and wrists, and I reciprocated, their tendrils intertwining and forming that spiritual connection I'd grown so addicted to. His love flowed into me like a tidal wave, coursing through my veins and every cell of my body.

"Parents, bind your children, and bless their union," Bron said.

Our mothers placed a hand on top of ours on their side, while our fathers did the same on the other side. As my parents didn't have *veris*, Oddai and Thilgra used theirs to bind all of our hands together. Unlike Helio and me, they didn't intertwine with us.

"Friends and family, you are the ring that will bring these souls back together should they ever lose their way. Let this ring be strong and unwavering in its resolve."

As soon as he spoke those words, our guests closed the two half rings on each side of us, forming two perfect circles. The smaller one, closest to us, was comprised of our non-Edocit friends, including Kaida, Cedros, and their children, all joining hands. Edocits formed the bigger circle, their joined hands further bound by their *veris*. Seconds later, I felt them rooting, their love and blessing feeling like a massive surge of energy and power, like a conduit enhancing my connection with the land. Simultaneously, the leaves in the trees surrounding us began to wave and whistle, while a flock of alibelles began dancing around us.

"Maeve and Helio, receive this blessing of those who hold you dear to their hearts. May this forever strengthen the unbreakable bond between your hearts, your land, and all the plants and creatures that dwell within. Let it be the foundation upon which you stand tall through the trials and tribulations of life. Let its roots grow ever stronger with each passing day, and rise undaunted and unbent, like an ancestral tree."

He gently placed his hands at the back of our heads and brought our faces closer so that we could rest our foreheads against each other's. As if with a will of their own, the vines in our hair connected, further deepening our spiritual link.

"Just like the seasons, may your love be constantly renewed. Whether it burns bright with the passion of summer, cools under the gentle breeze of autumn, or rests in the stillness of winter, let it always bloom again with the thawing of spring. With one voice, we bless you."

In response to this last sentence, the voices of our Edocit guests rose again, my skin erupting in goosebumps at the haunting melody.

"May your love be as strong and unbreakable as myrdian wood, as vibrant as the wildflowers, and as everlasting as the land itself. May your union be blessed and flourish for all times."

I barely heard those last words. Gently rocked by the voices singing and the leaves whistling, I gave myself over to Helio's spirit flowing through me and the call of the land claiming me.

EPILOGUE
HELIO

For the hundredth time, I stole a glance at Maeve, huddled on the couch across my desk, her portable computer on her lap. Her hair was a complete mess as she mumbled to herself while trying to solve a problem. Despite designing the perfect desk just for her, lovingly growing it out of nuvean wood, my mate systematically plopped herself at the same spot on the couch.

I didn't understand how she could be so focused on her work when I was feeling like a complete wreck. Maeve was eight weeks pregnant. I'd been expecting our little sprout to come out for the past three days. As a human, she should be the one freaking out, calling the healer every other minute, or dropping by our healing room to make sure everything was still fine.

But nope, not my mate. To her, this was all business as usual.

I turned my attention back to my screen, the words blurring before my eyes. What was taking him so long? Granted, there wasn't a specific number of days. Some sprouts, overly eager to feel the rays of the sun on their skin, came out early in the seventh week. Others would linger well into the ninth week, the worst cases taking up to ten or eleven weeks.

You better not take eleven weeks…

I'd go crazy, and Maeve would probably strangle me in aggravation. I glanced once more in my mate's direction only to see a decorative pillow coming hard and fast at me. I failed to dodge it, and it smacked me straight in the face.

"Hey! What was that for?" I exclaimed.

"I'm trying to figure out how to track down a major sleaze ball, and you're making it impossible for me to concentrate," Maeve replied, glaring at me with annoyance.

"WHAT?! I haven't said a word!" I said, outraged.

"No, but you're sitting here making yourself sick with worry for no reason. You freaking out upsets the house. And the house being upset messes with my concentration," she explained in a tone that clearly implied I was dumb for not realizing it.

And I did feel dumb.

I grimaced, feeling helpless. "Sorry. I just can't help it. How the hell are you so… 'Zen' like you call it? How can you be so calm?"

Maeve shrugged. "I'm calm because the alternative is pointless. You've been a mess for the past few days. You barely eat. You're exhausted because you can't sleep. And you haven't done jack shit on the task Tedrick gave you. What has that accomplished? Nothing. Lucky for you that this isn't an urgent case."

I gave her a baleful glare, unable to argue with a single of her statements. Of course, she was right. Maeve was almost always right.

She plucked a leaf from a vine in her hair and waved it at me. With her hormones going into hyperdrive during her pregnancy, Maeve's down leaves were almost as potent as those of our juveniles.

"Instead of stressing non-stop, how about you go make yourself a tea out of this and give the poor house a moment's peace? You'll make it age before its time with all your fussing," Maeve said as if talking to a particularly troublesome child.

I grimaced again, annoyed with myself, with my mate, and with that wretched sprout that just wouldn't come out. Maeve gave me a 'Come on, move it!' look while waving the leaf again. With an aggravated grunt, I got out of my chair, circled around the desk, and came to get the leaf.

Before I could take it from her, Maeve pulled her hand away, tapping the leaf twice against her lips. Despite my irritation, I couldn't help a smile. I leaned down and gently kissed her.

"Good boy," Maeve said mockingly when I straightened, then gave me the leaf.

I grunted in a non-committal fashion. I'd no sooner turned around to leave than Maeve slapped my butt, making me yelp. She'd put some energy in it, the sting reflecting the loud clapping sound it had made.

"What the…?"

"That's for not taking the initiative of managing your stress properly," she said matter-of-factly, her gaze already back on her screen.

I glared at Maeve, but her fingers were already flying over the keyboard. On my way out, I muttered under my breath, which only made her laugh.

As I prepared the tea, my annoyance with myself grew another notch. Maeve shouldn't have had to tell me this. *I* was the pureblood Edocit. It should be *me* reminding *her* of all the wonderful ways we could achieve inner peace, whether by chewing our own leaves, making tea out of them, connecting with the land in the healing room, or seeking comfort directly from Myma. But then, Myma was also beside herself with impatience at receiving our little sprout.

We already knew he was a boy. By connecting with Maeve, I'd been able to get a weak feel of his emotions. But as that contact had to go through my mate, who wasn't a pureblood Edocit, the link wasn't as strong. Once inside Myma's maturing knot, we would be able to connect directly with our son.

My entire being vibrated with impatience. If I were honest, the burning need to finally see my son and touch his soul directly mostly fueled my restlessness. Heaving a sigh, I poured the boiling water onto the leaf, giving it a moment to infuse while trying to picture what he would look like. Would he take after me or his mother? Would he be the perfect mix of us? I'd like that.

Bringing the cup to my lips, I blew on it to cool it a bit before taking a sip. A wistful smile stretched my lips as I began picturing again all the activities we would do together and all the things I would teach him. As I started heading back to the office, a violent shudder coursed through me, echoing throughout the house.

Our son is coming!

My cup slipped out of my hand, crashing onto the floor. I barely registered the burn of the hot tea splashing over my foot. I ran towards the office, only to see Maeve yank the door open and barge out. She stared at me with bulging eyes, the stress I'd been feeling for days finally reflecting on her face.

"Now would be the right time to panic," she said, genuinely looking on the verge of doing exactly that.

Closing the distance between us, I swooped her up and dashed out of the house. As I ran past the kitchen, I addressed a silent thank you to the Maker that the cup hadn't shattered. Stepping on glass and ending up bleeding half to death had absolutely zero place in my plans right now.

I stormed out into the garden to find Myma already spreading her thick roots to create a path closer to her, a section of them elevating into a low birthing bench for Maeve to recline in. Her branches were lit up from the over one hundred alibelles that had bonded with my land.

I carefully sat Maeve on the bench. She placed her legs on each side of the wide root that curved up into a ramp going up Myma's trunk. Despite what a mess I'd been lately, an odd sense of peace had washed over me during my run over here. My mate was now the one trying to fight her growing panic. She needed me to be strong and appease her.

Whispering soothing words of encouragement, I lifted the skirt of Maeve's short dress and removed her slip, then wrapped an arm around her shoulders.

"He's coming," Maeve said, her body tense and her voice filled with worry.

"Relax, my love. Just breathe. When he'll need your help, you will know. He will tell you. All is well. Feel the calm in the air, the elated peace from the land. Our little one isn't in distress."

"Right. Right," Maeve said, taking a shuddering breath.

I took her hand in mine and kissed her forehead. The seconds ticked by with little happening. Her stomach suddenly quivered, once, twice, and then she gasped.

"Now!" I said, sensing more than I felt an undefinable tug.

Judging by Maeve's reaction, she had felt it too and began pushing. Moments later, I opened my mouth to tell her to stop, but she already had. My heart filled with love and pride for my woman. I'd feared that with her being human, she wouldn't have been able to fully perceive the needs of our son during his birth.

By the third push, his tiny head came out. Unlike human babies, there was no blood and gore, no waters breaking, only a bit of sap that made him look like he'd been covered in oil. His tiny hands came out second, and he started pulling himself forward as he wiggled free. And just like that, our little Oziel was born.

My throat painfully constricted, I stared in wonder at our beautiful little sprout. In a fetal position, he wouldn't even fill the palm of my hand. This was why our females didn't go through the long and torturous labor many other species did.

By the way Maeve's hand tightened around mine, I could feel her burning urge to reach out for our son. But this was his journey to conquer. I kissed her temple, and my arm around her shoulders drew her even closer.

He crawled at first, as he familiarized himself with his tiny legs and arms. It wasn't until the alibelles began hovering in front of him that he pushed himself up on shaky legs. At this early stage of development, his eyes had not opened yet. A thin layer of skin—that would eventually turn into eyelids—covered them. Although he wasn't exactly blind, he couldn't see clear shapes. But the warm glow of the alibelles' tails served as guiding lights as he climbed the ramp towards Myma's knot.

"He's so beautiful," Maeve said in a choked voice.

"He's perfect," I replied with fervor.

And he was. Despite his still sketchy features and the absence of hair, his little body was perfect. Two plump vines already dangled from his bald head, healthy *veris* swirled beneath the semi-translucent skin of his arms and legs.

As he continued his journey upward, Myma shifted some vines and small branches on her trunk creating steps for our sprout, and creating a small net of vines behind him that would catch him should he slip. In the last stretch, the alibelles took turns caressing his spine with their tail lights, giving him the boost of energy he needed to get across the finish line.

Tears of joy were freely rolling down Maeve's cheeks when our little Oziel finally entered the gaping hole of Myma's maturing knot. Exhausted, our son all but collapsed inside, the vines in his hair and the *veris* in his arms and legs immediately extruding to connect with the vines lining the inner walls of the knot. A thick sap began forming in front of the opening of the knot, creating a protective dome that would shield Oziel from the elements and any possible harm, while allowing us to see him.

As soon as it was done, I placed Maeve's hand on the swirling patterns of the wood framing the edges of the knot, then settled my own next to hers. The vines that poked through the bark expanded, seeking a connection. I extruded my *veris*, Maeve imitating me.

"Oh, my God!" Maeve exclaimed. "That's him! I can feel him!"

I nodded, beaming at her. As if in response to her comment, the little buds in the vines surrounding the knot blossomed.

"He's happy. He feels warm and safe. And he's happy," Maeve said, half laughing, half crying. "He's going to dream now, isn't he? He's going to enter a beautiful dream, like I did?"

"Yes, he will dream and bond with the world that will keep him safe," I said, my heart full to bursting.

"I love you so much."

"I love you too, Maeve."

I kissed her, expressing all my love and devotion for her through it. We broke the kiss to gaze once more at our perfect little boy, Maeve leaning against me, and my cheek resting on top of her head.

As we continued to pour our love into Oziel through our link, the alibelles danced and the tree leaves whistled their welcome to the new member of our land.

THE END

IDOVA

HARSTAG

ALIBELLE

SKIFF

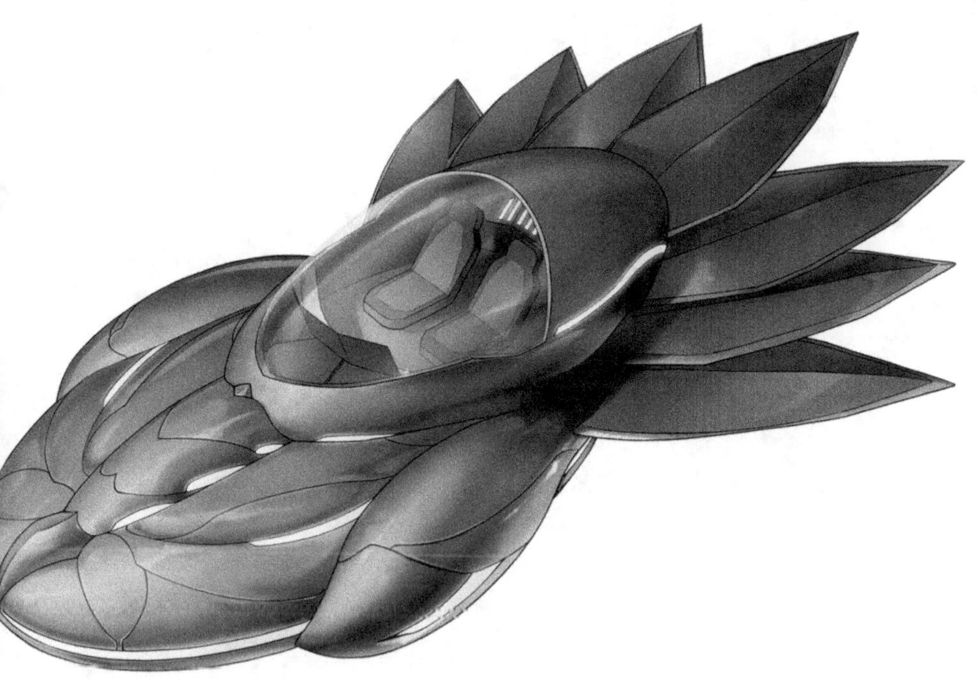

WEEPING FAIRY

ARZIG

SAYEEF

KRONOS

ALSO BY REGINE ABEL

THE VEREDIAN CHRONICLES

Escaping Fate

Blind Fate

Raising Amalia

Twist of Fate

Hands of Fate

Defying Fate

Imperial Fate

BRAXIANS

Anton's Grace

Ravik's Mercy

Krygor's Hope

Keran's Dawn

XIAN WARRIORS

Doom

Legion

Raven

Bane

Chaos

Varnog

Reaper

Wrath

Xenon

Nevrik

Rogue

Doom: A Graphic Novel

BLOOD MAIDENS OF KARTHIA

Claiming Thalia

ALSO BY REGINE ABEL

PRIME MATING AGENCY

I Married A Lizardman

I Married A Naga

I Married A Birdman

I Married A Minotaur

I Married Wonjin

I Married A Merman

I Married A Dragon

I Married A Beast

I Married Krogal

I Married A Dryad

I Married An Incubus

I Married A Mothman

I Married A Catman

I Married Amreth

I Married Kayog

THE MIST

The Mistwalker

The Nightmare

DARK TALES

Bluebeard's Curse

The Hunchback

THE SHADOW REALMS

Destined to the Wraith

Destined to the Reaper

Destined to the Lycan

VALOS OF SONHADRA

Unfrozen

Iced

ALSO BY REGINE ABEL

EMPATHS OF LYRIA

An Alien For Christmas

OTHER

True As Steel

Alien Awakening

Heart of Stone

Oops! I Summoned a Liderc

ABOUT REGINE

USA Today bestselling author Regine Abel is a fantasy, paranormal and sci-fi junkie. Anything with a bit of magic, a touch of the unusual, and a lot of romance will have her jumping for joy. She loves creating hot alien warriors and no-nonsense, kick-ass heroines that evolve in fantastic new worlds while embarking on action-packed adventures filled with mystery and the twists you never saw coming.

Before devoting herself as a full-time writer, Regine had surrendered to her other passions: music and video games! After a decade working as a Sound Engineer in movie dubbing and live concerts, Regine became a professional Game Designer and Creative Director, a career that has led her from her home in Canada to the US and various countries in Europe and Asia.

Facebook

https://www.facebook.com/regine.abel.author/

Website

https://regineabel.com

Regine's Rebels Reader Group

https://www.facebook.com/groups/ReginesRebels/

Newsletter

http://smarturl.it/RA_Newsletter

Goodreads

http://smarturl.it/RA_Goodreads

Bookbub

https://www.bookbub.com/profile/regine-abel

Amazon

http://smarturl.it/AuthorAMS

www.ingramcontent.com/pod-product-compliance
Lightning Source LLC
Chambersburg PA
CBHW071419200726
48294CB00002B/444

* 9 7 8 1 9 9 8 8 5 7 7 4 6 *